A woman's body has been found on a street in Unif, a town on Lasho, a newly constructed moon. She's a victim without any ID that was shot in the back of the head with a laser beam. Detective Brin has been sent to Unif to solve this case.

Tavo Is Dead
Copyright © 2019 Thadd Evans
ISBN: 978-1-4874-2406-0
Cover art by Martine Jardin

Published by eXtasy Books Inc or
Devine Destinies, an imprint of eXtasy Books Inc

Look for us online at:
www.eXtasybooks.com or www.devinedestinies.com

TAVO IS DEAD
MICHAEL BRIN, HOMICIDE DETECTIVE

BY

THADD EVANS

DEDICATION

Rene Magritte

CHAPTER ONE

It was the year 4023. As the interplanetary transport craft I was in went into orbit around the planet Cirok, preparing to land, Tesk's face, an incoming call from my supervisor, appeared in my contact lenses. He frowned. "A few minutes ago, a Qio humanoid found an Aito woman's body on a street in downtown Unif and called Precinct Nine. Because its department is understaffed and inexperienced, they want our help.

"Your flight for Lasho leaves in four hours. According to the victim's ID, her name was Tavo. It didn't mention anything else."

I frowned. "Didn't mention anything else? Somebody must have deleted her address."

"Unfortunately, most of Lasho's towns, villages, settlements, and outposts don't have enough hospitals, police, doctors, nurses, fire stations or other basic institutions. That makes it difficult to help most of the recently arrived refugees. Your new partner, Sultra, will provide more information regarding Tavo."

Text, the result of a search engine's recent probe, scrolled through my lenses. According to it, for unknown reasons, Sewo and other Unif Peace Officers in Precinct nine hadn't sent me any other details regarding Tavo. "Why didn't you bring in utility androids to solve this case?" 80 percent of the time, these robots, ones that worked day and night, solved them 90 percent faster than humans or Aito humanoids.

"Five weeks ago, when we first heard about a shooting in downtown Unif, we sent in three utility androids. Two hours after they arrived, in the late morning, Officer Henn, who noticed they weren't responding to her calls, started looking for them.

"That evening, she found all three. A hacker, somebody she didn't know, had sent computer viruses into their minds. The viruses destroyed every bio-circuit. Unfortunately, because Henn had only studied HTUC viruses' computer code for eleven weeks along with the fact that her wrist scanner wasn't designed to figure out how the code compiled data, she didn't know how or why these viruses were so effective."

My jaw muscles tightened in an irritated response to Henn's terrible situation.

HTUC, hypertext utility code, one that millions of humans and humanoids on many planets, moons, and spacecraft used to create software, helped just about everybody communicate with each other via 3D holograms, text messages, and videos.

I stepped inside the spacecraft and sat down. Sultra's text file appeared in my lenses. However, for unknown reasons, a 3D holographic replica of her face did not. I bit my lip, disappointed.

Nine years ago, while she was at Boon's Police Academy, a school on Cirok, this undercover detective, an Aito humanoid, began studying thirty kinds of networked computers, forty types of forensic software, and psychology. Three years later, after getting straight A's in every course, she was assigned to precinct D. Within eight months, she had arrested four drug lords and six hit men. All but one was convicted.

After the last trial ended, she was sent to Unif, an attempt to help its understaffed department. Within seven months, she had arrested six murderers, men who killed women because they wouldn't work as sex slaves in Jeen, a dangerous town on Cirok. Unfortunately, all six broke out of their jail cells and escaped before they went to court.

During this time, four of Sultra's partners disappeared. Ten officers and four detectives searched for them for seven months, using face-to-face interviews, neutrino probes, and wrist scanner analysis. Unfortunately, these professionals couldn't find any trace of her missing colleagues.

I winced, shocked that so many of her former partners were still missing and sent her an email, introducing myself.

Her reply scrolled through my lenses. She was impressed by my ability to break through sixty-four types of cross-platform firewalls. She had worked with sixteen other detectives, colleagues who knew a lot about IT, Information Technology, but they could only break through fourteen kinds of these barriers.

She was also excited because I had cracked six-thousand-nine encrypted messages, making it possible to read sixteen drug lords' files, eighteen murderers' text messages, thirty-nine kidnappers' emails, and fifty-three robbers' holographic ID photos.

However, to some extent, this professional was disappointed with me. I hadn't spent enough time learning more Nusp, the Aito language. This race's speech, alphabet, and their numbers made it easier for them to study fractals, motion, Chaos Science, and DNA manipulation.

Her message scrolled. *I look forward to working with you. However, I'm late for a meeting.*

I blinked, irritated, wishing we could talk, not exchange text messages and sent this new partner one, saying that I looked forward to meeting her.

The screen went black, end of the call.

Although 91 percent of any police officer's wrist scanners examined a computer, a robot or a spacecraft's shape, and compared this information with eighty billion archives, the scanners could only store and analyze 900 terabytes of data. The other 9 percent broke down every few days for a variety of reasons.

I started thinking about my qualifications for this tough assignment. Six months ago, after I killed Veil by destroying his platinum spacecraft, my supervisor at MPStation-4's homicide division, had transferred me from a moon called Wacev to Cirok for several reasons. First, I knew more about breaking through firewalls than most of this planet's detectives. 80 percent of the time, drug lords and other criminal's text emails, 3D holographic logs, video emails, phone call records, and files were hidden behind firewalls. As a result, it was difficult for most homicide detectives to figure out if a mining company or any kind of business was a front.

Second, three months ago, war had broken out on Roov, Maen, Yat, Grend, and Coam, all five of Cirok's continents. During that time, Tesk received a 3D holographic message from Commissioner Frus, the head of Zy's largest police department. The city of Zy was on National Territories' north coast. NT was nine million square miles, Grend's largest country. In the message, Frus pointed out that since every homicide detective on Cirok had been assigned to 30 percent more murder and missing person cases than usual, every police department on Lasho needed more homicide detectives. They needed experienced professionals who could work in jungles, frontier outposts, new towns or villages, places where many robbers and drug lords operated in the open, didn't have to worry about being arrested.

According to my lenses, astrophysicists used Genetic Technology and Moon Construction Spacecraft to build Lasho. This technology altered DNA. As a result, in a few years, jungles, grassy plains, and forests would cover Lasho, a barren moon's surface. If everything went according to plan, six hundred animal species would roam these lands, creating a well thought out ecosystem.

The GTM spaceships, a nine-year-old invention made it possible to build these celestial bodies, places where refugees could live safely, didn't have to fight or die in wars or live in crowded tenement buildings, two huge problems on Cirok.

The spacecraft touched down on a dirty rooftop. I stepped out, entered an unmarked police vehicle and sat next to the driver, a bronze humanoid robot. The vehicle rose, then took off. On a dashboard-mounted screen, hundreds of refugees, all of them sixty feet below us, shuffled down a sidewalk, a busy route partly covered by garbage.

I winced, shocked by their filthy clothes and dirty faces. "Do most of Unif's refugees look and live like this?"

The android replied in a monotone, "Yes."

"Why?"

"There aren't enough housing or jobs."

Farther down the sidewalk, six Qio women, females with turquoise skin, all dressed in skintight catsuits, were talking to each other. One spoke to a passerby, asking, "Honey, would you like to party? It only costs twenty oons."

He smiled. "Yeah."

Moments later we landed next to a drab high-rise, Unif Police Station Four. I climbed out and entered the building.

I stepped inside room 17, Ron Frank's office. He, my new supervisor, announced, "Go talk to Dr. Meff."

I hurried into an autopsy room, a space on the third floor and stopped next to a waist-high platform, one with Tavo's body on it. On my left, Meff, a six-foot-tall human in white scrubs glanced at me, his brow tight. "Brin. We started this scan and organize probe thirty minutes ago."

I nodded. During this procedure, thousands of nanorobots sent neutrinos into a corpse, retrieved the data, and compared the results with six hundred trillion medical databases to determine the cause of the death.

To my right, a ten-foot-tall humanoid Medical Assistant Robot, designed to perform autopsies, took more high-resolution pictures of the victim's blue forehead with its chest-mounted camera.

I asked, "What killed her?"

Meff replied, "Somebody or perhaps an android, shot her in the back of the head with a pulsed laser beam."

I frowned. These beams could punch holes in skulls in one-fortieth of a second. "Do you have any new information regarding the killer?"

He glowered. "No."

I blurted, "Why not?"

He frowned. "There are at least eight types of robots on Lasho. Only one type is on our database. Tavo's DNA isn't on any of our Lasho resident archives. There are four-billion-six-hundred refugees on Lasho, recent arrivals. Their DNA, names and snail mail addresses aren't on any databases.

"Figuring out who did this will be difficult. According to a statistical collection of suspects, there is a twenty-five percent chance of finding the killer."

I bit my lip, frustrated by this lack of information. In my lenses, text indicated that there wasn't enough forensic analysis staff on Lasho to update every resident's background archives within the next few days. It would take about four months for a forensics' team to finish the task.

Although the statistical collection of suspects software was helpful, a computer model pointed out that if detectives didn't come up with any more clues, there was a 60 percent chance that it would take that software six months to figure out which suspect was at the scene of the crime.

The eight types included battle-ready, security guards, medical assistants, pilot machines, database assistance, personal assistants, construction workers, and home care providers.

He frowned.

My stomach muscles tightened, a shocked reaction. "When will Human Resources hire more forensic analysis staff?"

"That's hard to say. I'm too busy to ask or sort through all my new emails, voicemails or holographic messages."

I made a fist, annoyed. "What about internet enabled computers?" The machines were used to share photos, 3D holograms of suspects, and their DNA files with every data processing machine on Lasho.

Meff blurted, asked, "Don't you get it? I don't know what the enabled computers are doing because I, along with all three staff members, are overworked trying to catch up."

My jaw muscles tightened in a frustrated response. "Let me know when you have more information."

"Definitely."

I left the room. Voice mail messages came out of my earplugs. According to the messages, Precinct Nine's computer server had broken down four days ago, couldn't accept or relay any calls. My jaw muscles tightened.

I reached a crowded street corner, next to dirty graffiti-covered apartments. To my left and right, men and women, humans, Aito, and other races, all in torn clothes, shuffled by. A human male with missing teeth glared at me. "Got any spare change?"

"No."

He blurted, "Asshole," and moved on.

I blinked, irritated.

A six-foot-tall chrome humanoid robot in a tight dress, an altered personal assistant model, strolled up to me. "Would you like to buy some ente?"

"No." Ente, an addictive drug, made you feel better.

She whispered in my ear, "Let's go meet Sultra."

I followed the robot.

Within minutes, we entered a shabby room, one on Hotel Deluxe's third floor. As a roach scampered across a stained rug, the robot departed, not making a sound. In back of me, clicking heels grew louder. I turned, wanting to know who had arrived.

A slender Aito woman with turquoise skin, a stranger in a black catsuit, black thigh-high boots, and indigo sunglasses, strolled up to me. "Would you like to party?" Behind her, the door buzzed shut.

I blinked, wondering why this prostitute was here. "No."

She took a few steps, sat on a bed, then offered a forced smile. "I'm Sultra."

I nodded. My pulse started racing, reacting to this gorgeous woman's looks.

She frowned. "Valuable cargo will arrive in Neib in two weeks. My guess, based on a recent conversation with a contact, is that Tavo was murdered because she knew too much about the shipment."

I paused, thinking. "Did your contact tell you what the cargo was?"

"No."

Neib, a village, was eight miles from Vot's north coast. A jungle, the Munt, covered most of Vot, a continent in Lasho's western hemisphere. "When and where will it arrive?"

She glowered. "I don't know."

My stomach muscles tightened in an irritated response. "Will somebody pick it up after it arrives or will the messenger take it someplace else?"

She bit her lip, a sad expression on her face. "I'm not sure."

I rubbed my chin, disappointed. "Who's your contact?"

She frowned. "Daon."

"Daon isn't much to go on. Tell me more."

She blurted, "I'm doing my best. Quit bitching."

I rubbed my chin, wanting to believe that Sultra had better data. "What does Daon look like?"

"She's five-foot-six, average build. She, a human, usually wears baggy sepia pants, a tight, gray jacket, and sunglasses."

"Did your lenses photograph her?"

"They tried to, but all six images were fuzzy."

I exhaled, irritated. "Why were they fuzzy?"

"Some Unif drug dealers' earphones have jammed my lenses' cameras. My guess is that her earphones were doing that."

"What about your wrist scanner?" If lenses broke down, these scanners, tools that used sound and body-shape recognition to locate missing persons or fugitives, created images of suspects and other objects. Unfortunately, these scanners couldn't find missing persons or fugitives if they were behind a wall or inside a building.

"They jammed that, too. As a result, all six images of Daon were hazy, useless."

I rubbed my chin, angry. "Does she have any distinguishing features?"

Sultra paused, her brow tensed. "Her chin almost comes to a point. Other than that, she's plain, nondescript, not pretty, not ugly."

"Where and when did you meet her?"

My new partner glowered. "I met her a month ago in Gerts, a bar in the Sorn District."

"Keep going."

"Five weeks ago, during a meeting at a fast food restaurant called Joey's, an uncover cop, who was posing as a john, told me that some informants hang out at Gerts. Four weeks ago, after visiting Gerts six times, Daon walked up to my table, told me she hadn't seen me before. Then she asked me if I wanted to make some money. I said I did. She paused for a few seconds.

"At that point, I asked her if she knew anything about some stolen phones. She glared at me and said if I gave her eighty oons in cash, she would give me some valuable information. I gave her the money. Then she pointed out that her friends called her Daon and mentioned a human named Wo Ta. I asked her if she knew anything about Tavo. She flinched. Within a few seconds, she explained that any information regarding that would cost ninety oons in cash. I gave her the money. Much to my surprise, she mentioned the valuable cargo.

"I asked her if it was an ente shipment. She said she didn't know and commented that the shipment would arrive in eighteen days. I asked for more information. This broad said she had to go. I told her I wanted to talk to her again about Tavo and the shipment. She explained that we would meet again at Hogs, a cafe, within two days at dusk.

"She arrived at Hogs thirty minutes after I did. A moment before I popped a question, she said that she was paying attention to a friend's comments. I demanded that she give me more information regarding the shipment. Who was receiving it? Much to my surprise, this gal told me she had to leave. I asked why she had to go, and she took off. I haven't seen her since."

I bit my lip, frustrated.

My new partner bit off a fingernail with a gloomy expression on her face.

"Can you trust anything that Daon says?"

She grabbed a cigarette, lit it, took a puff, then exhaled. "Good question. Time will tell. The problem is that Daon is my only lead."

I bit my lip, wanting to know more.

Behind me, a humming, barely audible, grew louder.

Sultra got up, then whispered in my ear, "There is a tiny

intensive probe drone behind you. Let's get on the bed, you on top, then we'll kiss. If you won't get on top of me, and we don't kiss, whoever sent it will know what we're doing."

I nodded, my mind racing.

She lay face up on the bed, then put her cigarette in an ashtray.

I got on top of her, and we locked lips. An intensive probe drone could fly through one-thirty-second of an inch-wide cracks. At the same time, it would send pictures, videos and sound images of its surroundings to a computer server at another location. Every sentient being, machine, room, hall, and street made sounds, ones that matched a huge Assemble and Analyze, archive. As a result, ASA's sound images had an 80 percent chance of determining where the drone was and what was taking place at that location.

To my left, the drone stopped inches from her cheek. On its top, a camera lens whirred.

As sweat poured down my forehead, a nervous reaction, the drone flew toward me and halted close to my eye. I moved a couple inches away from Sultra, worried that the drone might shock me. Without warning, it took off.

Sultra grabbed my shoulder and pulled it until my lips were an inch from hers. She whispered, "Kiss me again."

I complied, my adrenaline pumping.

She murmured, "Fuck me."

CHAPTER TWO

She whispered, "Stop. Although you feel good, the drone left, probably isn't watching us."

I got up, then sat on the bed.

Sultra wiped the sweat off her face. "Let's hope it couldn't hear our conversation before it entered this room." My new partner stood, walked toward the door, and halted. "According to my wrist scanner, the drone is outside this room, more than fifty yards from me."

"Hopefully, it isn't in a hall on this floor, ready to follow us when we leave this room or this building."

She did an about-face, glowering. "Hopefully."

"We need better leads."

Sultra frowned. "Let's leave separately and meet in a few days. I might have better information then."

I sighed. "Will you contact me or should I call you?"

"I'll contact you."

I nodded.

Two days later, not long after dawn, while I was walking down a nearby alley, examining the neighborhood, I noticed Sultra. She was behind a ten-foot-high garbage bin. She put on a dildo, then started fucking an Aito, a woman in a tight dress.

I bit my lip, irritated that she was doing this, not searching for leads. Then I hurried away.

The following evening, twenty minutes after her text message, one telling me to meet her here in person at 202 Trimson, scrolled through my lenses, I halted between a parked truck and a wall, a narrow space near the middle of a dark alley, four blocks from the Ven. As clicking boot heels grew louder, it started drizzling. A seven-foot-tall Aito man in a tan suit strolled by. Not far behind him, Sultra turned and walked toward me.

I blinked. "Why do you want to meet face-to-face? That's dangerous."

She glowered, rain dripping off her nose ring. "According to my communication update, somebody started monitoring my lenses two minutes ago."

My jaw muscles tightened, a horrified reaction. "Are you sure?" Communication update, our lenses' utility, could detect hackers or other intruders who were listening in our phone calls or reading our emails. This update examined our lenses' connections every four minutes.

The crunching became louder. A battle-ready robot's three-fingered hand grabbed my new partner's head, threw her into the middle of the alley and she landed on her back.

She screamed, "Help!"

I yanked out my automatic weapon. The half-inch-long gun expanded.

The battle-ready android punched her forehead.

I fired. Bullets struck the left side of its chest. The robot turned toward me with its fist raised. I squeezed the trigger. More hit its smooth face. I ducked while it punched the wall, barely missing my shoulder.

I stood, then turned, blasting, my adrenaline pumping. My weapon's laser beam struck the robot's neck. The android spun around.

I jumped to the left. Its fist grazed my ear. My gun's beam struck its neck. The android began shaking. Without warning, it ran away.

I shouted, "Nine Two," telling a nearby hospital that a police officer was down, probably dead. My lenses' Probe and Evaluate, application, a tool that could only detect somebody or any robot if they were outside, within a quarter mile of my current location, initiated scanning. Within three seconds, it determined that it couldn't find the robot.

Chapter Three

Within thirty seconds, an air ambulance touched down in the alley, its back door open. A stretcher flew out, slid under Sultra, then rose, her on it and went inside the vehicle. As I blenched, shocked by this tragedy, the door hissed shut, and the ambulance sped away. I raced toward my car.

I entered the emergency department, my holographic ID in front of my chest.

A physician in blue scrubs walked up to me. "Detective Brin, I'm Doctor Ru. Sultra is on NA life support. We have three hours to replace her head with a new PSCR. If we don't, she will die. Can any member of her family sign an LR authorization slip?"

My stomach muscles tightened, a shocked response. "No. Her only surviving relative is a brother and too far away. Can any judge use a TOC to handle this?"

She frowned. "Good question. I should have an answer soon." She hurried away.

NA, nanite assisted, life support was designed to keep a patient alive for a few days. During that time, a team of robots would use Pluripotent Stem Cell Replacement technology to create a new head. 80 percent of the time, this body part was as good as the previous one.

LR, life recovery, law required that a member of her family had to sign this form. If they couldn't be reached within seven-two hours, a Temporary Override Consent form, one that a doctor had to sign, made it possible for a medical team to go ahead with the operation.

My mind started racing, an attempt to figure out what my department could do if a judge wouldn't sign a TOC.

Ron Frank's face appeared in my lenses. He said, "I just placed a bulletin on an internet billboard, one that asks the public to contact my office if they have seen a BRR that matches your description."

I thanked him and his face vanished, end of call.

The next sunup, I woke up in a cold sweat. In my nightmare, Sultra's head jerked, responding to the battle-robot's punch.

Hours later, in the afternoon, when I was walking down the street, searching for anybody who had seen the robot attack Sultra, Ru's face appeared in my lenses.

She offered a quick grin. "Judge Gom just signed a TOC."

"Great."

"Your partner can return to duty in four days."

I thanked her for the update. Ru's face vanished, end of the call.

Frank's face appeared. "A few seconds ago we received an anonymous email. According to it, four hours ago, somebody noticed a BRR that matched your description. The robot was close to two-zero-two Trimson."

I asked, "Can you track down the anonymous email's source?"

"No. IT staff tried eight times and failed."

I thanked him, then headed for that location.

A list of names, women and men, who lived in buildings that were close to 202 Trimson appeared in my lenses. I dialed the first name, Gail Fose. A gray rectangle, not their face, appeared. For unknown reasons, this potential eyewitness didn't want anybody to know what she looked like. Voicemail switched on. I left my name, phone number and told her why I was calling.

The next day, several minutes before noon, after twenty-three failed attempts to speak to anybody whose name was on the list and since nobody on it had returned my calls, I waved my hand over an apartment door's face recognition screen.

An Aito male with a big nose opened the entrance a few inches. My badge materialized. I told him about my search.

He explained that about fifty battle-robots had entered or left 202 Trimson within the last month. He overheard one of them say that they were headed for 140 Elm Way. Without warning, he slammed the door.

My stomach muscles tightened, an irritated response.

Within forty minutes, I stood in front of a fourteen-foot-high, filthy gray door at 140 Elm Way, which was an entrance on a dead-end street, five miles from 202 Trimson. Although its face recognition device chimed, nobody opened the door. My mind started racing, attempting to figure out if there was a faster way of speaking to these potential eyewitnesses. I departed.

At dusk, after talking to thirty more neighbors, all close to 202 Trimson, I rubbed my chin, aggravated. All of them told me they didn't see or hear any battle-robots during the attack. Within seconds, I left their apartment building, climbed on a motorcycle, the only vehicle that other officers of this cash strapped police department weren't using and drove away.

Were all of these people afraid of me or somebody else? Did any of them care about my search? I wasn't sure. However, it was odd that they didn't hear or see the battle-robot when it assaulted us.

Mara Dox's, my new partner, file along with her 3D holographic ID enlarged. Soon the hologram started rotating, making it easier to recognize her from different angles, a standard procedure. At the age of fourteen, she, a human, began studying Inves, an object programming language as a hobby. Inves made it easier to locate just about any address on Cirok.

She received a Bachelor's degree in Criminology from Opel University, a school on Maen's north coast. Maen was crowded. After three years, the Dedr War had claimed forty thousand lives.

In the last five years, during her time at Precinct Eight, a police station located in Zaas, a city near Maen's south coast, she photographed, then scanned forty-eight crime scenes and discovered melanocyte particles. These particles, skin cells, all left by suspects made it possible for her and a partner to convict nine murderers. According to her partner, Mara grasped forensic science much faster than anybody he had ever known.

The next dawn, after Judge Kin gave me a warrant, I stood in front of 202 Trimson accompanied by Dox. A garbled message came out of a door-mounted speaker. *If you . . .*

I announced, blinking, "We have a warrant. Let us in."

Silence, the resident didn't respond.

I squeezed the trigger. My gun's beam destroyed the lock. Dox kicked the door open. Both of us rushed inside. This warehouse was empty, stripped bare.

In my lenses, text and videos, the result of insect pattern software analysis popped up. According to the text and the videos, the floor mites were gray, or 50 percent black. These insects, which had been hiding under furniture, had been exposed to ultraviolet light within the last three hours because somebody had removed every chair, desk, and cabinet. If the mites hadn't been exposed to UV during that time, they would be 100 percent black.

Both of us left and started talking with neighbors.

Forty minutes later, an older Aito woman explained that she had seen three battle-robots, all with cyan blue heads and orange arms, leave 202 Trimson twenty minutes before dawn.

I flinched, wishing my partner and I had arrived at that address forty minutes earlier.

Dox thanked her and sent out an all-points bulletin.

Within four hours, as we knocked on neighbor's doors, all of them without face recognition, a woman's face, an incoming call, came out of my lenses' background. She, a 412 Nota Way resident, a human who responded to the bulletin, told me that she saw a cream-colored battle-robot when it arrived at 403 Nota Way, a warehouse, six hours before she noticed the bulletin. I thanked her. Dox and I left.

We reached 403's huge entrance. A recorded statement came out of its wall-mounted speaker, announcing that the current resident didn't want to be disturbed, but leaving a message was acceptable. I offered one and sent a text email to Kin, asking for a search warrant. Knowing that we had to wait for several hours before he would give us the document, both of us departed.

Minutes later, after discovering that more neighbors weren't answering their doors, we went down the curved street and stood in front of another, 811. An incoherent message came out of a wall-mounted speaker. *Thank you . . .*

Detective Inq's face, an incoming call, appeared in my lenses. He frowned. "Somebody, they wouldn't give their name, just sent us a text email. Unfortunately, their email address was blocked. According to their message, five minutes ago, a battle-robot with a chrome body walked out of a warehouse located at twenty-four Cas Way."

"That email sounds suspicious."

He glowered. "Yes."

I told him about our current situation.

He nodded with his brow scrunched up.

My jaw muscles tightened, a frustrated response. "The android at twenty-four Cas Way might not be the one we're looking for."

He frowned. "That is correct."

Dox said, "We'll go to twenty-four Cas. It's our only lead."

We stood in front of its entrance, one with old flaking paint. At its top, a camera hummed, signifying that it had just scanned my retina. Then it announced incoherently, "We . . . Call . . ." On a cracked door-mounted screen, a man's ear, the only part of his head that wasn't covered by dots, flickered.

Dox blurted, "Another failure. Damn it."

I nodded, agitated. Nobody opened the door. We left.

My partner and I returned to 811. Its door, an entry made of suspended particles, vanished, revealing an Aito man with gray hair.

Dox's badge materialized. She told him about our search.

He flinched. "About ten minutes before you arrived, I heard a loud grinding. It might have come from eight twenty. But I'm not sure. It could have been eight twenty-four."

Dox asked, "Did you go outside to find out what was making the noise?"

He shook his head. "No. Going outside is dangerous. A robber might assault me."

I blinked, annoyed that he couldn't tell us more and thanked him for his time.

My partner pointed out that if he remembered seeing or hearing any battle-robots, he should call us.

This frowning resident said he would.

Dox's wristwatch sent her phone number, email address, and badge number into his ear-mounted phone. We left, then knocked on eight twenty. Nobody answered. Both of us tried eight twenty-four. A muffled voice, an incoherent statement, came out of a wall-mounted speaker.

She commented, "My guess is that the android used the email as a diversion. The robot wanted us to go to twenty-four Cas so it would have enough time to escape."

"I agree. The diversion worked. There is another problem. My Probe and Evaluate Application can't find any battle-robots."

Dox gnashed her teeth.

The next morning, I parked in front of 13 Appian Street, two blocks from 24 Cas. Yesterday, my new partner told me she would be standing in front of this sepia house at eight in the morning.

Where is she?

I waited, and my stomach muscles began to tighten because I was uneasy about her absence. I called her at home, using my lenses. Voicemail switched on, asking me to leave a message. I did. They dialed her office. Voicemail switched on. My lenses left one. I winced, shocked by her absence.

They dialed Frank.

His face came into view. He growled, "What's up?"

I told him about Dox.

He blurted, "Something is wrong. She's always on time. I just put out an all-points bulletin. I'll get back to you soon."

I thanked him, my adrenaline pumping. This bulletin would alert every police officer on Lasho. Unfortunately, because there were only six hundred of them, finding my missing partner would be tough.

Twenty minutes later, Frank's blurred face, a new call,

focused. He glowered. "Nobody has responded to the bulletin and four officers, her other partners, haven't seen or heard from her in the last twenty-four hours."

I thanked him for his efforts, chills running down my spine, a horrified response.

That evening, after speaking to eight Cas Way residents, and fifteen Appian Street residents, ones who said they didn't notice any battle androids, I gave them my email address, and told them to contact me if they had any information regarding Dox's disappearance. Without warning, Frank's face, a new call, came out of my lenses' background.

He glowered while telling me that there wasn't any new information regarding her.

I thanked him, my jaw muscles tensed, an alarmed response.

The next morning, when I was in Unif Police Station Four's parking lot, Sultra arrived, dressed in the sexy outfit she had worn before.

I said, "Your cheekbones are higher. You look more beautiful than ever."

She grinned. "My hearing is better, too. However, I feel a little dizzy, light headed."

Both of us climbed inside a new police cruiser. It rose, and we sped away. Inches above its dashboard, a foot-high 3D hologram of the battle-robot that had attacked us, enlarged and started rotating. This hologram, based on my testimony along with a new database and neighbor's descriptions, would help us find the android.

I told her about Dox's disappearance.

She gasped. "That's outrageous."

I nodded. In my mind's eye, one horrible possibility, a robot shot Dox in the back, and she keeled over, dead. We flew between recently constructed apartments, many with cracks in them. Although engineers and architects wanted to put up safe dwellings, they didn't have enough time to inspect each one. Our cruiser entered smog.

Sultra coughed. "My eyes hurt like hell and the air stinks." She spat out the window.

"Mine hurt, too. This pollution is out of control."

Within minutes, we flew over the Saal Ocean, fifty-three feet above it. I said, "According to echo-imaging software, the battle-robot is thirty miles ahead of us, riding an air motorcycle, headed due west." My echo-imaging software's maximum range was two hundred miles. There were problems. If a suspect's airborne vehicle or aircraft were two hundred feet above or fifty feet below my wrist scanner, echo-imaging wouldn't notice it. If I maintained an altitude of two hundred feet or higher, echo-imaging wouldn't detect the battle-robot. Air Motorcycles could travel four thousand miles before they needed more fuel.

"Good. Let's make love."

I switched the steering to automatic. As Dox's face, a haunting memory, popped into my head, I caressed Sultra's cheek.

We finished. She cooed, "That felt good."

I smiled. The engine stalled and the cruiser descended.

Sultra blurted, "Shit."

As my adrenaline started pumping, the vehicle hit the water. Then it bounced across whitecaps, stopped and began sinking. I waved my hand over the ignition screen.

I flinched. "The engine won't start. Damn it."

She hollered, asking, "Is there any other way to get it started?"

An image of the engine materialized in my lenses, an

automatic process. "I'm checking on it."

"Oh my god. Water is leaking through the floor."

My stomach muscles tightened, a terrified reaction. "According to my lenses, mutated amoebas have shorted out four of the engine's circuits."

She pointed out the window. "A Predu is sixty feet from us, coming this way. These fish eat flesh."

I glanced in that direction and noticed a five-foot-high fin. "I see it." The predator opened its huge mouth, then rammed its snout against Sultra's door.

My partner bellowed, "Lousy bastard."

The engine roared to life. The vehicle rose, lurched forward and sped up.

Sultra gaped at me, a horrified expression on her face. "Finally. That was shitty."

I exhaled, trying to calm down. "Yes."

Chapter Four

Within two hours, under a star-filled sky, our vehicle flew over a beach and went between two five-thousand-foot-high peaks. I steered to the right. Our cruiser descended, then stopped, hovering. Drill bits came out of the chassis' left side, then entered a four-thousand-foot-high cliff, boring fast and halted. My colleague's stiletto boot heels whirred as they retracted into her sole.

The two of us climbed out, shoved the toes of our boots into cracks, then placed them in other holes, moving to the right, a route that went around the cliff.

Within moments, we stopped. At the same time, our blue jumpsuits changed to mottled sepia and gray, camouflaging us.

Ahead, on the opposite side of a hundred-foot-wide gorge, a forty-foot in diameter camouflaged cave entrance appeared in my lenses, the result of a recent echo-imaging probe. According to the probe, the air motorcycle had entered this cave fifteen minutes ago.

Sultra murmured in my ear, "Let's hope that echo-imaging is accurate. That might be solid rock, not a cave door."

I nodded, my adrenaline pumping. Wanting to locate a natural bridge, a way to reach the entrance, I looked up, then noticed there weren't any and frowned. I raised my right arm. An arrow, a projectile with a tether on it, shot out of my sleeve, then hit the gorge's opposite side, next to the cave entrance. I grabbed this end of the tether, one with a tiny drill on it and placed it against the cliff. The tool bored into the cliff, attaching the line to the cliff. A hook dropped out of the tether. Gloves came out of my sleeves and covered my hands.

I grabbed the hook, and it started across the gorge, attached to the tether. As my adrenaline pumped harder, the hook stopped, halfway across.

CHAPTER FIVE

I looked up, teeth clenched, wondering why it had stopped. Then I raised my right hand, wanting to grab the tether, an attempt to reach the cave entrance by using a hand over hand method. As my mind sped up, trying to figure out what I could do if the thin cord cut through my gloves, the hook lurched forward. While my heart pounded faster, a nervous reaction, I reached a foot-wide ledge, next to the entrance. Within seconds, I let go of the hook, and it went across the line, headed toward Sultra.

She grabbed the hook, and it zoomed across the gorge. Behind her, a bat with a ten-foot-wide wingspan came out of a hole, one on the gorge wall. Without warning, it started flying around her dangling feet. She kicked at it. The bat hissed, saliva dripping off its fangs. Soon it departed, hissing.

As my stomach muscles tightened, a worried reaction, she reached the ledge, placed both feet on it, and let go of the hook. I stuck out my left hand, wanting to grab hers. Sultra took a step and plummeted.

I glanced down, my heart pounding, a startled response. My partner was forty feet below me, holding onto a branch, her feet dangling.

I murmured, "Line assistance." A tether popped out of my left sleeve. Soon the tether uncoiled, creaking, a barely audible noise. Sultra grabbed it, her face tensed and started up the cliff.

To my right, the entrance whirred. I looked in that direction as it opened. I blinked, surprised. A triangular planetary transport carrier, thirty feet long, flew out of it. The door hissed closed.

I stooped, glanced to the left, grabbed my partner's hand

and pulled her onto the ledge.

She wiped dirt off her face, her jaw muscles tensed.

I stood and turned right. In my lenses, information, the result of a recent echo-imaging probe, scrolled. *This hatch only opens when its Aircraft Shape Evaluator detects specific hull shapes.*

Sultra whispered in my ear, "More problems."

I nodded with teeth clenched. The Evaluator was designed to keep intruders out. The entrance opened. We rushed inside a poorly lit cave and crawled under a parked twenty-foot-long spider-shaped wall-crawler, a vehicle designed to scale mountains. To our right, in the middle of this dimly lit thirty-foot in diameter space, another planetary transport carrier, five feet longer than the first, flew by, engine droning and left the cave. Soon the droning was replaced by a whirring, the sound of the entrance closing.

To our left, a deep bass rumbling grew louder. Without warning, it stopped.

Sultra's message scrolled through my lenses. *There must be an entrance to another room nearby.*

I sent her a text response, signifying that she was probably correct. We stood and yanked out our weapons. They expanded. Both of us walked, moving toward the spot where the rumbling came from. My partner and I passed a stalactite. Close by, a poorly lit six-foot-tall humanoid, just a silhouette, darted toward us.

I squeezed the trigger. My automatic weapon clicked, wouldn't fire.

Sultra's weapon hummed, malfunctioning. She punched the stranger's face. His head lurched backward, responding to the blow. Without warning, he ducked. At the same time, he smashed his fist against her chest. She jerked backward.

I shot him in the neck. He keeled over. As Sultra rose to her feet, groaning, I dragged him toward the entrance. When both of us were close to it, he kicked my right leg. I fell and ended up on my side.

CHAPTER SIX

The entrance hissed open. A triangular planetary transport carrier flew inside and zoomed by us. A laser beam from my partner's weapon struck his back. He stumbled, then fell into the canyon, shouting, "Help." Within seconds, the door shut.

Sultra grabbed my hand and pulled me up. While my adrenaline pumped faster, both of us turned, then walked toward a doorway, and stepped inside a twenty foot by twenty foot dimly lit room, guns raised. In the near distance, a seven-foot-tall Qio jumped out from behind a wall, blasting.

To my right, Sultra disappeared, vaporized by this stranger's weapon.

I winced and fired at the shooter. A laser beam struck my left arm. As white-hot pain raced through it, he fell to his knees. I squeezed the trigger. Bullets ripped one side of his head off, and he dropped to the floor.

I said, "ODOS," sending a text message, Officer Dead On the Scene, to Frank. As images of my former lover, a fond memory, went through my mind, I took a deep breath, trying to calm down. Soon I glanced at my wound, a superficial cut. Medication came out of my sleeve, spread across the injury and the bleeding stopped. Within a few hours, it would heal. I raised my hand, wishing it would stop trembling. It did not.

Frank's response scrolled. *Sultra's replacement will arrive in the near future.* The message vanished, not offering any more information.

My lenses sent neutrinos into the dead stranger's lenses, wristwatch and one micron in diameter ear-mounted phone. The particles returned. According to them, his name was Ru Lem. His boss, Kolo, a stranger whose face or DNA wasn't on my database, had murdered Tavo because she overheard a conversation regarding Overton.

Was Overton a person, a city, a street or something else? My lenses' search engine began probing another database, one in Ru Lem's lenses. Results popped up. Half an hour ago, Kolo had left the northern end of the Munt, bound for Coet, a space station that was orbiting Lasho. I spun around and darted away. The door hissed opened. A planetary transport carrier entered. I rushed past the crawler's port side, inches from the cave wall, hoping the carrier's pilot didn't notice me.

I stepped inside my cruiser. It rose and accelerated. My lenses sent a message to Frank, telling him that I was headed for Coet.

CHAPTER SEVEN

In the near distance, two planetary carriers flew out of Coet, a globe-shaped space station. Lights around an entrance flashed. My cruiser decelerated, went inside, and touched down, then the hatch opened. My jumpsuit changed into a taupe business suit, clothes that many Coet residents wore. This new outfit would make it harder for any fugitives, bandits or Kolo to notice me. I exited.

In my lenses, text, a new message from Frank, scrolled. According to it, my new partner, Evers, a Qio humanoid from Af Wa, a town near Roov's west coast, would arrive in twenty minutes. Beneath this update, her background enlarged. At the age of eleven, after discovering a website with calculus on it, this new colleague figured out which equations could be used to determine how a spacecraft engine's Ion drives functioned. Her parents, who didn't have enough money to hire a teacher or send her to a better school, were amazed that she had picked up this information so much faster than any of her classmates.

One year later, in the autumn, during her first semester at Uip College, she read sixty books, titles that helped her understand how base pairs within DNA were used to create molecules, organisms that would ID a victim's ashes. Before this, other detectives couldn't ID them as quickly because these micron-sized particle's elements had been changed by intense heat along with the injection of mutated streptococcus, a technique that many criminals used to disguise their evil deeds.

Two days after receiving undergraduate degrees in Biochemistry and Police Science, she took the officer placement test, one that every applicant had to pass if they wanted to work for Af Wa's police department. Because she received an A, this rookie asked for and was assigned to the homicide division.

A month later, her partner, Nico, discovered a colleague's headless corpse. The assailant had vaporized the missing body part with a laser gun. Although they spent eight months on this case, Evers and Nico couldn't locate or determine who the killer was.

The following year, when both of them were inside a dimly lit warehouse, searching for a kidnapper who had abducted a surgeon's eight-year-old son, Nico disappeared. Evers and her new partner spent five months looking for him, but couldn't come up with any leads. As a result, her supervisor, Bex, assigned both to the Moolin case.

Six weeks later, in her spare time, when Evers was searching through 3D holographic files, an attempt to find out what happened to Nico, she noticed one that interested her. In it, Danae, a prostitute, an eyewitness, told the jury that Slock, a drug dealer had killed Nico at two in the afternoon by cutting her in half with smart bullets. Unfortunately, the jury decided that Slock was innocent because two of his friends stated that he had spent that entire day at a party, a gathering that was two miles away from 67 Brown Street, the spot where the murder took place.

Slock's attorney, Greb, told the jury that both of his client's friends were honest businessmen. However, Greb didn't mention that both businesses, grocery stores, were fronts, places where Slock's friends sold a lot of ente and morib, illegal, drugs.

Evers shared this information with her colleagues. Unfortunately, all of them told her there wasn't enough evidence to convict Slock.

Although Evers' testimony, along with 3D holograms and videos helped convict eleven killers, and fourteen kidnappers, 81 percent of her cases, the rest, unsolved ones, bothered this detective.

Two months ago, she was transferred to Precinct Nine. Many Qio, a race, loved Mandelbrot's equations. 80 percent of the time, these equations made it possible for some Qio detectives to identify robbers, murderers, rapists, and other criminal's techniques much faster than most humans could.

At the edge of a crowd, a five-foot-eleven-inch tall white human woman, a brunette in a gray spacesuit, an outfit that some Coet residents wore, strolled toward me.

In my lenses, her face, a hologram, vanished and was replaced by Evers' real one, a beautiful countenance. Like many Qio, her skin was tan, mottled with white streaks. At the bottom of her four-inch high triangular ears, lights on this new colleague's diamond-shaped phone flashed, signifying that she had just received another 3D holographic email.

She offered a forced grin, then frowned. "Judging by that look on your face, something is bothering you."

In my mind's eye, a fond memory, Sultra caressed my hand. I lied, "This case is getting on my nerves. At any rate, your file is impressive."

"Thanks. Unfortunately, according to my last message, Kolo jumped into crisis pod fourteen two seconds ago. The craft will eject in one minute."

I winced. A crisis pod was used if this space station was severely damaged, ready to fall apart. "Let's hop into pod twenty, the closest."

She blurted, "These pods haven't been thoroughly tested yet."

"I know." We sprinted through a crowd.

A woman yelled, "Don't push me."

The eleven-foot-long bullet shaped pod's transparent lid

whirred open and air rushed inside, whooshing. I climbed in its front seat, one of two.

Behind me, Evers said, "There isn't much room. It's hard to move my legs."

"Understood. Brace yourself."

"No Tep shit."

The lid clicked shut. Teps, a rat-like species, always stunk. The craft shot forward, rumbling. My body jerked backward, less than an inch, supported by the quivering seat. My lenses sent a video message to Frank, telling him we were inside a pod, bound for an unknown destination on Lasho. The lenses' receive field remained blank, indicating that he hadn't responded to my message.

Evers announced, "According to my lenses, Kolo is forty miles ahead of us, bound for the west side of the Munt."

My adrenaline pumped faster. I thanked my partner for the update and told her that Frank hadn't responded to my message. Although our lenses and wrist scanners were helpful, they couldn't create detailed maps of any jungle.

She called out, "He didn't respond to mine either."

To my left and right, cockpit-mounted touchscreens started rattling, a nerve-wracking sound. One broke off and whizzed by my left shoulder. Behind me, an object shattered.

My partner blurted, "That touchscreen missed my left cheek by an inch."

I sighed, teeth clenched while remembering that dangerous vipers and wild beasts roamed the Munt.

Evers announced, "The lid is shaking. If we're lucky, it won't break off."

I winced. "Yes."

Outside, on the pod's nose, a tiny antenna snapped off and bounced off the lid. I flinched. Within seconds, the smell of burned plastic become stronger.

She yelled, "Something might be on fire."

"Yes." I waved my hand over a touchscreen. "I just activated emergency monitor four." This tool was designed to spot malfunctioning equipment, switch it off and use other circuits.

She exclaimed, "The stench is getting worse."

At the bottom of the touchscreen, fuel volume dropped. The pod would run out of it in two minutes.

Evers barked, "According to my lenses, we have an eleven percent chance of landing in the Munt in one piece."

My stomach muscles tightened in a horrified reaction. "Thanks for the update."

Our craft shot between cliffs.

Evers yelled, "Tep shit."

It went between trees, ripping off branches. Soon it plummeted, hit underbrush, bounced, landed on more, kept going, and knocked down ferns. Without warning, the lid snapped off.

Evers hollered, "Yow."

I blenched. The pod came to a halt, its nose upward, six feet off the ground, on top of gigantic mushrooms, ones illuminated by early morning light. "Are you okay?" Helmets came out of our collars and covered our heads and faces.

"My neck hurts, but it isn't broken."

"Great." We climbed out slowly. Our suits and helmets turned sepia, mottled with ochre, camouflaging us. Two-inch long purple flies started buzzed around our helmets.

She announced, "This helmet and its face mask is blocking my peripheral vision." Both went back inside her collar. "That's better."

I swatted the insects. Some flew away.

My partner hit one. "If only we could get rid of these pests."

"I agree."

She frowned. "My lenses' receive field hasn't received any phone calls, text messages, three D holographic messages or emails from Frank or any Unif Police Station Four officers since we touched down on Lasho. According to Aito statistics, there is a thirty percent chance that hackers are blocking Frank or any Unif officer's attempts to contact me."

"Are you sure hackers are blocking them?"

"Hell no. According to a Qio computer model, there is a forty percent chance that solar winds in Lasho's stratosphere are destroying any messages or any calls from them. My Atmosphere Particle Detection software is checking these results, will provide an answer soon." She hesitated, an irritated expression on her face.

I paused, thinking. 40 percent of the time, Particle Detection software, one of my lenses' tools, would display helpful answers.

Evers moaned. "However, subatomic particles or something else, I don't know what jammed my lenses. As a result, a text warning didn't appear in them. A few minutes ago, when my other functions were scrolling, I noticed that the Alert Function was disabled. Normally, it repairs itself. This time, for unknown reasons, it didn't. With any luck, at some point, it will."

My stomach muscles tightened with an irritated response. The Alert Function, which had been tested in the Grend Police Academy's 3D holographic jungles for eight months, had only broken down three times.

Evers frowned. "Grend Academy IT staff should have tested it in the real world, not just in three D holographic jungles."

"Yes, they should have tested it in the real world." In an emergency, my lenses were designed to call Frank every two minutes.

"There is another problem. My Atmosphere Particle

Detection only functions eleven percent of the time. Frank should have given us a three D holographic map. We'll have to use terrain guide for the time being."

I said, "Yes, we'll have to." Terrain guide used our eye's cryptochrome to probe an area that was within a ten-mile radius of my lenses. Within seconds, cryptochrome, a sixth sense, would display a 3D holographic map, a tool that would show us which route was the fastest even if we ended up in a jungle, the mountains or at the bottom of a gorge.

"You look distracted. What's wrong?"

"Nothing. I'm weighing options."

My partner shrugged. "Understood."

"Somebody, I don't know who, just sent eight hundred computer viruses into my lenses' Alert Function. As a result, its text warning hasn't appeared in them. According to recent lenses' probe, a hacker started jamming my lenses' scans two minutes after we jumped inside pod twenty."

"Those hackers are a pain in the ass."

My stomach muscles tightened, an irritated response.

"I wish I knew why my Alert Function broke down. Its failure bugs the shit out of me. We'll have to wait."

I bit my lip, irritated. "According to terrain guide, there is a thirty percent chance that Kolo's pod touched down in Ool, an outpost. Ool is twenty miles north of us, two miles beyond the Doet Mountains."

My partner scowled. "That's a long way from here."

I blinked, shocked because she was correct. "When we reach Ool, there is a forty percent chance my echo-imaging can locate Kolo."

"My wrist scanner updated itself yesterday. When we reach Ool, it has a forty-two percent chance of finding him."

I bit my lip, upset by her condescending attitude. Then I lied, wanting to sound reasonable, "Good." We hiked past a four-foot-high pile of dung.

She glanced at the dung. "It stinks."

I coughed, reacting to the stench. "Yes, it does." In the near distance, many ten-foot-high bushes began shaking. Both of us yanked out our tiny automatic weapons. They expanded.

To my right, Evers glowered while pointing at them. "Something is hiding behind them, coming toward us. The problem is that my echo-imaging can't ID it because the bush's movement is confusing the imaging process."

Chills ran across my spine, a terrified response. 51 percent of the time, leaf movement overwhelmed the process. Without warning, the bushes stopped jerking.

"Whatever it is, it just changed direction, and is headed for that distant cliff."

I glanced in that direction. Eighty yards away, hidden behind several eighty-foot-high palms, a creature bellowed. *Oooona.*

"Shit. Whatever made that noise must be huge. Anyway, both my wrist scanner and echo-imaging can't ID that either."

I bit my lip, shocked by our equipment's shortcomings, and we trekked. In my lenses, text, the result of recent imaging probes, indicated that there weren't any humanoids within seventy yards of us.

"Judging by that look on your face, you're pissed off."

"That's true." Both of us came upon a fifteen-foot-wide stream, an obstacle with hundreds of sixteen-foot-long yellow millipedes in it. I winced. "According to my terrain guide, we'll have to cross here because the only bridge, a fallen tree, is nine miles to our right, not far beyond a five-thousand high, impossible to climb, mountain ridge, part of the Roog."

She grumbled. We raised our weapons above our heads, hiked into shoulder-high water, surrounded by the ugly invertebrates and kept going. To my left, two opened their jaws, croaked, then spit onto my left shoulder. As vapors rose out of the foul-smelling drool, my stomach started churning, reacting to the stench. We reached the opposite shore and trudged on.

After hiking over five sabal palmetto-covered hills, both of us went between towering ferns, a gloomy part of the jungle.

Evers wiped the sweat off her chin. "It's muggy."

"Do you want to take a break?"

"No."

All around us flies peeped. Far away, unseen creatures hooted.

My partner said, "According to my wrist scanner, two vipers, species that are forty yards from us, on my right, are talking about our loud footsteps."

I cringed. "Your scanner is sophisticated. Mine can't detect any snakes."

She offered a half-hearted grin.

"Does it have language conversion?" This software translated Qio humanoid speech along with that humanoid race's text messages and eight other languages into English and vice versa.

"Yes."

I smiled, impressed. Ahead, hidden behind a twenty-foot-high wall of creepers, gunfire rang out. Chills ran across my spine, a nervous response. "Somebody is firing M-eleven rifles." These only fired dumb bullets, projectiles without homing devices in them.

"Yes. The shooters must be poor." We stooped, wanting to avoid being hit and trekked.

In the early afternoon, thirty minutes later, my partner and I came upon the bottom of a four-thousand-foot-high cliff, part of the Roog.

She glanced to the right and left, glowering. "The shooters are gone. I hate climbing this, but the closest pass is fourteen miles away."

I nodded. My partner started up a narrow ledge, the best route available on the steep rock face, me behind her.

At noon, we sat on a ledge. Three thousand feet below us, somewhere in the jungle, gunfire rang out. I said, "My lenses just sent neutrinos into several spots below me, but they didn't return. Finding out who the shooters are and what they're doing will take more time."

"Yes, more time. Something, I don't know what's interfering with my lenses ability to evaluate returned neutrino probes."

I blinked, frustrated. "That something could be solar winds or phage. I wish I had more information regarding Lasho's atmosphere and microorganisms."

"I hate this. Yes, we need more information."

Fourteen thousand feet from my partner and me, a mortar shell struck a palm and tore it apart.

I said, "It would be nice to know who fired that."

My partner glanced at the jungle, squinting. "No doubt about it."

CHAPTER EIGHT

The next morning, after I woke from a nightmare, both of us resumed the journey.

Evers frowned. "Judging by that expression on your face, something is bothering you."

"Yes. Every night I dream about Sultra's death."

"If I can help, let me know."

I nodded, wincing. We headed downslope.

Just before noon, both of us reached a fifteen-mile-wide bamboo grove, an obstacle in another part of the Munt. Laser beams came out of our automatic weapons and chopped several of the plants apart, creating a six-foot-long path. My partner and I advanced as the beams sliced more.

Within two hours, we came upon a lone Qio, a twenty-something gaunt male in a tattered jacket who was standing between several kapok trees.

He glared at us. "Who are you?"

Both of us gave him our names, then asked him what his was.

He pushed sweat off his furrowed brow with a trembling hand. "Lonn. Those are well-designed outfits. Are you Special Forces?"

We didn't answer.

"Damn it, you won't tell me. Why did you come to this hell hole?"

Evers replied, "We could ask the same about you."

He spat on the ground. "Three weeks ago, after leaving Nipl, wanting to get away from the war, my wife and I fled and ended up in Last Chance, a peaceful outpost. Two days after we arrived, four Qio men with guns showed up. Two demanded that we give them our money. My wife complained, said we needed it to buy food. One of them shot her in the head, killing her.

"As tears rolled down my face, two of them took me to a clearing. When we arrived, they told me to turn around. I did while asking both what they were going to do and these assholes told me to keep quiet. Within minutes, somebody I couldn't see shot both, and I ran away. I've been hiding in different parts of the Munt since then."

Evers mentioned Kolo.

He glowered. "I don't know him or her. But I overheard some strangers. One said that Kolo was in Last Chance."

I asked, "Did they mention anything about Overton?"

Lonn frowned. "One said that it was a machine."

Evers scowled. "Did they say what kind of machine it was?"

He replied, a blank expression on his face, "No."

I blinked, disappointed by his answer. Then I offered a polite white lie, not wanting to make him an enemy. "Thanks for the update." Nipl, a town in Cirok's northern hemisphere, was in the United Territories, a country on Grend's east coast. Grend, a continent, was six thousand miles long, four thousand miles wide. My lenses sent neutrinos into his mind. The tiny particles didn't return. I bit my lip, frustrated.

Lonn blurted, "Are you going to kill me?"

Evers replied, "No."

The neutrinos returned to my lenses. According to the lenses, Lonn was from Nor, a small town on Coam and he was single. More text indicated that one of Kolo's men had sent this assassin to murder us. A Torp, a pistol that fired smart bullets, projectiles with homing devices, was underneath his armpit, hidden by this man's rumpled clothes.

He yanked out his weapon and fired.

My partner jumped to the right.

I jerked mine out, then pulled the trigger. Bullets struck his neck. He took a few steps and collapsed.

Evers stood, trembling. "That was an ugly surprise. Did you know Lonn had a gun?"

"Yes."

My partner glowered. "How did you know that?"

I mentioned my lenses' analysis.

Her eyes opened wider. "We're lucky yours functioned properly. According to my wrist scanner, mine aren't because wimbas and other trees are sending out electrons, particles that are jamming four of my lenses transmitters."

My stomach muscles tightened, a nervous reaction. "I've never heard of trees doing that."

"I didn't think they could jam them either. It's a shocking revelation."

I bit my lip, upset by this new challenge.

Evers scowled. "Did you think he would attack us so soon?"

"I wasn't sure. When the analysis first appeared in my lenses, it caught me off guard. Much to my surprise, he reached toward his armpit, wanting to use his Torp."

She blinked. "It happened so fast. I thought he was going to scratch his arm."

"He is quick, a skilled assassin."

My partner's brow tightened. "Why did your lenses' analysis work properly?"

"After seventy failures, their Neural Network figured out how to destroy viruses, phages, and bacteria, organisms that had recently shorted out some of my lenses' bio-circuits. As a result, my lenses blocked the particles that were jamming its transmitters. Unfortunately, I didn't know they had shorted out some until a few minutes ago."

My partner reached down, touched a hole on her

bulletproof jumpsuit's waistline and flinched.

I flinched, shocked that ammo had gone through her jumpsuit. "Are you injured?"

"Just sore. The pain will go away soon. Part of his ammo also tore a half an inch layer off my suit."

She blurted, "Check functionality," manually activating an application.

CF automatically examined lenses, searching for a breakdown. This time, for unknown reasons, this tool failed.

She hesitated, a distraught expression on her face. "Fifteen software apps are broken. Hopefully, check functionality can repair them within a few hours."

"Hopefully."

"Judging by that look on your face, you're just as shocked as I am by its problems."

"That is correct." In front of us, a one-inch long triangular shaped drone called the Incessant Search flew out of adjacent ferns.

Evers froze, wanting to stop making noise. She pointed at the drone.

I nodded, indicating that I noticed it while my stomach muscles tightened, a horrified response. In my lenses, her text message flashed. *Although it's designed to notice any strange attractors in the air, ones our bodies created, it hasn't spotted us yet.*

Strange attractors, temporary structures in the air, water and gas, changed every few seconds.

Without warning, it started circling her head. She blenched.

I touched my right thumb with my right forefinger, activating a command. My lenses sent a fake algorithm into the drone's sensor, telling the aircraft there was a 40 percent chance that a humanoid intruder was two miles from it, due west of this location. The drone took off, flying in that direction.

My partner offered a quick smile. "I'm glad your fake

message fooled it."

"So am I. It will probably return soon. Let's go." We marched.

Within minutes, as both of us stepped over lupuna roots, a rustling, about eighty yards ahead, coming from a spot that was hidden in shadows, grew louder.

My partner raised her weapon while murmuring, "My wrist scanner can't ID whatever it is that's making the noise."

I winced. "Mine can't either."

Not far above the ground, a three-eyed lemur jumped out from behind a wall of leaves, hooting. Without warning, it grabbed a branch, and swung away, bound for a distant palmetto.

Evers shook her head. "All that worrying for nothing."

"We were lucky. It might have been an assassin."

"Yes, we were. This humidity is awful, makes me tired."

I nodded. We trudged on, beneath two-hundred-foot-high acacias, trees that blocked out the sky while the stench of mucus, a red substance that an unseen creature had sprayed on nearby mushrooms, became stronger. My stomach began churning, responding to the stench.

At dusk, tiny compressed tents, both coming out of our sleeves, landed in the dirt. Soon both camping equipment that was hidden inside 3D holographic grass expanded. Tiny chairs dropped out of our sleeves. At the same time, both seats opened. We sat down.

Minutes later, a nearby rustling grew louder.

As hazy shapes, partly resolved images, appeared in my lenses, the result of an echo-imaging probe, both of us yanked out our weapons.

In the near distance, three Qio women in grimy pants and

ripped tops stepped out of towering bushes.

The tallest, a stranger with orange hair, said, "My name is Pre. All three of us are starving. Do you have any food to spare?"

My lenses sent neutrinos into her cerebral cortex and returned, signifying that she was telling the truth. The lenses repeated the procedure with the others, but nothing came back. My neck muscles tightened, a nervous response. I sent these results into my partner's lenses.

She blinked as her response scrolled through mine. *They won't send any neutrinos.*

I blenched, irritated that they wouldn't. "We don't have any to spare." I pointed to the right. "However, those succulents are edible. Break them open and eat the pulp."

Pre and her companions did.

I asked, "Do any of you know Kolo?"

All three shook their heads.

I paused, wondering what these strangers would do next.

Evers pushed a worm off her knee. "Do any of you live in Last Chance?"

The shortest sighed. "All of us used to."

Evers scowled. "Why did you leave?"

Pre frowned. "A week ago, a month after we arrived, a human woman told us to leave immediately because gangs, a group that would sell us into slavery, was hiking toward Last Chance. We fled and ended up in this area."

Evers frowned and thanked them for the information.

Pre nodded, hands trembling. "Sure. We need to leave now, before any Vablo, blood-sucking worms, arrive and attack." All three departed.

My adrenaline started pumping. "Is your tent equipped with halt intruder?" This tool, one of my tent's features, sent 2000 watts of electricity into anything that touched its outside wall.

Evers scowled. "Yes."

Moments after night set in, two Qio men with orange skin, both in torn, stained jumpsuits arrived.

Both of us pulled our weapons out.

The oldest, a thirty-something, flinched. "My name is Reod. Both of us are hungry. Do either one of you have any food to share?"

My lenses sent neutrinos into their cortexes and returned, pointing out that both men wanted to slaughter us, steal our money, and take any other valuables they could find.

Reod yanked out his Xi pistol and started blasting.

I dove to the ground, discharging my weapon.

Reod, took a few steps, staggering.

Behind him, the other one's Xi chattered, releasing a stream of bullets. As they whizzed past my ear, ammo struck his temple, ripping it off. He stepped back and fell.

While my mind sped up, wondering if anybody else would arrive, Reod sat up, his Xi aimed at me.

A laser beam, coming from Evers, struck his forehead. He screamed, "Iiii," then dropped to the ground.

I glanced to the right, sweating. "That's fancy shooting."

Evers blinked. "Thanks, but I'm getting tired of this shit."

I sighed, hands trembling. "Let's change our suit's appearance so that we resemble refugees." That way both of us would have a better chance of defending ourselves if we encountered more robbers or assassins.

"Good idea." Both suits became darker. At the same time, rips and dirt appeared.

She got up. "Now we look like them."

I offered a brief smile.

She walked toward Reod, her wrist scanner aimed at his neck. "No pulse." She pointed it at the other assailant.

"Dead?"

"No doubt about it."

Within minutes, we finished spraying fast drying polymers on the bodies. Soon acid inside the polymers started destroying both corpses, making it impossible for other assassins or robbers to figure out what happened to them. As a result, they wouldn't come after us, seeking revenge.

Moments before dawn, my partner and I departed.

An hour later, we came upon a gorge and started climbing down one its crevices. Ahead, three white human women, all dressed in rags, came toward us.

My lenses sent neutrinos into their minds. The tiny particles returned. But my lenses' Character Analysis Screen was blank. Beneath it, on another, text scrolled, indicating that five minutes ago mutated streptococcus had shut down Character Analysis' ability to process the particle's retrieved data. I clenched my teeth, disappointed.

The skinniest frowned. "They call me Truna. Who are you?"

Evers offered both of our names. Then she repeated our goal.

The other, a redhead with a huge scar on her nose, declared, "I haven't met him. My name is Nellie."

Truna squinted, an irritated expression on her face. "Brin and Evers, where are you from?"

Evers' brow tightened, but she didn't reply.

I remained silent, avoiding the question. If I answered and assassins tortured these women, wanting to know more about us, she might tell them. At that point, they would know for sure that we were detectives, not refugees. As a result, they would spend more time searching for my partner and me. My lenses sent neutrinos into Truna's hippocampus.

Nellie glared at me. "Why won't you answer? You're pissing me off."

Evers exhaled, a doubtful expression on her face.

Behind Nellie, the other, a short brunette with several missing teeth, wiped dirt off her big jaw. "I'm Wendy. Do you have any food?"

I said we didn't. My lenses sent neutrinos into Wendy's hippocampus.

Truna glowered. "All three of us are lonely. We want to come with you."

They sent neutrinos into Nellie's hippocampus.

Evers said that was fine with her and glanced at me, seeking my response.

I nodded. Although locating Kolo was my primary goal, the idea of leaving these hungry, desperate refugees behind struck me as being cold-hearted.

The particles returned. According to them, Wendy, a Naturalist who taught at Teto High School, had left Teto because gunmen were robbing her neighbors. She fled. Within hours she located a space vessel, one filled with refugees and climbed aboard. The ship touched down in the jungle, near Last Chance, and all the passengers exited, searching for food.

More particles came back. Nellie, a geologist, who taught at Zy City College, boarded a spacecraft because a neighbor warned her that a battle between sixteen Zy street gangs would break out soon. The craft landed near Last Chance, and all the passengers exited, searching for food.

Within the hour, our group reached the bottom of the gorge, a location filled with towering kapok trees and huge creepers. Hidden behind them, an animal shrieked. *Ohway.*

Evers glowered. "What made that noise?"

Truna started trembling. "That's a Gaoot. They tear off your flesh, then start eating you."

Evers and I yanked out our automatic weapons. They

expanded.

Nellie squinted, a suspicious expression her face. "You're either police or mercenaries."

I remained quiet, avoiding the statement.

Evers frowned. "Have you seen the Gaoot do this?"

Truna blurted, "Yes. Two months ago, one clawed my buddies' face off. I took off before it attacked me."

I cringed. "What do they look like?"

Wendy's forehead tightened. "They're ten-feet long, four-legged lizards, gray."

Evers blinked while our group advanced. To our right, hidden behind dangling vines, something cleared its throat, a raspy noise.

Wendy announced, "That's a Paxo. It's harmless."

I asked, "What does it look like?"

Wendy replied, "It's three feet long, hairy, with two long thin legs and skinny arms."

Particles returned. Truna was from Af Wa. She, a body nanite specialist, repaired these tiny machines, ones in the bloodstream, whenever they broke down. More information would be available later.

Everybody came upon the other side of the gorge wall, Wendy leading.

In front of me, Truna glanced to the right and left, scowling. "Sometimes Leet's men will rob you. Watch out."

Behind me, Evers asked, "Who is Leet?"

Truna responded, "He's a mean Qio, a refugee from Nipl, a city in the United Territories. Five star rises ago, he and several of his buddies, Naan supporters, found some body-sensing pistols and began robbing strangers."

According to my lenses, the city of Nipl was in Cirok's northern hemisphere. United Territories, a country, was on Grend. Four summers ago, during a street protest, UT Senator

Ang's followers and those who supported UT's President, Naan, started yelling at each other. Ang's followers complained that Naan's cabinet members needed to pass a bill that raised the minimum wage. A year later, these groups clashed on the outskirts of Nipl. A week after the conflict started, eight thousand of Ang's followers perished. Two days later, six thousand of Naan's supporters died.

Automatic body-shape sensing pistols' maximum range was four hundred yards. If a Qio, human or a member of the Aito race was farther away, this weapon's sensor couldn't detect them. A star rise was a term for one day.

Truna spun around, lunged at me and cut my sleeve with her knife. I did an about-face, blasting.

She pivoted, then stabbed Evers' stomach while my weapon's bullets hit this stranger's throat.

Truna screamed, tripped and ended up on her side, blood spurting out of her wound.

Evers took a few steps, staggering, her face contorted in agony.

I grabbed her arm, wanting to help my partner and she rested on her back. "The pain."

CHAPTER NINE

Evers' suit hummed, indicating that its medical nanites were suturing the deep cut. At the same time, they applied a combination of antibiotics and antigens to the wound. 52 percent of the time, the nanites saved a patient's life.

Chills ran up my spine, a horrified response.

Wendy glowered as she touched Truna's wrist. "She's dead. I didn't know she would attack you. I thought she was a harmless refugee."

Nellie exclaimed, "I met her two star rises ago. She was always kind to me."

Wendy flinched. "I met her eight star rises ago. She gave me berries."

I glanced at Truna. Her lips turned black. Without warning, nearby flesh became darker.

Wendy jumped up, pointing at Truna. "My friends call this horrible fungus, Awa. It's spreading, will cover her entire body soon. Then her flesh will begin falling apart. Let's get out of here. Somebody told me that Awa is contagious."

I stooped. The others placed Evers on my back, her chest against it. I grabbed her wrists, stood up, then walked.

My partner groaned.

"Are you okay?"

"Barely."

Twenty minutes later, in the early afternoon as we passed slimy bromeliads, all of them partly hidden in shadows, my partner groaned. "My stomach hurts like hell, but I'm alive."

I squeezed my partner's hand, trying to comfort her. "Would you like to spend the night here?"

She murmured, "Yes."

I halted and stooped. Others pulled her off, then placed my colleague on her back. A compressed tent came out of her sleeve and wrapped around my partner.

Wendy said, "I've never seen this kind of fancy tent before. Are you police or mercenaries?"

I remained silent, avoiding the question. If I answered and this acquaintance shared the information with refugees, marauders, bandits or Kolo's troops might hear about it and come after us.

Evers groaned.

Wendy's jaw muscles tensed up. "Why won't either one of you answer my question?"

I clenched my teeth, irritated by her inquiry.

Wendy's forehead tightened. She pointed at us. "Do you work for Kolo?"

In the far distance, hidden in darkness, a creature snorted. I flinched. "What made that noise?"

Wendy blenched. "A Gaoot."

In my mind's eye, a deadly possibility, it rushed at us.

At sunup, after Evers' tent and mine went inside our sleeves, Nellie glared at me. "Brin, Evers, are you Kolo's assassins or robbers?"

My partner gulped down seeds, ignoring the question.

Two Fen humanoids, five-foot-tall women with green skin, both in tattered coats, stepped out from behind towering bushes, their body-sensing pistols aimed at us. The fattest scowled. "Give us your money and guns."

Nellie glowered. "I don't have any."

Wendy shook her head. "I'm broke and don't got either one."

My partner and I handed them our automatic weapons and some coins.

The thin one shoved her gun barrel against my chest.

I blenched.

She glared at me. "Judging by your tents, you're probably mercenaries. Transfer your units into my phone."

I winced and sent them. Mercenaries carried units and cash. Units could be exported from lenses to ear-mounted phones or vice versa.

The fat robber aimed her weapon at Evers' temple. Without warning, she yanked out a knife and slashed my partner's wrist.

My colleague flinched while blood trickled out of the wound.

The fat robber snapped, "Yesterday, I shot two refugees, enjoyed listening to them beg for mercy while they bled to death."

Evers blinked.

I grabbed the thin one's gun barrel, then knocked it aside. A wrist-mounted knife popped out of my sleeve. I stabbed her neck with it. She stepped backward, screaming, "Yeeee," and stumbled.

My partner ducked while punching the fat one's stomach. At the same time, the fat one's weapon discharged. While bullets from her weapon struck my partner's ear, I spun around.

A knife popped out of Evers' sleeve. She stabbed the fat one's cheek. This stranger stepped backward, howling in pain, "Yooww."

As Wendy screamed, the fat one tripped and ended up in the dirt, face down.

Nellie started weeping.

I blinked, glanced over my left shoulder and noticed that the thin one was on her back, trembling. Without warning, she stopped moving. According to my wrist scanner, this stranger had died because she had fallen on a rock, one that crushed the back of her skull. I looked straight ahead while asking, "Evers, is your wound serious?"

She frowned. "No. Nanites will heal it."

I exhaled, trying to calm down. "Wendy, are you okay?"

She glanced at me, lips quivering.

I asked, "Wendy, are you injured?"

She coughed. "No."

Evers scowled. "Nellie, are you hurt?"

She shook her head while examining her shaking hand.

As my mind kicked into overdrive, trying to figure out how my partner and I could react faster to the next robber's arrival, I bit my lip, frustrated. Evers and I grabbed our automatic weapons.

My partner aimed her wrist scanner at both body-sensing guns. "These are equipped with genome sensing ID."

I nodded. 90 percent of the time genome ID would shut off if anybody but the original owners tried to use the firearm.

Nellie picked up a body-sensing gun, then squeezed the trigger. The weapon whirred. She blurted, "It won't fire." She tossed it away.

Wendy seized the other. "Are you sure?" She pulled the trigger. The weapon buzzed. "Junk." She cast it aside. All of us trekked. Above our group, a lemur-like creature came out of the shadows and began swinging from branch to branch.

Evers scowled while pointing at the creature. "What is that?"

Wendy laughed. "A Paxo."

Evers shrugged.

Two hours later as we slogged through a poorly lit area of the Munt, a bullet grazed my shoulder. I along with everybody else dove to the ground. A laser beam went past my ear. In my lenses, an echo-imaging probe indicated that a slender blonde Aito with blue skin had fired at me. Much to my surprise, this stranger, a woman with a huge nose, wide shoulders and a rapid discharge rifle dashed away and disappeared into the jungle. I whispered, "Evers, did you see the shooter?"

She murmured, "Briefly." My partner described the stranger I had just seen. "She took off before I could get a better look at her. If we're lucky, she won't return."

Chills ran across my spine. "Let's hope she won't. If we're lucky, she's alone." A quantum computer model's screen, a tool that my lenses invented within the last twenty-four hours, came out of my lenses' background. According to the model, 15 percent of Lasho's assassins owned rapid discharge rifles. 61 percent of its robbers used them as well. My lenses shared this information with Evers.

Nellie whispered, "I couldn't see her."

Wendy glanced at me. "I didn't see her either. Brin and Evers, how could you?"

Evers replied, fibbing, "It's our training."

Wendy glanced at my partner. "I wish I had that training." Evers shrugged.

I said, "Let's move on. If we do, it will be harder for that gunman or her friends to find us."

Soon our group started up a cliff, entering the Doet. Wendy announced, "Follow me. I know a great route."

Nellie said, "She's traveled through these mountains many times."

In my lenses, terrain guide information scrolled. *This area is complex. It will take thirty hours to create a map with safe paths.* I bit my lip, irritated by the results. Not wanting to annoy Wendy with more inquiries, I sent a text message to Evers, asking my partner if her terrain guide had provided a high-resolution topographic map of this area.

Her response came out of my earplugs, "No."

Within four hours, we reached an eight-thousand-feet-high

gap, a rocky area partly covered by snow.

Wendy huffed, then remarked, "This is the Deif Pass." All four of us descended. To our right, one hundred yards from our group, an avalanche started. Soon it rumbled louder.

Wendy bellowed, "It's coming this way."

I blenched as our crew veered left, hiking across loose rocks. Underneath Wendy's boot heel a couple of small ones rolled downhill. She tripped and crashed to the ground.

Nellie shouted, "We need to move faster."

I grabbed Wendy's hand and pulled this new friend up. She glowered. "We're going to die."

Without warning, the avalanche halted, several yards from us.

Evers called out, "That was too close for comfort."

Wendy groaned. "I agree."

Ahead, hidden behind a boulder, an animal shrieked. *Twaooo.*

Evers spat, "What made that awful noise?"

Wendy flinched. "I don't know, haven't heard anything like it before."

Nellie kept staring at the boulder, a terrified expression on her face. "Unknown. It's not a Gaoot."

I blenched, then yanked out my weapon, waiting for the unseen creature to strike.

CHAPTER TEN

As my heart beat faster, a terrified response, I walked toward the boulder, my gun aimed at it.

To my right, Evers frowned. Then she stepped over rocks, and her weapon pointed in the same direction as mine.

Behind us, Nellie called out, "Careful."

Evers passed the boulder and glanced behind it, her teeth clenched. "The creature left. There's a hole in the ground, a route it used to escape."

I exhaled, relieved. "Let's go. Forget about the creature."

Evers glanced at me with her brow scrunched up. "Okay."

Behind us, Wendy said, "Brin is right." Our crew advanced then entered fog.

I asked, "Wendy and Nellie, would you like some berries?" Both grinned.

I gave them some while the icy wind shoved us sideways.

Nellie glowered. "I hate crossing the Doet."

I sighed while flexing my cold fingers.

Wendy called out, "The Doet is a shitty place. It's freezing and scaling its cliffs hurts my back and legs."

Far away, a beast, hidden in the mist, screeched. *Wooeee.*

Evers blurted, "What made that sound?"

Wendy scowled. "A Ulo. It's a reptile that will rip your neck open, then suck your blood. If you see it, kill it."

I blenched. "Don't reptiles usually stay in the Munt?"

Wendy pushed snot off her runny nose. "Most of the time, yes. But, if they're hungry, they fly up here."

Within five hours, after climbing down slopes, our group came upon bamboo, another part of the Munt. We pushed them aside. To our left and right, somewhere behind poorly illuminated kapoks and towering vines, unseen insects chirped.

Evers' brow tightened. "Are crickets making that noise?"

Wendy blenched. "No, sigo worms are."

I blinked. "Are they dangerous?"

Wendy cleared her throat. "They don't bite. However, they spit. Their saliva will blind you."

Nellie blurted, "Sigos are a pain in the ass." We advanced, then hiked under a maze of eleven-foot-high roots. To our right and left, hundreds of three-foot-long slugs crawled over leaves.

I pointed at the mollusks. "What are those?"

Ahead, Wendy replied, "Foohs."

Evers scowled. "Are they edible?"

Wendy chuckled. "Yes, but they taste like shit." She grabbed one and shoved it in her mouth.

I cringed.

To my right, Nellie laughed. "Brin, you'll get used to the taste."

Evers seized one and took a bite. "Sour. Gooey."

I winced.

Evers swallowed. "Brin, does watching me eat this turn your stomach?"

I flinched, then lied, "No, go ahead."

Evers said, "Judging by the look on your face, it does. Oh well." She took another bite.

I looked away, wanting to examine something that wasn't repulsive.

After crossing three ridges, all of them partly covered by towering anthills, our party came upon ten huts, all made of branches and dirty wood planks.

Wendy bit off a fingernail and spat it out. "This is Ool. Several refugees used to live here. Marauders, Gaoots or something else must have scared them off."

I cringed. "Let's camp here."

Nellie scowled. "This place gives me the creeps. But I'm tired, need to rest."

Everybody else agreed with me. Evers handed out berries.

At dusk, when all of us finished eating, a rustling that was coming from a spot hidden behind towering ferns grew louder.

Evers murmured, "What's making that noise?"

Nellie mumbled, "It might be a Paxo."

Wendy hesitated, then whispered, "Whatever it was, it's gone."

I said, "I'll monitor this area until one in the morning." Although my echo-imaging alarm would wake us if an animal or a stranger came within fifty feet of our camp, it would take several moments for my partner and me to respond. Even if we did, spotting an intruder in the dark and hitting them with a first shot would be difficult.

Nellie said she would take over when my watch ended.

A few minutes after midnight, a pterodactyl-like creature with a ten-foot-wide wingspan, a barely noticeable silhouette in the darkness, silently glided by adjacent treetops, and disappeared behind a gigantic bromeliad.

To my right, Nellie whispered, "Another Ulo." She pulled out a long knife.

I flinched. "Thanks for the warning."

She offered a raised fist. In my lenses, the text became brighter. According to it, this gesture meant thank you. She rested her head on a backpack.

In the morning, our small group ate bland tasting mushrooms that Wendy had picked the day before. A helmet and a protective mask came out of my collar, then covered my face and head.

Nellie frowned. "You're a mercenary. Do you work for Leet?"

I bit my lip, ignoring the question.

Nellie spat, "You won't tell me."

Two hours later, Wendy and Nellie, who had taken the lead, yanked long knives out of their leg-mounted sheaths and started cutting their way through bamboo. Without warning, gunfire rang out.

Wendy blurted, "Somebody just shot me in the arm."

All of us dove to the ground. I crawled toward Wendy and placed a medical nanite bandage on her wound.

She murmured, "It hurts like hell."

I whispered in her ear, "Your arm will be . . ." Bullets grazed my left shoulder. My adrenaline pumped faster.

To my left, Evers crawled toward the noise. In my receive field, her message came out of the text filled background. *I'm going to crawl to the right, outflank them.*

My lenses responded, pointing out that her plan was a good idea. She went behind three-foot-high rocks, kept going and disappeared, hidden by thick underbrush.

On my right, Nellie shoved aside bamboo, then advanced and vanished, hidden in the shadows.

I looked straight ahead, then squeezed the trigger, assuming my smart bullets would detect our attacker's infrared heat signature and hit it.

Ammo struck the top of my helmet, tearing off pieces. I flinched, then ducked.

Wendy murmured in my ear, "Are you injured?"

I glanced at her, then whispered, "No," and put one finger over my mouth, telling her to keep quiet.

She glared at me as bullets sliced locks off this new friend's hair. She jerked her head down.

Chills ran down my spine, a horrified response. I looked straight ahead.

More shots tore off nearby branches. I blenched while discharging my weapon.

Evers shoved aside ten-foot-high grass and walked toward us, two rapid-fire rifles in hand.

I blinked. "This is a surprise."

My partner glowered. "I just killed two Qio women, the ones who were shooting at us. These are their weapons. After sixteen attempts, I figured out how to use self-same equations to switch off their genome ID. We should teach Wendy and Nellie how to use these guns."

I nodded. "Good idea. Did you spray the bodies?"

"Yes. Unfortunately, I used up all the polymers. Do you have any?"

"No."

She glowered while handing a rapid-fire rifle to Wendy.

Wendy frowned. "What does spraying the bodies mean?"

Evers replied.

Wendy scowled. "I've never heard of that technique."

To my left, Nellie came out of towering weeds. "I heard all that. Teach us how to use a rapid-fire."

Evers gave her the other weapon and pointed at screens, panels that were floating above the barrels.

Nellie's brow tightened. "Using this will be complicated."

Evers said, "You'll get used to it."

Wendy gnashed her teeth. "We'll see."

Nellie inspected her weapon. On its screen, one that was floating above the barrel, a purple grid changed into viridian, indicating that her rifle was scanning the adjacent jungle. She aimed it at a sabal palmetto and fired. "Missed. Shit."

Evers said, "Keep trying."

Nellie added, "Let's get the hell out of here. An assassin might have heard us."

Wendy remarked, "The easiest route is through the bottom of the Tret Canyon, a spot in the Munt that is between two steep, hard to scale cliffs. We'll have to climb the Ro Hom, a low mountain with a gradual slope to reach the Tret."

Evers announced, "Lead the way."

Tesk's blurred face, the result of a weak signal, appeared in my lenses. He scowled. "Can you . . ." His face vanished. At the same time, his voice faded and was replaced by static. I sent Evers a text message, telling her about his call.

Her response scrolled. *It materialized in my lenses for less than a second. The only thing I heard him say was you.*

My jaw muscles tightened with an angry response. Was he telling us to give up, end our mission? It was impossible for me to know.

At noon, as our group slogged between towering mushrooms, most of them in the shadows, Wendy called out, "We're a poto from the Tret."

According to my lenses, a poto was about the same length as a mile.

Ahead, in the far distance, hidden behind banyan roots, shots rang out. I flinched. "Nellie, Wendy, who is firing?"

Wendy pushed sweat off her face with a trembling hand. "Hard to tell. It's best to keep going."

Nellie flinched. "It could be Deng and his men. They live in this area."

Wendy clenched her teeth. Our group reached the bottom of a mountain slope and started climbing another. To our right, far away, hidden behind underbrush, a creature squawked.

Evers frowned. "What made that noise?"

Wendy blurted, "A Ulo."

Evers flinched.

Our group came upon the Tret's south rim and started

down a fissure, one among many on a cliff.

I winced. "Is this the easiest route? It's dangerous, full of loose rocks."

Wendy glowered. "It is the easiest. Quit complaining."

Evers glared at her.

To our left, in the near distance, five gray scorpions, all six inches long, crawled out of holes. They raised their pinchers while rushing toward us.

I pointed at the arachnids. "Are they dangerous?"

Wendy grabbed one, smashed it against the cliff, and shoved the corpse into her pouch.

Nellie crushed the others with her fist and stuck them into a pocket.

Wendy said, "After they, Xan, pinch you, venom shoots through your body. Within eighteen seconds, you feel faint. Then you pass out, don't recover. Kill them, rip off their pinchers, throw the pinchers away and eat the rest of the Xan whenever you like."

Evers exhaled, a blank expression on her face. "Thanks for the information." Our crew tramped on. To our right, about fifty feet away, eleven more Xan rushed out of holes.

Wendy pointed at the arachnids. "There are too many to kill. Move faster."

I flinched. Our group continued on.

We hiked across knee-deep muddy rapids, ones at the bottom of the Tret. A cloud of bees arrived. Without warning, they started circling our heads.

Evers blurted, "These insects are drones."

Wendy gasped. "I've never seen anything like them."

Nellie announced, "They give me the creeps."

The drones flew away.

I said, "Although they left, I'm not sure why."

Nellie glowered. "Evers, how did you know they were

drones?"

My partner frowned. "Experience."

Wendy scowled. "That's a vague answer. You're secretive. Are you an assassin or a government agent?"

My partner blinked.

Nellie glared at her. "Evers, your silence makes it hard for me to trust you."

My colleague glanced to the right and left. "We should pay close attention to this area. It's dangerous."

Everybody else agreed.

Our troop came upon the canyon's north end and marched through knee-deep grass, a narrow spot between steep, hard to scale cliffs. Ahead, far away, hidden behind gigantic thorn trees, a thrumming grew louder.

Nellie blurted, "I can't see what's making that strange noise. It gives me the creeps."

Wendy blinked. "I can't see it either. The noise is unfamiliar, nerve-wracking."

Fifteen feet above us, two ten-foot-long hornets arrived and stopped, their wings thrumming.

Nellie announced, "They're ugly."

Wendy exclaimed, "Mucus is dripping out of their mouths. It stinks."

Both insects descended slowly, their jaws open.

Nellie raised her weapon. "Uh oh."

One of the hornets spat. The gooey liquid ended up on my shoulder. I announced, "Their saliva smells like dead rats." My lenses sent neutrinos into the gigantic insect's minds.

Wendy, Nellie, Evers and I fired. Both hornets screeched. *Reeeee.*

As their drool landed on Evers' chest, they ascended and flew away.

Wendy announced, "Good riddance."

Evers' brows furrowed in concentration. "Wendy and

Nellie, have you seen these hornets before?"

Wendy's eyes opened wider, a terrified expression on her face. "Never."

Nellie spat, "No." Our troop hiked.

I exhaled, trying to calm down. "They look real, aren't drones." The particles returned. According to them, these gigantic hornets didn't match any insect species on my lenses' databases. I bit my lip, irritated while my lenses automatically sent this information to Evers.

Her text response scrolled, pointing out that her lenses' Insect Identifier, had only provided scrambled, useless results.

My jaw muscles tightened, an annoyed reaction. 80 percent of the time, her Insect Identifier offered helpful information.

Evers jaw muscles tightened. "They do look real. But who created them?"

Nellie replied, "I don't know."

Wendy raised a trembling hand, then wiped the sweat off her chin. "Hard to tell."

I clenched my teeth, exasperated. Did geneticists, Kolo's friends, make them?

Evers said, "Brin, judging by that look on your face, something is bothering you. What is it?"

"If there are hundreds or thousands of those hornets, they might kill us before we find Kolo."

Evers winced. "Good point."

Wendy cringed. "I don't want to think about this anymore. We have enough problems."

Nellie scowled. "I agree with Wendy." Our group hiked uphill and passed boulders.

Soon we reached a gap, then started downslope, an area partly covered by strangler figs. The wind started blowing.

Two hours later, as the wind died down, our crew entered a dimly lit part of the Munt, an area with three-hundred-foot-tall acacias, all with huge leaves that blocked out the sky. On adjacent trunks, striped snails crawled over orange slime.

Ahead, Nellie wiped sweat from her neck. "This heat is wearing me out."

Next to her, Wendy glowered. "It's disgusting."

A bullet grazed my sleeve. I winced as all of us dove to the ground.

Evers' message came out of my lenses' background. *Can you tell who is shooting and where they are?*

I replied, using text, saying I couldn't answer either question.

CHAPTER ELEVEN

More ammo struck the top of my helmet, tearing pieces off.

In the near distance, a woman who was hidden behind towering weeds called out, "Surrender or die."

Nellie announced, "Clua, it's me."

Ahead, six Qio women with green skin, strangers with rapid discharge rifles, stepped out from behind the plants. The tallest, a gaunt female in a soiled coat, announced, "Nellie, long time no see. What have you been up to?"

"Clua, staying alive." Nellie mentioned our names and the group's destination.

Clua lowered her barrel. "Good luck reaching it. My clan stays here because the area around Last Chance is too dangerous."

My lenses sent neutrinos into Clua's telencephalon, the most advanced part of her brain.

Wendy stood. "Why is it so dangerous?"

Clua glowered. "Every few minutes, snipers fire at you."

Nellie rose, scowling. "Could you see them?"

Clua replied, "No."

Nellie mentioned the gigantic hornets.

Clua exclaimed, "You must be joking. We haven't seen any."

The rest of her friends laughed.

A short brunette snickered. "Nellie, you're tired, seeing things that aren't there."

Nellie sighed. "We need to keep going."

Wendy, a disgusted expression on her face, shook her head.

Clua announced, "See you later."

Our group departed. Wendy complained, "They should have listened to us. Those hornets are dangerous."

I said, "You provided a detailed explanation. If they didn't listen, that's their problem."

Nellie blurted, "I like Clua, don't want her to get hurt."

Wendy frowned but didn't say anything.

Evers said, "Brin, you look upset. Did Clua's reaction to Nellie's story regarding the hornets irritate you?"

"It did." My stomach muscles tightened, a shocked response.

Nellie glared at me. "Brin, why didn't you back me up? Clua might have believed you."

In my mind's eye, a horrible possibility, the hornet tore us to shreds. Chills ran up my spine, a terrified response. "I'm not her friend. She wouldn't have."

Nellie's mouth contorted into a frown. "I should have tried harder. Her life is rough."

Evers added, "You did your best. Forget about it and move on."

Nellie clenched her teeth, then grumbled incoherently.

In my lenses, the received field remained blank. For unknown reasons, Frank and Tesk hadn't contacted me. I sent a text message to Evers telling her about this.

Her response scrolled through my lenses. *Them not contacting us is dangerous. Unfortunately, for unknown reasons, since my lenses' receive field is blank. I'll have to rely on probability of reaching your goal software.*

This application offered two types of statistics, ones that would rate our chances of locating Kolo based on the current amount of information available. In my lenses, the first, which used fractal, self-same numbers analysis, indicated that there was a 30 percent likelihood of finding him. The second, based on quantum mechanics, explained that there was a 28 percent chance. The quantum mechanics' analysis, which used a subatomic particle's most energy efficient path to reach a goal, was 4 percent more reliable than a fractal analysis. Unfortunately, 70 percent of the time, quantum mechanics' rules didn't work in the macroscopic world.

I sent a text message, a memo that included these results to my partner.

Her response came into view. According to it, for the time being, the quantum mechanics' analysis was the best way to find Kolo. However, if Frank or Tesk responded, telling us to use another technique to locate Kolo, we would follow their orders.

I sent her another text, explaining that using the quantum solution was a good idea.

The neutrinos returned. Professor Clua, a Pran College teacher, used to live near Imm, a town on Coam's south coast. She along with her daughter, Mindy, boarded a spacecraft that landed near Pran. The ship, filled with refugees, touched down close to Last Chance. Not long after it arrived, eleven gunmen showed up. All the refugees scattered. Clua sprinted into a crowded house, then called out her daughter's name. She didn't answer. Gunmen rushed into the building. Clua and several others darted outside. Then Clua started wandering, trying to find Mindy.

Soon we entered a field of opium poppies. Nellie and Wendy grabbed some and placed them in their pockets.

Evers frowned. "Are you going to smoke those?"

Nellie glared at my partner. "No, I'm going to sell them."

Wendy exclaimed, "These are worth a lot of money."

I said, "Turning refugees into addicts is a bad idea. Is that what you want?"

Nellie gave me a dirty look, pulled them out of her pockets and threw the poppies away. "Shit, I need money."

Wendy paused, then yanked the plants out and tossed them.

The wind started blowing. Further forward, about ten-feet away, not far beyond Nellie and Wendy, the ground cracked open, creating a two-foot-wide chasm.

Nellie bellowed, "What the hell?"

Wendy exclaimed, "Why is this happening? I hate it."

Evers called out, "Is Lasho falling apart?"

I flinched. "Good question." I took a few steps, then glanced down. On the chasm wall, dirt broke off and plummeted eight hundred feet.

Evers jumped over the abyss. "Let's move on. If it opens wider, we might fall into it."

Everybody else hopped over it, and our group trekked. In front of them, Nellie sighed. "Too many obstacles."

Wendy gnashed her teeth but didn't say anything.

After hiking through a huge kapok grove, our group reached the top of a gloomy ridge, a weed-covered area between towering acacias. A few steps from me, Evers stooped, pointing down. In front of her, several feet above the ground, flies buzzed louder. Her wrist scanner hummed, photographing and scanning an object that was hidden in the knee-high weeds.

Wendy frowned. "Why are you pointing?"

Evers replied, a disgusted expression on her face. "Come over here and see for yourself."

Everybody else did. My partner was standing next to a severed arm.

Wendy gasped.

Nellie exclaimed, "Oh my god."

As the smell of rotting flesh became stronger, my stomach muscles tightened in a mortified response. My scanner probed this gruesome object, storing the body part's DNA, an attempt to ID the victim.

Evers looked away, teeth clenched and stood. "I've seen

these things before but forgetting about this grotesque sight along with the stench will take a while."

Our group departed.

Within two hours, we sat in a small clearing, a spot surrounded by towering wimba trees, and started eating wild legumes, a species Wendy had recently picked.

Evers said, "These taste bitter, but they'll do."

Wendy frowned. "At least they're edible. If you don't like them, find something else."

Evers paused, her brow tight.

I chewed, my stomach churning, upset by the strange meal. It started raining.

Wendy sighed. "I hate being wet."

I added, "Every tree and plant on Lasho is less than one year old. Wendy, how do you know which plants are edible, not poisonous?"

She glowered. "If Zele monkeys eat them, I know they're edible."

In mind's eye, a bad memory, Sultra disappeared, vaporized.

Evers said, "Brin, you look upset. What's wrong?"

I fibbed, "My stomach hurts. That's all."

Evers said, "You're thinking about Sultra again. Aren't you?"

I lied, "No."

Evers paused. "If you want to talk to me about her, I'll listen."

In my imagination, Sultra grinned while touching her new cheek. This fond memory vanished. As droplets trickled down my sleeve, the rainstorm ended.

To my left, in the distance, hidden behind the grass, a droning grew louder.

Nellie jumped up. "What's making that strange noise?"

Wendy rose to her feet. "Something I can't see is coming this way."

Fifteen feet above the grass, a ten-foot-long hornet stopped, hovering above us. In its mouth, Clua's dangling body, covered with saliva, jerked as the insect bit her head off.

Wendy gasped.

I raised my weapon, flinching. The hornet swallowed Clua's corpse and flew away.

Nellie started crying. "I hated seeing that. If only she had listened to me."

Wendy blenched while grabbing Nellie's quivering hand, trying to comfort her friend. "I hated seeing it as well."

Evers bit her lip. "That was as horrible as watching a battle-ready robot tear one of my former partner's body in half."

I blinked. "When did that happen?"

Evers sighed. "That's all I'll say for now. I want to forget about it."

I said, "It's time to go. If that hornet is hungry, it will return." Our group departed.

Nellie wiped tears off her cheek. "Evers, what is a battle-ready robot?"

Wendy coughed. "Yeah, what is it?"

"I don't like talking about them. It's too painful."

Nellie paused, a hurt expression on her face. "I'm sorry to hear that it's so painful."

Wendy exhaled. "I want to know more about them, but don't want to upset you."

Evers clenched her teeth, then thanked her.

At dusk, we passed an old hut, a dwelling without any windows and stopped between fifteen more.

Wendy glanced to the right and left with a startled expression on her face. "This is Last Chance. It looks deserted."

A five-foot-eight-inch tall Qio woman with purple skin, a redhead in a rumpled tunic, stepped out of a hut, a structure made of carbon nanotubes, her rapid-fire rifle aimed at us. "Put your guns down, or I'll kill all of you."

We did. I winced. "We're looking for . . ." My lenses sent neutrinos into the redhead's mind.

She blurted, cutting me off, "Shut up. Put all your money and weapons on the ground, then go inside that." She pointed at a hut.

Evers and I placed what little we had, paper currency, in the dirt. Nellie and Wendy tossed several coins, their guns along with their knives at the same spot.

The redhead barked, "Hurry."

All four of us stepped inside. The redhead slammed the door shut.

Outside the building, a deep male voice said, "This won't buy enough. Execute them soon."

The redhead remarked, "Executing them soon is a good idea."

Nellie whispered, "What can we do now?"

Wendy frowned. "I'm not sure."

Evers' jaw muscles tensed up. Her message arrived in my lenses. *I don't know how to escape without being shot.*

As chills ran down my spine, my lenses responded, saying that I didn't know how to either. The neutrinos returned. The redhead's name was Ilia Lan. She, a robber, came from a town called Teto. Teto was on Maen's north coast. A year ago, after being released from a prison called Locda, she began repairing security guard robots, a minimum wage job. Two months later, when the Maen War, a conflict between two of its towns, Jeen and Teto, broke out, she left Teto. After crossing three rivers, she boarded a spacecraft full of refugees. Within days, it docked on another space vessel. This one touched down close to Fao. She left it, robbed two men, and they started chasing her. Not wanting to be captured and sent back to Locda, she fled and ended up in Last Chance.

CHAPTER TWELVE

The following dawn as my adrenaline pumped harder, Ilia flung the door open and barked, "Everybody come outside."

Evers flinched, and all of us left the hut.

Ilia shouted, "All of you stand next to each other, facing me."

My jaw muscles tightened, a terrified response.

Nellie called out, "What are you going to do with us?"

Ilia blurted, "Keep your mouth shut." She shot Nellie's pinky finger, cutting the end off.

Nellie screamed, "Oww."

Wendy blenched.

Evers scowled, and all of us turned, following Ilea's order.

Four Qio women, strangers with purple skin, stepped out of another hut, then halted, their rifles aimed at us.

Ilia glanced at them. Then she announced, "On the count of three, fire."

To my left, Wendy's lips started quivering. She spat, "What the fuck are you doing?"

Nellie burst out, "Stop."

A five-foot-tall Aito male with turquoise skin arrived. He pointed at Nellie. "Ilia, I know her. Don't shoot them."

All four Qio women lowered their weapons.

I exhaled, surprised and relieved by the firing squad's reaction.

Evers wiped the sweat off her chin with a shaking hand.

Nellie called out, "Siim, I'm glad to see you."

He walked toward Nellie. They shook hands. He said, "I haven't seen you in weeks."

She offered a weak grin, her eyes filled with tears.

Siim asked, "What brings you here?"

Nellie answered.

Siim glowered. "Kolo was here a few days ago. But now he's in Fao."

I thanked him for the information. My lenses sent neutrinos into his hippocampus.

Siim glowered. "Nellie, why are you looking for him anyway?"

I paused, chills running across my spine, a nervous reaction.

Evers lied, "A friend of ours wants to know if he's okay, not hurt."

Siim frowned. "Why didn't your friend come along?"

Evers responded, blinking, "He's busy."

Siim glanced at Nellie. He asked, "Are they telling the truth?"

She nodded, teeth clenched.

He paused. "Why would anybody's companion hike through this grotesque area to find out if a friend is okay?" He glowered while looking at the redhead. She frowned. Both of them walked away and started talking in hushed tones, a conversation I couldn't hear.

Nellie came over, then whispered in my ear, "Siim and I usually get along. I can't tell what he is doing."

I murmured, "Tell me more about him."

"He's a refugee from Dored, a village near United Territories' coast. He left when war broke out between two clans, the Gaod and the Mela. I met him six months ago in Last Chance. A few days later, he told me he made a few friends."

A slender blonde Aito woman with blue skin, the stranger Evers and I had seen before, arrived, her rifle raised. She glared at Siim. "Why are you here?"

Siim yanked out a pistol. The Aito woman shot him in the

forehead. He took a few steps and collapsed.

CHAPTER THIRTEEN

Ilia walked, then stooped, touched Siim's wrist and looked at the Aito woman. "CZ, he's dead."

CZ pointed at the body. "I told him not to come to the south end of Last Chance." She walked toward our group, her rifle aimed at us. "All of you will be sold in a few days."

Nellie exclaimed, "Why? We haven't done anything to you."

CZ grinned. "You'll fetch a good price." She took a few steps and punched Nellie's stomach.

Nellie lurched backward, responding to the blow. "Bitch."

CZ slapped Nellie's face. Then CZ barked, "Keep your pie hole shut, shithead. You're lucky I didn't kill you."

Nellie clenched her teeth.

Wendy spat, "Leave her alone."

CZ laughed and socked Wendy's jaw. She fell over. Evers grabbed her hand, then pulled our new friend up.

My lenses sent neutrinos into CZ's mind.

She turned toward Ilia while announcing, "It's time to leave."

Hours later, in the early afternoon, our group hiked past two-hundred-foot-high banyans, a gloomy part of the Munt.

The particles returned. Six months ago, CZ, a drug dealer, a refugee from Fota, a town in the United Territories, had beaten her husband to death with a hammer because she was in a bad mood. Within hours, she boarded a spacecraft. When it reached Lasho's outer atmosphere, it docked on a bigger one. She entered it and met two women. All three agreed that they needed more money.

At dawn, their space vessel touched down in the Munt, an

area that was two miles west of Neib. All three stepped out, then hiked. The next morning, all three attacked strangers, grabbed their rapid discharge rifles and robbed anybody they met.

Behind us, a member of the firing squad spoke to another, "I despise this area. The heat is unbearable, and there are too many Dwots."

Nellie whispered in my ear, "Dwot spiders bite. In a few minutes, after their venom paralyzes you, they rip your flesh off and eat it."

I cringed and shared this information with Evers via my lenses.

My partner clenched her teeth. Ahead and to the right, hidden behind towering ferns, a scraping grew louder.

Nellie glanced in that direction. "There isn't enough light. It's hard to see what's making that noise."

Further forward, CZ and the members of her firing squad halted. CZ pivoted and fired. A bullet grazed Evers' shoulder.

She winced.

CZ announced, "Brin and the rest of you, keep your pie holes shut. If anybody in your group tries to escape, we'll shoot to kill."

Nellie blinked. Wendy flinched. Evers glowered.

Chills ran up my spine.

Not far beyond CZ, a rustling, coming from behind adjacent bushes, grew louder. She pointed at them. "Mek, Otto, I can't see what is making that noise. Can you?"

Mek replied, "No. I'll take a closer look."

Otto aimed his rifle in several directions. "I can't hear it anymore. The creature, whatever species it was, left."

CZ barked, "This short route is poorly lit. Let's get a move on, before a Dwot or something else strikes."

Mek shoved a bush aside. "It's gone."

Faraway, hidden in the mist, something hooted.

Nellie stepped over a knee-high root. She whispered, "Ges make that noise."

Evers blurted, "A tiny worm just bit my cheek." She knocked the invertebrate off.

Wendy murmured, "It's a Jas worm. Minutes after they bite, the venom kicks in and you hear echoes."

Evers whispered, "What is a Ges?"

Nellie recoiled. "A foot-long snail that bites."

I cringed. "Is its bite poisonous?"

Wendy replied, "No."

CZ hollered, "Shut the hell up."

A laser beam struck Nellie's finger, creating an indigo burn mark. She yelled, "Ouch."

CZ snarled, "Keep quiet, or I'll shoot you in the eye."

Tears rolled down Nellie's cheeks as she touched the mark.

In the late afternoon as our group went between huge acacias, trees that blocked out some of the sky, a two-foot-long Dwot rushed out of gigantic weeds and bit Otto's leg. He cried out, "Ouch." The arachnid spun around, darted into the underbrush and vanished, concealed by it.

I flinched.

Otto took a few steps, fell and ended up on his back, lips trembling.

Mek frowned. "Otto is paralyzed, can't speak or walk." He stooped. Another member of the squad lifted Otto onto his back. Mek stood and trekked.

After we crossed two muddy streams, Nellie glowered. "I hope that Dwot doesn't come back."

Evers winced.

Wendy blenched. "Shit."

Further forward, CZ barked, "Keep your pie holes shut."

To our left, hidden behind huge succulents, all dimly lit, a faint scraping grew louder.

Nellie glanced in that direction. "What's making that noise?"

Evers squinted, "It's too dark to see it. Judging by that sound, whatever made it is close, a few feet from us."

I paused, teeth clenched, but only heard our crunching boot steps.

Without warning, the scraping moved away from us.

Evers murmured, "The creature that made that sound is headed toward those shrubs." She pointed to the left.

Nellie added, speaking in a hushed tone, "I hope it's leaving. My nerves are shot."

Within half an hour, while slogging through a kapok grove, an area partly obscured by mist, Mek stooped, and let go of Otto. Otto dropped to the ground. Mek took a deep breath. "I'm tired, need to rest. Otto is heavy."

CZ shot Otto's forehead.

Mek snarled, "Why did you slaughter him?"

She barked, "He was slowing us down, making it easier for a Dwot to attack. Move out."

A short Aito, a member of the squad, halted, a distraught look on his face.

CZ pointed at the short Aito. "NB, what the hell are you waiting for?"

NB sighed. "Otto was a close friend. I'll miss him." Everybody marched.

Not long before dusk, our group came upon six huts, all of them in a clearing, a poorly lit spot surrounded by towering palms. In the near distance, two Qio men with green skin and a female Qio with an eye patch, all with rifles in hand, stepped out of one. The female glowered. "CZ, what brings you here?"

She pointed at us. "Raya, I have slaves to sell."

Raya walked, grabbed my neck, then punched it with his other hand.

I flinched. My lenses sent neutrinos into her mind.

Raya laughed. "A stupid human with strong muscles and quick reflexes."

I winced.

CZ bragged, "These are outstanding tooloos."

According to my lenses, a tooloo was a healthy slave.

Raya walked, then seized Evers' neck.

She glared at Raya.

Raya smiled. "Blue eyes, your next owner will be pleased. If I was rich, I would keep you for myself."

Evers' forehead tightened.

Raya let go, took a few steps, grabbed Nellie's arm and raised it.

She blurted, "Let go, asshole."

Raya yanked out a knife and slashed her arm. "Be quiet, asshole, or die."

Nellie cringed while placing her hand on the wound. Behind her, one of the Qio men gave the other Qio male, a gaunt stranger, a severed finger.

I cringed.

Raya moved on, seized Wendy's hand and inspected it. "Good skin, no sign of Deig worm infestation. CZ, I'll give you sixty oons for all four of these tooloos."

CZ blurted, "Eighty."

Raya spat, "You're stubborn. Seventy."

"Seventy-five."

"Seventy-two."

"Seventy-two it is."

In my imagination, a desire, I shot CZ and Raya in the head, and both died, screaming.

Raya handed CZ several coins. CZ and the rest of her squad departed.

Raya smiled, then came toward me. "Your teeth are good."
I bit my lip, angry.

Raya aimed her rifle at my chest while pointing at a hut. "All of you tooloos go inside that."

All of us walked, entered and sat in the dirt. One of the Qio men shut the door.

Outside, a woman with an unfamiliar voice said, "Raya, I will pay one hundred oons for these tooloos."

"Good point. Let me think about it." Their voices moved away.

Nellie whispered in my ear, "I can't hear them anymore."

I murmured into hers, "I can't either."

Evers' message appeared in my lenses. *What do we do now?*

I replied, using text, saying all four of us needed to wait. During that time, we could plan our next move.

Evers spoke to Nellie and Wendy in a hushed tone, repeating my plan.

Nellie murmured, "Evers, I couldn't hear him mention it. How could you?"

Evers lied, "He used body language."

Nellie frowned. "I didn't notice it. Anyway, his idea is good."

Wendy said she agreed with Nellie. A two-inch-long turquoise spider darted out of a hole and scampered across the floor.

Wendy stomped on it. "I hate the Kwa. After they bite, you get a headache and die within a few minutes."

I flinched. The neutrinos returned. According to them, Raya, a drug dealer, was from Oxo, a town on Maen's west coast. Four months ago, after deserting her husband and daughter because she was bored with them, she boarded a spacecraft, one filled with refugees. It came to rest two miles north of Last Chance. Within days, she robbed four women and fled, wanting to find others she could steal money from.

This information shocked me. My lenses shared this data with Evers.

She frowned. Soon my partner replied with a text message, telling me that her lenses' neutrinos came up with the same information as mine regarding Raya.

I nodded. If I shared this information with Nellie and Wendy, and they asked me how both of us knew so much about Raya, Raya or one of her guards might hear the conversation, and slaughter all four of us.

Did Raya own lenses, tools that were the same as ours? I hoped not.

Just before midnight, faint voices moved toward our hut. A stranger with a baritone voice said, "Raya, two of the females will make great slaves. I'll give you one hundred fifty oons for both."

"Acceptable."

A gaunt seven-foot-tall Qio male, his silhouette illuminated by starlight, flung the door open. At the same time, he aimed his shoulder-mounted infrared scanner at us.

My lenses sent neutrinos into his neocortex. The stranger pointed at Wendy and Nellie. He barked, "Come with me."

Both glowered, stood, left the room and he slammed the door shut.

Wendy yelled, "Let go of me."

The gaunt male barked, "You talk too much, whore." The crunching sound of boot heels stepping on dirt moved away from us.

Evers sighed, an angry expression on her face.

I flinched. The neutrinos returned. The gaunt male's name was Vin. Seven months ago, he, a convicted murderer, escaped from Reen, a prison on the outskirts of Imm. Imm was on Coam's east coast. Three mornings later, he joined a crowd of refugees. They entered a spacecraft. When it reached

Lasho's outer atmosphere, it docked on a larger one's belly. Then every refugee and he entered the larger one. After it touched down close to Neib, just about everybody stepped out.

Feeling desperate, Vin robbed two refugees. Both screamed at him. Not wanting to be sent back to Reen, he murdered both with a knife and ran into the jungle. Within days, he met Raya.

At sunup, my stomach growled. A four-inch-long centipede emerged from a hole, pinchers on its jaws twitching. It squealed and rushed toward Evers. She stomped on it, and her jaw muscles tensed. Orange mucus poured out of its crushed head. On the invertebrate's tail, a stinger uncoiled and dropped.

I exhaled, relieved. "Thanks for killing it."

She offered a thumbs up. A foot centipede crawled out of the hole, spitting.

As chills ran up my spine, a horrified response, it jumped toward Evers. She dodged to the right and smashed it with her fist. The pest squealed. *Seeoooo.* Evers crushed it with her boot heel. The invertebrate rolled over, yellow mucus pouring out of its mouth.

Outside, the approaching sound of Vin's voice became louder, "That is all I will pay."

Raya said, "Acceptable."

He flung the door open, then aimed his rifle at Evers. "Both of you come with me."

We left the building, and he handcuffed me. My stomach muscles tightened in an angry response. A text message from Tesk, one with an attachment called android develop, scrolled through my lenses. According to the message, android develop would transmit itself to a plant. Within minutes, it would alter the plant's DNA, and create a robot.

Vin placed shock engage handcuffs, on Evers' wrists. If she moved the shackles more than six inches away from her torso, they would send hundreds of volts through her wrists. He snarled, "Raya, I don't trust them."

She blurted, "Vin, I don't either." She aimed her rifle at my eye. "Follow me, or I'll shoot you." She yanked out a knife, then slashed my neck, creating a superficial wound.

I flinched.

Raya did an about-face and marched, everybody else behind her.

Vin struck my shoulder with a rifle butt.

I blenched.

He exclaimed, "Try to escape, and I'll put a bullet in your eye."

Chills ran across my spine, a terrified response.

Within minutes, our group, Raya, Vin, Evers and I, hiked between waist-high mushrooms, gloomy shapes, all beneath the jungle canopy. At the same time, the stench of rotten plants became stronger. My stomach churned, reacting to the stench. It started raining. Soon it turned into a downpour. Ahead, Raya, a barely visible silhouette, climbed over a waist-high root.

As the wind started blowing, I blinked, wishing the storm would end.

In the late morning, when the wind died down, all four of us pushed aside weeds and walked toward six tents, all of them in the middle of a clearing, a spot surrounded by gigantic banyans.

A six-foot-tall bearded human male in a ripped, camouflaged jumpsuit, stepped out of a tent. "Raya, new recruits. Impressive."

"Yes, new recruits."

He looked at me, then glanced at Evers. "Fight for us, or we'll chop your heads off."

My partner blurted, "Why should we help you?"

Raya shouted, "Shut your trap, asshole."

Vin punched Evers' stomach. She jerked forward, teeth clenched, responding to the blow.

The bearded male squinted while he stared at my arms, chest, and legs. He walked and examined Evers' wrists, arms and hips. "Both of you are healthy. Why did you come to the Munt?"

Evers blinked, but she didn't answer. It stopped raining.

I exhaled, my body tensed, waiting to be hit. My lenses sent neutrinos into the bearded male's cerebrum. They returned. His name was Nate Doen. He was a heroin dealer. For unknown reasons, no more information was available.

Vin frowned. "They won't talk." He kicked Evers' leg. My partner keeled over, wincing.

Nate looked at Vin. Vin glowered.

Nate walked, then kicked Evers' hip. She winced. He announced, "We need good fighters. The battle at Blo Glun is raging." He turned, took a few steps, punched my stomach, then slapped my face.

I jerked, responding to the blows.

Nate scowled. "I'll give you two hundred oons for both."

Raya blurted, "Acceptable."

Nate placed coins in her outstretched hand. He said, "Vin, I'll pay you thirty oons to guard them."

He glowered. "How long will I have to do it?"

"A week at the most. They'll die before then."

"Thirty is fine."

Nate gave him coins.

A six-foot-tall Qio woman, a stranger with one eye missing, stepped out of a tent.

Nate glanced at her. "Una, I'll pay you twenty-five oons to

guard them for a week."

"Give me thirty or fuck off."

Nate frowned. "Thirty it is." He gave her coins.

Una walked and kicked Evers' leg. My partner winced.

Una snarled, "You miserable piece of shit." She yanked out a knife and stabbed my partner's right eye.

Evers screamed. A nanorobot-filled bandage came out of a sixteen-inch in diameter housing, one on the bridge of my colleagues' nose, and went over her eye.

I winced.

Una snapped, "What is that thing that just covered your eye?"

Evers flinched.

Una spat, "You won't tell me. I don't give a shit. You'll be dead soon." She chuckled.

Nate bellowed, "Everybody follow me single file. Una, you take up the rear." Nate, Vin, Una, Evers and I hiked.

Behind me, Una complained, "Nate, I hate the Blo Glun."

"You won't take part in any battle."

Una grumbled incoherently. In the far distance, bombs went off.

I blenched, worried that a mortar shell would strike us any second. Evers scowled. "Brin, I enjoyed meeting you. We don't have much time left."

I nodded. "Is the bandage working?" 60 percent of the time its nanorobots would repair this severe wound.

"It's too early to know. Let's hope so."

I offered a weak smile, frightened that Una and the others might stab us and laugh as we bled to death.

Una barked, "Both of you, shut the fuck up."

I bit my lip, angry.

My colleague scowled.

More neutrinos returned. Eight months ago, the morning

after Nate, a drug lord from Nor, a town on Coam's north coast, shot and killed a gang leader named Moss, he boarded a spacecraft. Although he didn't want to leave Nor, he knew that if he stayed, Moss' friends would gun him down. The ship touched down near Fao. After entering this outpost, he robbed four Qio men, refugees. Two complained. He killed all four, and came to this location, wanting to find a better place to make money.

The following afternoon, our group halted between towering kapoks. In the near distance, a hatch near the top of a fort's ten-foot-high wall, a six-hundred-foot in diameter barrier, opened, then closed.

Nate pointed at it. "That is Blo Glun. According to my spies, there are twenty Qio men and women inside. All of them have rapid discharge rifles or automatic body-sensing pistols."

I winced.

Nate removed our handcuffs, then gave Evers and me rapid discharge rifles. He snarled, "Both of you must attack Blo now."

I flinched. "Will anybody else help us?"

Nate snapped, "Do it immediately, or we'll shoot both of you in the forehead."

Evers flinched.

Both of us rushed toward it. Ammo struck the front of my bulletproof shoulder pad. My adrenaline pumped harder. Evers and I veered left, darted into the jungle, and jumped over knee-high undergrowth, trying to escape.

Behind us, Nate shouted, "Kill them."

I flinched as bullets grazed my left hip.

Evers ducked. It started raining.

Two hours later, not long after the storm ended, my

partner and I reached a tiny spot between towering shrubs. As distant parrots squawked, we halted and spun around, covered in sweat. Within seconds, both of us peeked between leaves. At the same time, we aimed our weapons at nearby dimly lit ten-foot-high underbrush, a precautionary measure. I whispered, "Let's take a short rest."

Evers bent two fingers, saying that she agreed with me.

To our right, in the near distance, hidden in the gloom, Nate yelled, "Drop your weapons, then walk toward my voice or we'll shoot."

I remained silent, my heart pounding, a tense reaction. Both of us took a few steps and crouched behind a waist-high fallen tree. Evers' message came out of my lenses' background. *I can't see them. If they move, I can.*

I nodded, teeth clenched. In my lenses, text, the result of a recent echo-imaging probe, scrolled. *Assailant's location cannot be determined.*

Why had this tool failed?

They started firing. *Zing, zing, zing.* Bullets struck the fallen tree and pieces of bark rained down on our shoulder pads.

My partner and I blenched. Evers' message scrolled. *If both of us fire, they'll know exactly where we are.*

I sent her a text response, telling my partner that although there was a 40 percent chance their rapid discharge rifle's weapon shape detectors software had spotted our rifle barrels, I didn't want to shoot at them either because firing our weapons would make it 98 percent possible for their detectors to determine our exact position.

More ammo struck the same area, ripping off more bark.

CHAPTER FOURTEEN

Within minutes, they stopped firing. Nate yelled, "Surrender."

Evers and I remained silent, ignoring the request. As chills ran across my spine, a scared to death response, my partner scowled.

Zing, zing, zing. Bullets destroyed adjacent leaves. Both of us cringed.

Evers' message popped up. *Only two of them, not three, are shooting at us. Are the others tired?*

I sent her a text response, agreeing that only two weapons were being used. However, the other's silence baffled me.

After our attacker's bullets tore several limbs off the trunk, their rifles went silent.

Her message scrolled. *Why did they stop firing?*

I texted her, pointing out that although the question was a good one, providing an accurate answer was impossible.

Another materialized. *I'm going to find out why they stopped. Cover me.*

I flinched and rose half an inch while squeezing the trigger. *Tat, tat, tat.*

My partner stood until she was in a crouched position. Out of the blue, Evers turned left, took off and went around a bush. In my lenses, her figure, a red silhouette, the result of echo-imaging, shoved aside underbrush. Beneath her figure, text and coordinates indicated that was she was twenty feet from me. She raised her right hand, saying I should join her.

I stood, then walked, stooped, my rifle aimed, and circled the bush, my stomach muscles tensed. In the far distance, hidden behind thorn trees, a parakeet chirped. I shoved aside six-foot-high underbrush. Several feet away, Evers was standing next to Nate and Una's corpses. A Dwot had bitten off Nate's right cheek and ripped out his right eye. The left side of Una's head was gone, chewed off.

I flinched.

In the near distance, hidden behind poorly lit bromeliads, Vin screamed.

My partner blenched, then whispered, "Let's get out of here."

Both of us took off and jumped over a log, moving to the left, away from Vin. Behind us, rustling leaves grew louder. Was a Dwot chasing us? It was hard to tell. To our right, somewhere in the dark mist, an unseen parakeet whistled. I flinched, scared that a Dwot was making that sound, trying to fool us.

After rushing between vines and crossing four streams, we slowed down. I said, "Although Dwots probably killed Vin, going back to find out for sure is a bad idea."

"It is a bad idea."

"We should head for Blo Glun to find out if anybody there can tell us which route to Fao is the safest."

Her brow furrowed in concentration. "I don't want to head for it. But according to my echo-imaging's computer model, somebody there might know which is the safest."

Terrain guide had mapped the first part of our journey through the Munt. At the same time, this tool had produced a computer model. The model's statistics indicated that both the first and second parts were flawed, didn't include Dwot movement, robber's locations, Gaoot hunting grounds or many other obstacles.

CHAPTER FIFTEEN

We stopped about thirty feet from its wall. Evers mentioned our goal.

At the bottom of the wall, a two-inch in diameter hatch popped open. A woman yelled through it, "Put your rifles down."

I flinched. Both of us did.

Evers whispered in my ear, "If we're lucky they won't shoot."

I winced. "Yes."

A gate opened. Two Qio men with purple skin, stepped out, their rapid discharge rifles aimed at us. They advanced slowly, grabbed our weapons, and motioned with their hands, beckoning us to follow them. All four of us entered Blo. A six-foot-four-inch tall black human woman with a scarred cheek announced, "My name is Tira. Several star rises ago, a friend told me that Kolo might be in Fao."

I thanked her for the information.

Behind her, a Qio male with a broken ear frowned. "Tira, they're assassins, working for CZ."

She drew a circle in the air with her finger. The Qio male pointed at us. "Come with me."

Evers blurted, "Why?"

Tira barked, "Go with him, or we'll shoot you in the face."

I cringed. Both of us followed him. He led us to a hut. We entered. He slammed the door, locked it and departed.

Evers shook her head. "More complications. Tep shit."

I rubbed my face, irritated. "We'll have to wait." Outside, a group started arguing.

Evers sat on the dirt floor. "Are they talking about us? These walls are blocking my lenses' probes."

I clenched my teeth. "Good question. They're blocking my mine, too." Far away, an incoming mortar shell screeched louder.

Evers exclaimed, "It's coming this way." My partner and I hit the dirt. The shell exploded.

She cleared her throat. "That struck an area somewhere outside Blo, too close to it."

I flinched. "That's my guess." Another screeched. Outside the hut, men and women yelled incoherently.

"This one is closer. Tep . . ." It went off, and the walls jerked.

CHAPTER SIXTEEN

Minutes after the shelling ended, Tira flung the door open. She motioned with her hand, asking us to step outside.

In the near distance, a gaunt Qio woman with orange skin, a five-foot-tall stranger, pointed at us. "Yes, those are ones that Nate, Vin, and Una tried to kill."

A Qio male placed his clenched fist in front of her eyes. At the same time, he called out, "Sylvia, as usual, you don't know what you're talking about."

She announced, "Yes I do. I saw all three shoot at them."

He shook his head. "Sylvia, you're a fucking moron."

She glared at him. "Get out of my face, ass wipe." He lunged at her. She stepped aside, and he crashed to the ground.

Tira paused, frowning. "No more fighting."

He wiped dirt off his chin while grumbling.

Sylvia glared at him, then crossed both arms across her chest.

Tira announced, "Brin, Evers, it's a three-day hike to Fao. The area around it is occupied by Dwots."

Evers said, "Thanks for the update."

Tira gave her a paper map. Tira continued, "We could use your help. Last week, ten gunmen, six Qio and four humans, attacked and killed two of our friends. We drove them off. Unfortunately, chances are that they will return."

I frowned. "Did the gunmen attack Blo itself?"

Tira spat, "No doubt about it."

Evers blinked. "We understand. However, Kolo might be involved in a plan to destroy all of Lasho. We have to find out if that's true."

Tira scowled. "Very well. Search for Kolo." She told others to give us our rifles.

In the late afternoon, not long after we left Blo, Evers glowered. "I wish we could help Tira and her friends."

"So do I."

She pulled the bandage off her eye.

I cringed. "Can you see out of it?"

My partner glowered. "Not yet." She placed it back over the optical organ.

I winced, frightened that the nanorobots might have failed.

My partner's brow furrowed in concentration. "I haven't heard from Frank or Tesk yet."

"I haven't either." My jaw muscles tightened, a frustrated response. We were on our own until our lenses could receive phone calls or any kind of messages.

Two hours later, as we crossed a knee-deep swamp, Evers said, "I can't see them, but I hear somebody talking." We reached the shore, and stopped, hidden behind a ten-foot-high wall of vines.

A recent echo-imaging probe analysis scrolled. *Cannot detect stranger's shapes because adjacent wimbas' conversations are drowning out echo-imaging's ability to ID any humanoid's shape.*

I blenched, shocked that wimbas' dialogue could do this and shared this information with my partner via a text message.

Her response materialized. *They drowned it out? I don't believe it.*

I pushed aside vines, wanting to see the strangers. In front of us, in the near distance, a stout male, one of four white human gunmen, bragged, "I shot the bitch in the temple. Then the broad fell over, dead. She had forty-nine coins in her pocket."

The tallest chuckled. "It's a good thing we killed all three of those bitches. They whined too much."

My jaw muscles tightened, an angry reaction.

Evers' message scrolled. *These men disgust me.*

All four walked away, laughing.

I said, "They're gone. Let's go." We trudged on.

Within minutes, my partner and I stepped over knee-high anthills. Ahead, not far away, the stout male and a tall man, two of the humans we had just seen, stepped out of the shadows. The stout one pointed his Torp at us. At the same time, he blurted, "Throw your rifles down."

I winced, and both of us complied.

The tall human walked, then grabbed both weapons. The stout one shot Evers. She collapsed.

I blenched. The fat one's weapon went off. A bullet hit my stomach. I fell backward and ended up on my side, flinching.

Evers jumped up, tackled the tall human, and he fell on his back. The fat stranger's Torp chattered. *Tep, tep.* Bullets from his weapon hit the dirt, inches from my partner's leg.

I sprang to my feet, raced toward the fat one while he turned toward me. As bullets struck my hip, an area protected by my vest, I punched his face. He fell backward, then hit the ground. I kicked his groin. He screamed. I stomped on his chest. He cried out and went silent, and then both eyes closed. I seized the Torp and shot him in the neck.

While blood gushed out, I glanced to the right. Evers fired a rifle. Bullets struck the tall stranger's forehead. His body jerked, and he stopped moving. She got up.

The Torp and a rifle shrank until they were the size of a coin. We shoved them in our pockets, grabbed our rifles, then resumed the journey.

I said, "If we're lucky, the other robbers aren't nearby."

"Yes."

"Are you wounded?"

"No, my bulletproof vest protected me."

After hiking through a huge palmetto grove, an area partly obscured by mist, we climbed over waist-high banyan roots. To our left, about twenty yards away, a ten-foot-long four-legged beast, a poorly illuminated silhouette, crept silently between huge leaves. I cringed. In front of us, something buzzed. I glanced in that direction and noticed nine drones, ones that resembled mosquitos, as they flew out of nearby shadows, coming this way.

I flinched. Without warning, all four veered to the right, bound for distant bushes.

Evers whispered, "That was close. If those motion detection drones spotted you or me, somebody would chase us."

I mentioned the beast.

She winced. "I didn't see it. According to my recent echo-imaging probe, it's gone."

I bit my lip, worried that the creature would return. We trudged on. 80 percent of the time, when motion detection drones were in grasslands or the desert, they spotted moving humans, Aito or other humanoids that were within a fifty-foot radius of them. The rest of the time, if the drones were in a dense jungle, there was a 40 percent chance that they would recognize moving objects such as humans, Aito, or Qio.

Moments after crossing a swamp filled with four-inch long leaches, my partner and I stepped over rotten leaves, flora that smelled like death. To our right, hummingbirds placed their beaks in flowers.

Within the hour, my colleague and I passed hundreds of three-foot-high mushrooms, all barely visible in the gloom. As a canary, one that far away, hidden in the darkness, whistled we reached a wall of fifteen-foot-high weeds. Not far beyond them, unfamiliar voices mumbled incoherently. In my lenses, text, the result of a recent echo-imaging probe, enlarged. *Four lupunas' recent conversations have destroyed a thorough analysis.*

I clenched my teeth, irritated and shocked that lupunas could do this and shared this information with my partner via text.

Evers whispered in my ear, "I can't see who is talking."

I murmured in hers, "I can't see them either."

She pushed weeds aside. Her message appeared in my lenses. *It's two Qio men. One says he is hungry.*

I nodded.

Another popped up. *They don't have any weapons. I'm going to talk to them, find out if they know anything about Kolo.*

I sent her a text response, telling her to do it while my mind raced, hoping I could return fire fast enough if they shot at Evers.

She took a few steps and pushed weeds aside.

I shoved more out of the way. At the same time, my partner walked toward the strangers. They kept talking to each other, ignoring her. The tallest glowered. "I hate this heat."

Evers said, "Hello. Have you met Kolo?"

The tallest frowned. "We should leave here soon."

My partner shoved her right hand through him. At that point, she placed her left hand inside his partner, another 3D hologram.

I blinked, surprised.

Evers glowered. "I don't know why anybody placed these here. Let's go."

"I don't know why either." We departed.

Minutes later, after inspecting a dark area between kapoks and noticing there weren't any tents or huts, both of us moved on. Ahead, far away, hidden in thick fog, gunfire, rapid discharge rifles, rang out.

I flinched. "Be careful."

My partner gnashed her teeth. "Let's go to the right, around the spot where somebody is fighting."

I nodded. We passed corpse lily flowers and came upon three Aito skeletons. All of them were on their backs or sides. Two of their skulls were missing.

Evers stooped. "Figuring who killed them and why they did it is impossible. These victim's DNA isn't on any of my databases."

I flinched, surprised and outraged by this gruesome sight. "Good point. Their DNA isn't on mine either." My partner and I resumed the journey.

As the stars came out, we bedded down for the night.

Sultra kissed me. Then she grinned. "Meeting you was the best thing that ever happened to me." I woke up in darkness, sweating, wishing she were still alive.

At dawn, Evers glowered. "Did you dream about her again last night?"

I blenched, nervous about my condition. "Yes."

Evers paused, a worried expression on her face. "If there's anything I can do to help, let me know."

I offered a weak grin, not sure what else to say. We trekked. Soon both us came upon three utility androids. All of them were face up on the ground, their torsos partly covered by mold.

Evers stooped, her brow furrowed in concentration. "According to my wrist scanner, eight minutes after they arrived, mutated streptococcus destroyed their bio-circuits."

I winced. "Four of my computer models indicate that if we want to know how deadly this streptococcus is, they need more information regarding its mutation."

She sighed. "Figuring how deadly they are might take months."

I blinked, scared. "Does this happen to every utility android that comes to Lasho?"

Evers frowned. "Unknown. We must go. They're beyond repair." My partner and I departed.

Within thirty minutes, both of us stopped close to a thicket. In the near distance, beyond this barrier, somebody we couldn't see was sobbing.

I blenched, worried. "Is a hologram making that noise?"

My colleague looked over the thicket, frowning. "No, it's a Qio girl, about fourteen."

We went around it.

Several feet away, she, a stranger in a soiled multi-environment pantsuit, looked up at us, her eyes filled with tears. She whispered, asking, "Who are you?"

I replied, "We're looking for Kolo."

The girl cocked her head to one side, a baffled expression on her purple face. "I've never heard of him."

Evers asked, "Why are you here, all alone?"

"It's a long story. I'll tell you later."

Evers commented, "Come with us. We'll try to help you."

I asked, "Did your family abandon you?"

The girl's lips started trembling.

Evers glowered. "She's nervous. Let her relax."

I paused, not wanting to scare the girl.

Evers spoke softly, "What's your name?"

She glanced at her hair and twisted it. "Yinnie. I'm lonely, glad that you found me."

Evers said, "Glad to meet you."

In the far distance, hidden in the jungle, rapid discharge rifles fired. At the same time, a thrumming grew louder. I winced. "Somebody might have fired at a hornet. Unfortunately, they're too far away. My echo-imaging can't ID them or their surroundings."

Yinnie asked, "Why did they fire at a hornet?"

Evers told her about our experiences with the gigantic insects.

Yinnie blurted, "That's scary." She began fidgeting, a terrified expression on her face.

I said, "Yes."

Evers complained, "I don't want to deal with the hornets anymore."

Yinnie grimaced. "I'm hungry, haven't eaten in four days."

Evers gave her berries, ones we had collected recently.

Yinnie ate a few. "These taste weird."

Evers said, "They're safe to eat. Where do you come from?"

"Vewa, a village near Roov's south coast."

Evers asked, "I don't mean to be rude, but why did you come here?"

Yinnie's brow tightened. "My dad, Glenn, told me a battle was headed toward Vewa. We packed our bags and went to Uncle Joe's house. Then all three of us left and hiked across grasslands. Within a couple of hours, we boarded a ship. It took off. It landed near Neib. We got off. All around us crowds were scattering. Several men with guns dragged my dad and uncle away." She paused, lips trembling. "I followed several women, hoping they would assist me. When they were a couple of miles from here, a loud one told me they didn't have enough food. I complained. She told me I should find some on my own. I hiked and ended up here."

I blenched. "Stay with us as long as you like."

Yinnie remarked, "Thanks."

When Yinnie finished her meal, our small group hiked between towering succulents. Further forward, about eighty yards from us, fourteen one-inch long red canaries, drones with echolocation, flapped harder and rose. Without warning, they halted. Out of the blue, they veered to the left, peeping softly, a noise designed to fool many observers.

My partner and I aimed our rifles. The drones, search, probe and analyze models, stopped, hovering several feet above nearby dirt.

As chills ran across my spine, a horrified response, the drones rose, went between nearby bushes and vanished in the darkness. Within seconds, the peeping moved away from us. I complained, "If we shot the drones down, a bandit or somebody who sent them here would probably have come after us."

Evers frowned. "You could be right. At any rate, I'm glad they're gone."

I paused, blinking, irritated that she had questioned my comment.

Yinnie blurted, "The drones scare me."

At dusk, sleeping bags came out of our sleeves.
Yinnie grimaced. "I wish I had one of those."
Evers said, "The two of us can sleep inside mine."

At dawn, after eating berries, we hiked. Frank's email appeared in my lenses. At the top of it, text indicated that an attachment should be exported onto a nearby bromeliad. Below the text, meaningless icons scrolled. I clicked the attachment. The plant became taller. At the same time, it changed into a six-foot-tall white human woman, an attractive blonde. She said, "My name is R Eight." She took a few steps and dissolved.

Evers frowned. "She was unstable."

I said, "It's time to try again." I repeated the process. Within seconds, after R Nine mentioned her name, she lowered her left hand and fell apart.

Yinnie blinked. "What is she?"

I replied, "A robot."

Evers complained, "It's probably a waste of time, but do it again."

I did. The plant became taller, then transformed into a woman who was identical to the last female. "I am Y Ten. Frank's IT department sent me to help you in any way I can." Her right hand changed into a rapid discharge rifle.

I said, "You'll need that weapon. Let's go."

Evers asked, "Y Ten, are you stable enough to help us find Kolo?"

"Time will tell. I'm a prototype. IT tested earlier versions of me in three D holographic rooms. However, there wasn't enough time to do that in the real world."

I flinched, shocked that IT had sent me this partially tested model.

After trekking through a maze of banyan roots for half an hour, our group reached the top of a cliff. A thousand feet below us, in a half of a mile-wide valley, thousands of ten-feet long hornets bit corpses' legs and arms off. I winced. "This area smells like death."

Evers blurted, "What a horrible sight."

Yinnie placed both hands over her eyes and vomited. Evers put one arm around her, comforting our new friend.

I raised my arm. An arrow wouldn't come out of it. I flinched, stunned by this problem. Text scrolled through my lenses. *Arrow instrument has failed because airborne amoebas have destroyed its circuits.* I shared this information with the others.

Evers glowered. "Tep shit."

Yinnie said, "Don't use naughty words."

My partner shrugged.

Y Ten said, "It's time for me to change into a glider. When

I'm finished, climb onto my fuselage, and I'll fly over the valley."

Evers frowned. "Are you stable enough to retain that form?"

"There is a forty-two percent chance that I can." She morphed. All of us crawled onto it. The aircraft lurched forward and went over the edge.

Chapter Seventeen

As shivers raced across my spine, the glider plummeted fifty feet. Below us, the thrumming grew louder.

Behind me, Evers said, "At this rate, we'll crash in a few seconds."

Next to her, Yinnie screamed.

Evers announced, "Keep your voice down. If you don't, the hornets will hear you and come after us."

Our young friend, a terrified expression on her face, shut her mouth.

Three hornets took off.

I flinched. Suddenly, all three flew down the valley.

Yinnie murmured, "They're going someplace else."

Evers said, "We were lucky."

I exhaled, relieved. The glider rose. I said, "That's better."

As the wind howled, Evers said, "Yes."

To our right, a hornet came toward us.

Evers murmured, "Complications."

I cringed.

Yinnie whispered, "It's carrying a body. Yuck."

My body went cold, a terrified response. Without warning, the hornet descended.

Evers scowled. "That was too close for comfort."

I took a deep breath, trying to calm down. Ahead, another hornet rose.

My neck muscled tensed up, a mortified response. It came toward the glider, flew over it and kept going.

Evers complained, "One of those is going to attack us."

Yinnie blurted, "Don't say that."

Evers murmured, "Keep your voice down."

Yinnie blinked, then shut her mouth.

The glider reached the top of a cliff, a spot that was on the opposite side of the valley, and touched down. We climbed off. Evers wiped sweat from her forehead. "I'm glad that's over."

Yinnie glanced at her trembling hand. "So am I."

I exhaled, trying to relax. The glider changed into Y Ten.

I said, "Let's get a move on." Our group trekked and went around thorn bushes. Within seconds, a crunching grew louder.

Evers asked, "What's making that noise?"

I blurted, "Speak up. It's difficult to hear you."

She yelled, "It's coming . . ."

I called out, "I only understand part of what you're saying." In front of us, not far beyond grass, a six-hundred-foot-wide by five-hundred-foot-long chunk of land shot upward and kept rising.

Yinnie exclaimed, "Wow."

Evers grimaced. "Part of Lasho is falling apart. If we're lucky, the rest of it will remain intact."

I flinched. "If we're lucky." Our group stepped over thorn-covered leaves.

Y Ten's wrist-mounted computer hummed. "Where are we're going? Frank and IT only detected three percent of your recent messages."

Evers replied, "I just exported that information into your lenses."

Y Ten said, "Thanks. I sent that to Frank and IT the moment I received that export. But they aren't replying. Something is interfering with my lenses."

I mentioned that for unknown reasons they weren't responding to ours.

Y Ten spoke, a blank expression on her face. "Understood. My search and resolve software is trying to overcome the problem." A tiny satellite dish popped out of her shoulder pad.

Evers frowned. "Y Ten, will the dish help you communicate with Frank or IT?"

"According to my quantum computer model, there is a thirty percent chance that it will."

I flinched, disappointed by the low odds.

Y Ten said, "So far my dish hasn't received any messages from Frank or IT."

Evers scowled. "Tep."

After we trekked over several poorly lit hills, a droning became louder. I looked up. Further forward, in the near distance, a thirty-foot-long police cruiser descended and vanished behind towering palmettos.

Y Ten said, "My dish picked up a faint, garbled voice mail message."

Evers scowled. "Can you understand any part of it?"

"No."

I announced, "Let's find out what happened to the ship."

Evers said, "This bamboo patch is in the way." Both of us grabbed our rifles.

I squeezed the trigger, but a laser beam or bullets wouldn't come out of the barrel. "What a mess," I mentioned the problem.

Evers frowned. "They won't come out of mine either. Shit."

Yinnie asked, "What can we do now?"

Evers shook her head. "Good question."

My stomach muscles tightened, a frustrated response.

CHAPTER EIGHTEEN

Y Ten's hands retracted inside her wrists. A huge blade popped out of each wrist, and she began cutting her way through the ten-foot-high patch, everybody else behind her.

Yinnie shouted, "Hooray!"

Evers said, "Impressive."

Within half an hour, Y Ten reached a grass-covered area. Not far away, smoke rose above the wreckage. All of us rushed toward it, then stepped over scattered carbon nanotube parts.

To my left, hidden behind a chunk, Evers grimaced. "I just found a body. The head, arms, and upper torso are gone, torn off. According to my wrist scanners' DNA probe, this was Detective Lo, one of Frank's staff."

I winced. "Let's keep looking."

Yinnie blurted, "Gross."

Not far beyond Evers, Y Ten announced, "I discovered a severed head. According to my DNA probe, this was Detective Aan, one of Lo's colleagues."

Chills ran across my spine, a horrified response.

To my right, Yinnie exclaimed, "Eww." Then she stared at us, her body trembling.

Evers walked toward our new friend and hugged her. Evers said, "You should go over to those trees, an area where you can't see any more bodies." My colleague pointed at them.

Yinnie flinched and walked, her hands shaking.

Within minutes, we discovered three more corpses. Two were detectives, Lo's colleagues. The other was a pilot named

Coza.

Y Ten announced, "Brin, according to Aan's lenses, Frank sent this team to help you."

Evers grimaced. "What a waste."

Y Ten said, "I used my dish to send a three D holographic message to Frank. He hasn't replied. Quantum probability graphs indicate that there is a two percent chance that he received it."

Evers frowned. "Why didn't he receive it?"

Y Ten's wrist-mounted interferometric telescope, a sixteenth of an inch in diameter tool, hummed. "According to my latest scan, Lasho's atmosphere is thin. As a result, solar winds from the star Alpha Centauri A have destroyed ninety-five percent of our messages and keep doing it."

I scowled. These telescope's evaluations were 80 percent more accurate than my lenses' or wrist scanner probes. Lasho orbited Alpha Centauri A, a main sequence star. "Y Ten, is your telescope just as effective as the dish in terms of figuring out if the winds have destroyed them?"

"It is sixty-two percent more effective."

Evers asked, "Why isn't it one hundred percent more effective?"

"Because my software created the dish twenty minutes this morning, hasn't had enough time to get rid of all the bugs in the programming."

Evers shook her head. "Complications."

I said, "We must find Kolo." Everybody trudged on.

Within twenty minutes, our group hiked between shoulder-high mushrooms. Evers flinched. "According to my lenses, these are poisonous, filled with neurotoxins. Twenty minutes after taking a bite, you come down with a headache."

Yinnie blurted, "Yuck. But I'm hungry."

Evers continued, "Then you pass out."

I cringed. "Do you ever wake up?"

Evers replied, "No."

To our left, a green Dwot, one that was barely visible because it was the same color as the weeds, rushed out from behind a bush, never making a sound. I pointed at it, blenching and told everybody else about the spider. It darted away and went back to where it came from.

Evers called out, "I only see a bush. Are you sure it was a Dwot?"

I bit my lip, annoyed by her ignorance. "Yes."

Evers' brow tightened. "You're probably tired, seeing things that aren't there."

Yinnie commented, "This area is dark, creepy."

Y Ten kept staring at the bush, her telescope whirring. "Brin, are you sure it was a Dwot?"

I blinked, irritated. "Yes." Our hiking party marched through ankle-deep mud, all of it filled with maggots.

Yinnie exclaimed, "These icky things are all over my boots. They stink."

Evers said, "I don't like them either."

In the far distance, rapid discharge rifles rang out. I scowled. "Y Ten, who is shooting?"

"Unknown. Kapoks are blocking my telescope's scans."

Evers grimaced. "This violence is getting on my nerves."

My hand itched. I looked at it. Two of my fingers were brown, covered by mold. I flinched, yanked out a tiny bottle, sprayed the mold, and it began disappearing.

Evers came toward me, frowning. "According to my lenses, this mold was created by amoebas. These organisms aren't on my database."

I cringed. "They aren't on mine either."

Y Ten walked toward us. "According to my DNA archive, the Munt's high humidity makes it possible for them to thrive."

Evers flinched. "Thrive? Tep shit."

Our group slogged on and went between huge acacias. To our right, in the shadows, a rustling grew louder.

Evers asked, "What's making that noise?"

Y Ten replied, "Unknown. Undergrowth is blocking my probes. There is another problem. My left hand is gone, destroyed by protozoa."

I blenched. "Will it grow back?"

"According to a probability graph, there is a twenty-four percent chance that it will. Unfortunately, since the protozoa keeps evolving, that prediction is premature."

Behind me, Yinnie called out, "This is scary. Y Ten, I like you, don't want you to get hurt."

Y Ten said in a monotone, "I like you, too."

Evers grimaced. "We'll have to be patient. With any luck, your hand will grow back."

At dusk, Y Ten ripped legumes out of the dirt. Microwave nozzles popped out of her chest. She cooked the legumes with them and handed the meal to everybody. Yinnie said, "Mine tastes like weeds. Wow, your hand has grown back."

"Yes."

Evers announced, "Wonderful."

I said, "Amazing."

Moments before sunup our group departed. Soon we came upon a huge spider web. In it, a falcon's corpse jiggled.

I cringed.

To my left, Evers pointed up. She blurted, "A Dwot is coming."

I glanced in that direction while my stomach muscles tightened, a frightened response. The arachnid jumped, came to rest on my sleeve, and bit into it. I shoved the creature a few inches.

It wouldn't let go.

As it hissed, I aimed and fired. The arachnid screeched. *Eeeeoon.* Then it hopped off and scampered across the web.

The others shot at it. Bullets struck its thorax, tearing the creature apart.

In the near distance, eight other Dwots rushed out from behind a wall, an opaque part of the web. At the same time, some of them whistled.

Evers shouted, "Let's get out of here."

All of us veered to the left and darted around huge thorn bushes, all of them partly covered by the edge of the web. To my right, four Dwots leaped. Y Ten, Evers and I discharged our weapons. Three of the arachnid's corpses dropped. The other sprayed a yellow mist. It ended up on my sleeve, and Y Ten's right hand, missing Yinnie by inches. A blade popped out of the robot's other hand. She chopped the Dwot's head off. Everybody jumped over a pile of rocks.

On our right, a large clump of the arachnids, just a blur, scampered in this direction. Three of us fired. *Eeeeoon.*

Yinnie screamed.

I looked straight ahead, my adrenaline pumping. Within seconds, our group went under banyan roots.

Behind us, whistling became softer.

On my left, Evers blurted, "They're slowing down, can't keep up with us."

We came upon an ankle-high wall of creepers, sprang over them and kept going.

After rushing through waist-deep grass, a small area surrounded by kapoks, we slowed to a walk.

To my right, Y Ten announced, "We've left them behind."

I nodded while glancing at my sleeve. Part of it was eaten away, destroyed by the Dwot's spray. My body went cold, a horrified response.

Evers glanced at my sleeve. "Horrible. I'm glad it missed Yinnie."

Our young friend rushed forward and examined the same spot. She burst out, "Eww."

Within minutes, our group stepped over a ridge, most of it covered by two-inch long beetles.

Yinnie exclaimed, "They're ugly."

Evers said, "According to my wrist scanner, droplets, all of them filled with neurotoxins, were coming out of their jaws. If they bit you, you would end up with a stomachache."

I cringed.

Ahead, far away, artillery fired.

Y Ten announced, "Ninety-threes are making that noise."

I nodded. A ninety-three cannon fired two hundred shells per second. Each shell, equipment with a homing device, had a 69 percent chance of hitting the target. If your opponent's lenses were transmitting signals, ones that jammed the device, the shells missed the target 80 percent of the time.

Evers called out, "I hate ninety-threes. Dek's Armies used them to destroy part of Af Wa, my home town."

Yinnie blanched.

Y Ten's satellite dish hummed.

To our right, eighty yards away, several ninety-three mortar shells hit strangler figs. Pieces of bark rained down on our group. I winced as everybody dove to the ground.

Yinnie screamed.

Y Ten called out, "Another shell is coming."

I shuddered with horror. "We better get out of here."

Evers asked "Where do we go?"

I replied, "Another spot." Our group jumped up, sprinted to the left and went between palmettos. Behind us, shells hit nearby strangler figs, a deafening noise. *Craaaak.*

Chills ran down my spine, a mortified response.

Yinnie shrieked.

CHAPTER NINETEEN

After passing hundreds of wimbas, the noise of shells blowing apart huicungos, trees that were far behind us, became softer.

Evers exclaimed, "I'm surprised that the shells didn't hit our group."

Y Ten announced, "They didn't because my telescope sent computer code into the homing devices a hundredth of a second after each shell left a ninety-three. As a result, they hit targets that were forty or more yards away from us."

I asked, "Are you telling me that if our group stayed in the same spot, every shell would have missed us?"

Y Ten replied, "If we stayed there, the devices would have adjusted. As a result, there would be a seventy-nine percent chance of them hitting us."

Evers asked, "Why aren't they hitting us now?"

"According to my telescope's last evaluation, the homing devices in nine-three's shells can't find us because we keep moving."

I blinked, worried. "Are the devices looking for our infrared heat signatures or using echo-imaging to find us by detecting our voices?"

"It could be both or just one of those. I'm not sure. My telescope is trying to answer your questions. Unfortunately, at this point in time, locating their shells is hard because trees and other plants are in the way."

Evers frowned. "We should communicate via text messages, not talk. If we speak, the ninety-three's devices are more likely to spot us."

Yinnie asked, "What about me? I don't have any lenses."

Evers murmured, "The next time you want to

communicate, whisper in my ear or use hand signing."

Yinnie formed an X with her fingers, signifying that some of the time she would use hand signing from now on if she wanted to communicate to us.

I acknowledged her statement while forming a zero with two fingers, indicating that using hand signing was a good idea.

Evers and Y Ten copied my gesture.

Yinnie smiled.

I drew three horizontal parallel lines, asking Yinnie what she wanted to do at night when we couldn't see her hands.

On this young ladies' forehead, some of her skin became brighter, creating glowing icons, shapes that were identical to hand signing.

I blinked, surprised and amazed, and drew an oval, pointing out that her ability to do this was impressive.

After hiking between hundreds of shiringas, our crew reached a curved river. To our left, in the near distance, three Aito men fired at us. We dove to the ground and crawled behind a dirt mound.

A text message from Y Ten appeared in my lenses. According to it, she wanted to know if I would use experimental red blood cells, organisms that made it possible for me to hold my breath for thirty minutes. If I were interested, she would export them into my lungs. As a result, I could swim downriver, come up behind the gunmen and shoot them in the back.

I responded, telling him that using the cells was a good idea. Her text message materialized, telling me she had just exported them. I crawled past bushes, entered the water, then turned while pushing algae aside.

CHAPTER TWENTY

A head, sunken tree roots blocked my way. I glided around them. To my right, a seven-foot-long worm opened its mouth, one lined with teeth. Without warning, it rushed toward me. As my adrenaline pumped faster, a knife popped out of my sleeve. I stabbed the creature's jaw. It lunged at my shoulder pad and sank its teeth into the material. I yanked out the weapon and shoved the blade into its neck. The creature began shaking as muscles gushed out of the wound. I kicked and went forward.

In front of me, several feet away, two more worms came in this direction. To my right, a three-eyed alligator lunged toward them. Soon it reached one, and its jaws snapped shut. Between its teeth, the worm jerked its head, trying to escape.

I went underneath the reptile, my heart pounding — a terrified reaction — then jerked my head above water. To my right, in the near distance, all three men were discharging their rapid discharge rifles. If I raised my weapon, they might see it out of the corner of their eyes. I kept going.

Within minutes, I paddled toward the bank and crawled onto it. Not far away, all three men were facing the opposite direction. I yanked out my rifle. It expanded. At the same time, its waterproof covering went inside the butt. I squeezed the trigger. Ammo struck all three men. One bellowed, "Help," and all three collapsed. I exhaled, relieved.

Within five minutes, Y Ten, Evers and Yinnie walked up to me.

Evers offered a thumbs up.

On Yinnie's forehead icons formed asking me how I got

here.

I hand signed, pointing out that it was a long story and there wasn't enough time to explain.

More formed, indicating that Yinnie didn't understand.

I frowned, disappointed by my inability to communicate with her.

We trudged on. Evers turned toward her while hand signing, answering our new friend's question.

Y Ten's text message scrolled through my lenses. According to it, she was surprised that the blood cell tool, a device that needed more testing, had worked. Our crew slogged on. Within seconds, she announced, "According to my latest telescope evaluation there aren't any humanoids or ninety-threes within a mile of us so we can talk."

After hiking through a dried-up lake's ankle-deep mud, we came upon a huge grove of towering wimbas. A crunching sound grew louder. I winced.

Evers asked, her voice almost drowned by the racket, "What's making that noise?"

Y Ten replied, "Good question."

Ahead, in the near distance, the ground cracked open, creating a six-hundred-foot-long, fifteen-foot-wide, thousand-foot deep chasm.

Yinnie screamed.

On the opposite side, several wimbas fell over and dropped to the bottom. On this side, more toppled over and went into it. Without warning, the crunching stopped.

Evers frowned. "Hiking around this will take a day or two."

Y Ten said, "I'll change into a helicopter. The rest of you climb aboard, and I'll fly over the chasm. Crossing it will only take a few minutes."

Evers' brow tightened. "Are you sure you can do it?"

"Yes." She changed into the flying machine. Everybody else hopped on. It took off. As I watched in horror, the aircraft dropped.

Y Ten's message scrolled through my lenses, indicating that since two of the helicopter's blades had broken off, every passenger should prepare for a crash landing. I flinched. A door opened.

Evers blenched.

Yinnie sobbed. "I don't want to die."

CHAPTER TWENTY-ONE

Evers said, "Don't let go." She grabbed Yinnie's hand, and both of them jumped out.

I leaped, my adrenaline pumping. Parachutes came out of our shoulder pads, and we glided downward. Below us, Y Ten changed into a glider and crashed landed in a three-foot-wide, thirty-foot-long patch of dirt, a spot at the bottom of the chasm.

The gusting wind shoved me sideways. As I flinched, the right side of my parachute rose. It missed a protruding rock. I exhaled, relieved. Without warning, an updraft pushed me in the opposite direction. The left side of the parachute hit a branch and tore the branch off. I cringed. Underneath my boot heels, the ground was rushing toward me. I clenched my teeth. My heels struck it, and I rolled. As chills ran across my spine, a terrified response, I stood. Then I flexed my fingers, bent each leg and took a step, trying to find out if anything was broken. Although my legs were slightly numb, they were intact.

In the near distance, Evers and Yinnie walked toward me. Yinnie blurted, "That was creepy."

Above us, a cracking grew louder.

While chills raced across my spine, I looked up as a boulder bounced off a chasm wall, headed this way. We rushed in several directions. It crashed to the ground.

Evers flinched as Yinnie's hands shook.

The broken glider changed into Y Ten. She said, "My jamming transmitter updated itself in the last two seconds. Now robbers and others can't hear us if they're close by, within fifty yards or less of our group."

I thanked her. Helmets came out of Evers' shoulder pads

and mine and covered our heads. At the same time, face masks slid out of the headgear.

Yinnie remarked, "I need something to protect my face and head."

I pulled a tiny square off my sleeve. It expanded and changed into a helmet. I gave it to our new friend, and she put it on, a worried expression on her face.

Evers scowled. "Climbing out of here will take hours." Above our crew, a grinding became louder.

I looked up, wincing as pebbles rained down on us. "The cliffs are falling apart."

Y Ten said in a monotone, "I can't fix that."

Evers scowled while pointing up. "That cliff is stable."

Y Ten's wrist-mounted scanner hummed, processing data. "I'll change into a Wall Climber. After I do, get on my back and hold on."

Evers grimaced. "It sounds like a bad idea, but I can't think of another plan."

Y Ten morphed. We crawled on. Straps popped out of the vehicle's back, then wrapped around everyone's arms and legs.

Yinnie blurted, "I'm scared."

Evers sighed. "That makes two of us."

The Climber started up a cliff. At the same time, our bodies jerked downward. Soon it passed a crumbling section.

My stomach muscles tightened, a horrified response.

Evers called out, "I hope Y Ten knows what she is doing."

A branch crashed down on the top of my helmet and fell off. My adrenaline pumped faster.

Yinnie screamed.

Evers asked, "Brin, are you hurt?"

"No."

Falling dirt rained down on us.

Yinnie hollered, "This is scary."

Evers flinched. "It is." She pushed some of it off her sleeve.

Above the Climber, a snapping became louder. My jaw muscles tightened, a scared to death response. The Climber veered to the right. To our left, a section of the wall broke off and plummeted.

Yinnie wailed.

Evers spat, "Wow."

I blenched. "That was too close for comfort."

Evers announced, "No shit."

The cliff began shaking. The Climber moved to the left. On our right, the steep rock face crumbled.

Evers shouted, "Oh my god."

I examined my hand, wishing it would stop trembling.

Yinnie started crying.

The Climber went over a branch and kept going. Below us, the limb snapped off.

I exhaled, trying to calm down as gusting wind shoved me sideways. Soon falling dirt landed on my left wrist. I winced. Below us, the crag fell apart.

Evers snapped, "Our luck is running out."

I exclaimed, "I hope you're wrong."

The Climber reached the top of the chasm, went over it and lurched forward.

Evers called out, "We made it."

The vehicle went by palmettos. Behind us, a grinding became louder. I glanced in that direction. Inches from us, the top of the cliff broke apart and plummeted into the chasm.

CHAPTER TWENTY-TWO

I cringed.

Evers blurted, "Tep . . ."

Yinnie screeched.

The Climber sped up. All around it, a snapping became louder. The ground along with the surrounding palmettos plummeted about five feet. The Climber went uphill, reached a patch of dirt, a spot between strangler figs and jerked forward.

Yinnie's entire body twitched.

Evers burst out, "Oh my god."

The ground began shaking—then a rumbling grew louder. To our right and left, palmettos fell over. Several missed us by inches. I winced.

Yinnie shrieked.

Evers shouted, "Not again."

The rumbling was replaced by the sound of gusting wind. I took a deep breath, trying to relax.

Evers called out, "The ground has stopped shaking. Finally."

I nodded. "Yes. And the trees aren't falling down."

The vehicle halted. On our arms and legs, the restraints popped open. All of us hopped off the Climber. I said, "We lost our rifles."

Evers shoved dirt off her sleeve. "More complications."

The Climber changed into Y Ten. She commented, stony-faced, "Brin and Evers, I just exported DNA enhancement code, a new invention, into the skin on your wrists. As a result, twenty cells have been converted into tiny guns, weapons that fire one sixty-fourth of an inch in diameter grenades or a stream of one-sixteenth of an inch-long bullets.

Use your lenses' trigger to fire them. A grid in your lenses will help you hit a target."

I blinked, surprised and thanked her.

She stared at me, a vacant expression on her face.

Evers glanced to the left. In the near distance, a grenade went off, destroying a bush. She burst out, "Amazing. I hit the target on the first try."

I exclaimed, "Fantastic."

Evers examined her arm. "I can't see the tiny gun with the naked eye, have to use my lenses' microscope to find it. Is the gun stable, won't break down?"

Y Ten replied, "There is a fifty percent chance that it will malfunction."

I sighed. "It will have to do."

Yinnie took a deep breath while examining her trembling hands. Evers walked and hugged her. Yinnie offered a weak smile. "Thanks, I needed that."

All of us sat on fallen trees. Evers handed out berries, and three of us ate.

Y Ten's left wrist fell apart. At the same time, her hand dropped to the ground. A new wrist grew out of her arm. She grabbed the hand, attached to her wrist, then straightened out her fingers. "My hand's functionality has returned."

I blenched. "What happened to your wrist?"

"Mutated streptococcus destroyed it. Although my bodies' antigens eradicated the lethal microorganisms, for the time being, more streptococcus will attack my body soon."

Evers glowered. "That's horrible. Can your body destroy the microorganisms before they attack?"

"No, the air in this location is filled with them."

My stomach muscles tensed up, a shocked reaction. "Why are our legs along with the rest of our bodies intact, not covered by the streptococcus?"

"According to my quantum computer model, your

antigens and white blood cells are strong enough to fight it off."

Yinnie spat, "The air is dirty. Eww." She examined her wrists and hands.

I said, "Yinnie, I don't want you to get sick."

Evers announced, "Yinnie, if that happens all of us will help you in any way we can."

Our young friend grinned.

I glanced at my hand, then looked up. "The mold is gone."

Evers smiled. "Great."

Far away, ninety-threes fired.

Evers announced, "I hate that sound."

My stomach muscles tensed up. "I don't like it either."

Y Ten's wrist hummed. "According to my telescope, the ninety-threes are four miles from this spot, between us and our destination."

Evers stood. "My terrain guide has created an alternate route, a path to get around them."

Y Ten's wrist-mounted computer hummed while it was processing algorithms. "According to my latest telescope evaluation, there is a seventy-four percent chance we can use that route to avoid those weapons."

I rose to my feet. "Can your telescope point out who is fighting?"

"No."

Evers frowned. "Will it ever do that?"

Y Ten replied, "I'm not sure. At this point, it has determined that thirty-six percent of the fighters are either moving or stationary. It will take at least twenty minutes for my telescope to recognize their faces and DNA. The rest of these strangers are hidden in bunkers and trenches. It just figured out that the moving humanoids are difficult to probe. In other words, it can't tell if they're Kolo's men, Frank's team or somebody else."

I tightened my fist, disappointed.

Y Ten added, "Also, some are transmitting computer code, syntax that is designed to confuse my telescope's evaluations."

Evers asked, "Some of them are IT?"

Y Ten's telescope clicked. "Yes."

I asked, "Are IT personnel scanning our group?"

Her tool clicked four times, processing files. "Good question. It will take a few hours for my telescope to evaluate that."

Evers' forehead tightened. "More complications. That bugs the shit out of me."

I bit my lip, annoyed by the lack of information. A memory of Sultra kissing me popped into my head. I rubbed my chin, wishing the haunting recollection would go away. The left side of Tesk's face, an incoming call, one that was distorted by something, appeared in my lenses. He said, "Brin . . ." His voice trailed off and was replaced by static. Without warning, his face vanished, end of the transmission. I told everybody else about our short conversation.

Evers' brow tightened. "More complications. Y Ten, can you update our lenses so that we can keep in touch with Frank and Tesk?"

"Not yet. I'm working on it."

Yinnie glanced to the left and right. "The jungle smells weird."

Evers scowled. We slogged on and stepped over tiny bones. I pointed at them. "Did Dwots kill these creatures?"

Y Ten responded, "No. Amoebas did."

Ahead, a beautiful woman and a tall male, twenty-something humans, both dressed in rags, stepped out of the shadows. My lenses sent neutrinos into their cerebrums.

She grinned. "I'm Linda. What are your names?"

All of us answered.

The male put his arm around her. "I'm Dan. I met my girlfriend ten days ago. Isn't she gorgeous?"

Evers nodded.

Yinnie blurted, "Sure. She has pretty eyes."

Linda winked at our young friend.

I offered a weak smile, worried about our challenges.

Y Ten's telescope clicked, processing data.

Linda caressed his hand. They walked toward our group, and all of us sat down.

Evers asked, "Where are you from?"

Linda replied in a sexy voice, "Cody. It's a town on Maen's east coast."

Evers nodded. "Why did you come here?"

Linda sighed. "It's safer than Last Chance. That place is disgusting, filled with thieves. I don't want to think about it anymore."

The neutrinos returned. This stranger was telling the truth.

Dan frowned. "I was a farmer, worked on a Robot-Human Operating Farm near Soha, a village close to the Heg Mountains, near Coam's interior. Like my girlfriend said, it's safer than Last Chance. What a shitty place. Too many fights and gun battles."

The neutrinos came back. He was telling the truth.

Linda pulled a bag out of her belt-mounted pouch. "I have berries to share." She handed it to Evers.

My colleague thanked her and shared the food with the rest of us.

Not long after the stars came out, Linda and Dan told us they were going to sleep and went behind huge bushes. Moments later, they laughed.

I rested on my back. "It's amazing that they can forget about their problems."

Evers yawned. "Yes. I envy them."

Yinnie asked, "Can somebody tell me a story?"

In the far distance, a rustling became louder. I flinched. "According to my wrist scanner, two vipers are passing through, bound for a succulent patch."

Evers said, "My mother told me three. This is the best tale. A young girl hears a violinist and asks him to become her teacher. At first, he argues, says he is too busy. Then he agrees. A month later, he tells her that she is one of his best students."

Yinnie blurted, "Wow. That's a great story."

I closed my eyes and fell asleep.

CHAPTER TWENTY-THREE

Suddenly, a crunching woke me. I sat up, flinching. Beneath a full moon, Linda rushed toward us. She called out, "Muggers just stabbed Dan to death, robbed us and ran away."

Evers, Y Ten and I darted behind the bushes. On Dan's blood covered neck, flies buzzed.

Evers said, "According to my wrist scanner, somebody slashed his neck eight minutes ago, and he bled to death."

Y Ten stooped. "Linda, boot prints that lead away from the body match yours."

She exclaimed, "A lot of muggers wear boots that are like mine."

Y Ten said, "All four cracks in the heels match yours. Those are your tracks."

She jumped backward, firing. A blast struck Y Ten's chest.

Evers discharged her weapon. Bullets struck Linda's cheek. She hollered, blood gushing out of the wound. Without warning, she stumbled and ended up on her side.

I walked toward Linda. "According to my scanner, she's dead." I cringed. "My neutrino scans were wrong."

Evers announced, "So were mine. Y Ten, are you injured?" She rushed toward her.

Y Ten sat up. "My chest hurts, but the pain will subside."

I said, "Y Ten, I assume that your neutrino analysis failed. You didn't know that Linda was an assassin or a bandit."

"Your assumption is correct."

Evers grimaced. "This stranger's transmitter cloaked her identity. I don't know how the device worked."

Y Ten said, "I don't know either. According to my computer, an analysis may be available soon."

My jaw muscles tightened in an irritated response. "The sooner, the better."

Yinnie darted toward Evers, the young girl's lips trembling. My partner hugged her.

My mind sped up, trying to figure out who Linda was.

Evers frowned. "Why didn't Linda kill Dan before they met us?"

Y Ten replied, "My theory, based on a computer model, is that if she killed him, she couldn't pretend to be his lover. As a result, refugees without scanners, those she could rob a few minutes after she met them, would be more likely to believe her lies."

Evers paused, eyes shifting back and forth. "Y Ten, although I never thought about that, it's feasible." Our group went back to bed.

In the morning, after crossing an area filled with orchids, our collective reached a Pallas grove. On their trunks, thousands of butterflies flapped their purple wings. Yinnie darted up to one while several of the insects touched down on her wrists. She grinned. "Aren't they pretty?"

I offered a faint smile. Above us, far away, hidden in the jungle, a barely audible droning grew louder.

Y Ten announced, "Leopards are coming."

Evers glanced upward. "Are you sure? The only things I see and hear are butterflies. My scanner and echo-imaging can't detect the Leopards."

"I'm sure. According to my telescope, they're jamming your scanner."

I kept looked straight ahead, into the distance, but only noticed towering dimly lit palmettos. Quite often Leopards, also known as Sixty-Eights, were parked on spaceships. 80 percent of the time bullets from a Leopard's smart gun hit a target.

As I watched in horror, seven Sixty-Eights, black aircraft, shot out of the dark.

Everybody darted behind a huge Pallas tree.

Above us, all seven fired. *Zing, zing, zing.* In front of them, ten white Leopard's guns went off. *Zing, zing.* Two black ones exploded. At the same time, three white Leopards blew up.

Y Ten announced in a monotone, "The pilots are skilled."

Yinnie whimpered, "I'm scared."

Evers hugged her. Carbon nanotube chunks hit adjacent strangler figs, ripping them apart.

I flinched.

Evers and Yinnie dove to the ground. More chunks struck nearby Pallas. Above us, a white Leopard swooped down and went between towering wimbas. Behind it, a black Leopard fired. The white aircraft exploded, and pieces flew in every direction. The indigo one rose. Eighty feet from its starboard side, a white Leopard discharged its weapons. The indigo aircraft broke apart, struck by laser beams. The white Leopard shot upward, engines droning. Not far behind it, an indigo 68's weapons blasted. *Zing, zing.* The white Leopard's port wing disintegrated. The aircraft plummeted, hit Pallas and blew up. Soon rising flames spread. At the same time, the smell of burning fuel grew stronger.

Y Ten said, "A distinctive odor."

A white Leopard zoomed over our heads, thirty feet above them. Not far behind it, an indigo 68 sprayed bullets. Some hit palms. Others struck the white Leopard, tearing off its antennae.

I blenched while the droning moved away. "They're fighting in a different spot. Let's search the wreckages. If a pilot is alive, we should help him or her."

Y Ten spoke, a blank expression on her face. "Shouldn't we move on, try to find Kolo?"

I snapped, "If a pilot is hurt, it's our duty to help them."

Evers blurted, "Brin, I agree with you."

Y Ten commented, "I'll do it. However, if any of those black Leopards return and kill us, don't blame me."

My stomach muscles tightened, an angry response. "I won't." Our group advanced and stepped over severed arms and legs. A few yards away, blood trickled out of a chopped off head. Chills ran up my spine. Within seconds, the stench of death became stronger.

Evers put one hand over Yinnie's eyes. Evers said, "Don't look."

Yinnie stammered, "I wa won't."

To my right, inches above a pilot's intestines, ones that partly covered her stomach, flies buzzed.

Evers spat, "Getting over this horrible sight will take a long time."

Yinnie vomited.

I said, "Take Yinnie to another area. Otherwise, she will throw up again."

The girl nodded.

We kept going. Y Ten announced, "According to my telescope, every pilot is dead. However . . ."

An aviator jumped out from behind a torn off wing, blasting.

Y Ten and I discharged our weapons. The aviator limped toward us and collapsed.

I announced, "According to my scanner, she's dead."

Y Ten said, "Yes."

I burst out, "Y Ten, you're hit."

"The wound will heal in two minutes." We hiked.

Not long after we hiked over a ridge, Evers commented, "I've never seen a wound heal that fast. Did you get rid of the streptococcus?"

Y Ten said, "Yes."

Evers exclaimed, "You keep evolving."

"Yes. I do it faster than four prior models."

I blinked, amazed by Y Ten's ability.

Evers added, "Brin, judging by that look on your face, Y Ten's feat surprised you."

"It did."

Our group slogged on.

CHAPTER TWENTY-FOUR

Evers exhaled, blinking. "With any luck, I'll get over that, won't have any nightmares."

Y Ten said, "I'll never understand why humans, Qio or any other race cries or gets so upset when they see corpses or the severely injured."

I grimaced. "That's the way we are."

Y Ten's hip-mounted camera whirred.

Evers paused, a curious expression on her face. "Y Ten, what are you doing?"

"I'm taking pictures that will help us understand how likely it would be for a Dwot to attack our group. According to one statistic, forty-two percent of the time, they hide in kapok and lupuna groves."

I nodded.

Evers frowned. "I have mixed feelings about robots. Some are helpful. Others get in the way."

Y Ten spoke, a blank expression on her face, "It's my job to help."

Evers' brow tightened. "I keep telling myself that. However, relying on a machine like you bothers me."

A floating screen appeared above Y Ten's hand. She examined it, never responding to Evers complaint.

Evers remarked, "Y Ten, why don't you argue with me? I could be wrong."

She replied in a monotone, "I have other duties to perform."

A memory of Sultra kissing me popped into my head. I blinked, wishing the haunting memory would go away.

Evers announced, "Brin, you look irritated. Am I getting on your nerves?"

"No. I'm just a little tired."

Evers' brow tightened. "Do you think about Sultra anymore?"

I lied, "Once in a while."

Y Ten added, "Romance is an interesting topic. When we have more time, somebody should tell me how it functions."

Evers glared at her. "I will."

Y Ten kept staring at a floating screen. "Tell me more about this later. I need to organize this file."

In my mind's eye, Sultra caressed my cheek. At the same time, she pressed her hips against mine.

Evers said, "Brin, you're thinking about something else. Talk to me."

"Okay, what do you want to discuss?"

"Whatever is bothering you."

My stomach muscles tightened, an annoyed response. "Don't worry about it. We need to find Kolo."

Evers' brow tightened. "All right. I was just checking."

Yinnie grabbed my colleague's hand. The girl frowned. "Don't let go. I'm scared."

My partner offered her a quick smile. "I won't."

A grinding became louder. I asked, "What's making that noise?"

Y Ten shouted, "I can barely hear you."

In front of us, about eighty yards away, part of the jungle rose. Soon wimbas and palms toppled off this five-hundred-foot-high ridge.

Chapter Twenty-Five

Minutes later, when the ridge was four thousand feet high, it stopped rising.

I blinked, awestruck. "Lasho keeps changing. My guess is that this is an unplanned event."

Y Ten said, "According to three computer models, the change is unplanned."

Evers called out, "We'll have to cross that. Shit."

Y Ten reported, "According to my telescope, there is a pass. I'll call it the Qenta Gap, after a famous human geologist. It's four miles away."

Our group reached it, a spot with several boulders on it and descended. Further forward, below us, somewhere in the Munt, gunfire rang out. My body went cold, a shocked response. "More battles."

Y Ten said, "Yes. Unfortunately, since wimbas and other trees are blocking my telescope probes, I can't tell who is fighting."

We entered another part of the jungle. In the near distance, a tall Qio male with a rapid-fire rifle stepped out of the shadows.

I winced.

He rushed toward us.

Y Ten asked, "What do you want?"

He grabbed her shoulder and tried to kiss our colleague. She pushed him away.

He discharged his weapon. Bullets ripped strands of Y Ten's hair off. She jerked her right hand upward. Her gun clicked, malfunctioning.

He spat, "If you resist, I'll kill you."

I glanced at the center of my lenses' grid, then blinked. Unfortunately, my tiny gun hummed, but it didn't fire.

To my right, beyond my peripheral vision, Evers remained silent.

Y Ten kept staring at him, not moving an inch. He stepped forward, shoved the gun barrel against her chest and kissed her on the mouth. Soon he stepped back, grinning. "You're beautiful, would make a great sex slave."

She grabbed his barrel with her right hand, then shoved it aside. At the same time, her other hand changed into a knife. She stabbed his neck. He staggered backward, a shocked expression on his face, tripped and fell on his back.

Yinnie screamed.

Y Ten kicked his stomach. He didn't move. She announced, "He's dead." Our new partner stooped, seized his gun and stood. At the same time, her knife reverted into its original shape.

Two Qio men, both dressed in filthy, ripped spacesuits, arrived. The fat one pointed at the corpse. "Who killed him?"

Evers replied in a businesslike tone, "We arrived a few minutes ago, don't know who did."

Yinnie trembled.

The other, a gaunt newcomer, frowned and pointed at Y Ten. "There's blood on your chest."

Y Ten remarked in a deadpan tone, "I killed a Dwot a few minutes ago."

The fat one walked toward her. He snickered. "I want you." He jumped and kissed her on the mouth.

She pushed him away. "I'm not interested."

He grabbed her shoulder, then kissed her in the same spot. Our colleague shoved him aside. He laughed. "I love a fighter."

Our new partner kept staring at him, a blank expression on

her face.

The gaunt stranger aimed his weapon at Yinnie. He announced, "Don't move or I'll shoot all of you."

My stomach muscles tightened, an angry response.

Evers spat, "Leave the girl alone."

Yinnie wept.

The fat one looked at Y Ten while announcing, "You got beautiful tits."

She kept staring at him, a blank expression on her face.

The fat male shot the ground between her feet.

Y Ten raised her chin, a vacant look in her eyes.

The fat male pointed at her. "Don't push me away again or I'll shoot you in the eye." He giggled.

Our new partner shrugged.

The fat stranger spat on the ground. "You won't talk. Fine." He lunged forward, then kissed her lips. Her right hand changed into a knife. She plunged the weapon into his throat, grabbed his arm and yanked his limp body in front of her chest.

Fifteen feet from our new partner, the gaunt male fired. Bullets struck the fat stranger's back. Y Ten threw her knife. It struck the gaunt man's throat. He dropped his weapon, then collapsed. Our new partner flung the fat one's body to the ground.

Evers and I rushed toward the gaunt male. My colleague stooped, then seized his gun while he flinched. He started choking.

As my adrenaline pumped faster, I said, "According to my scanner, he'll be dead soon."

Evers blenched and stood.

The gaunt man's head stopped jerking.

I exhaled, relieved that he wouldn't kill us. "According to my scanner, he just flatlined."

Evers scowled. "Good riddance."

I turned and pointed at the other male. "Y Ten, is he dead?"

"Affirmative." She walked, then stooped, yanked the knife out of the gaunt male's throat, and placed it on her right wrist. The weapon reverted into its prior shape, her hand. She grabbed his rifle and stood.

Evers rushed toward Yinnie and hugged our young friend.

I said, "Y Ten, you moved a lot faster than those men. They never had a chance."

She glanced at the gaunt stranger's body, a blank expression on her face. "I'm designed that way."

I frowned. "You're supposed to thank me."

She glanced at me, a vacant look in her eyes.

I scowled. "You don't care about compliments."

Y Ten announced, "Thank you."

I said, "You sound like a recording . . . don't really care."

"It's the best I can do, part of my programming. Next time I'll do better."

Evers announced, "We should move on. If any of these bandit's friends show up, they might kill us."

After hiking around several hundred dimly lit strangler figs, our group stopped behind a ten-foot-high wall of vines. Beyond this opaque barrier, men we couldn't see spoke, their voices barely audible. Evers and I pushed the dangling plants aside, a few inches. In the near distance a group of nine armed strangers, six Qio men, two human women, and one Qio woman, all dressed in wrinkled coats, kept talking to each other.

Next to them, six human women in torn dresses, a group that was on the ground, sitting close together, frowned. A Qio man shot one of the six in the head. As blood spurted out of the wound, she keeled over.

I winced. The other five human women shrieked. My lenses sent neutrinos into the tallest Qio male's brain. The particles didn't return. My stomach muscles tightened, an irritated response.

Evers whispered in my ear, "According to my recent neutrino probe, the shortest Qio male is going to shoot the remaining five soon. Then everybody in his group will rob the corpses."

I nodded as my teeth clenched. My lenses sent a text message into hers, telling my colleague that my neutrinos had failed.

Evers murmured, "There are too many gunmen. We can't kill all of them."

Y Ten's text comment scrolled through my lenses. *When night comes, I'll sneak up on every bandit, then kill them.*

I sent her a text message, telling Y Ten that we should go around the robbers immediately, and find Kolo because that was my primary goal.

Evers whispered in my ear, "We can't let the remaining five die."

I bit my lip, irritated and murmured into her ear, "Okay, but I think it's a bad idea."

Moments before midnight, Y Ten changed into a green, camouflaged tiger, then crept toward two of the bandits. Everybody else was asleep.

One, a male with a missing eye, yawned, then walked around a boulder.

Next to him, the Qio woman, a stranger with a huge scar on her chin, sat, inspected her rifle, then glanced over her left shoulder. She glowered. "Did you hear that crunching?"

He snickered. "It was me, stepping on leaves."

"Maybe." She turned, then glanced to the right, her weapon raised. "Listen." This stranger's shoulder-mounted flashlight switched on, then moved left to the right, illuminating her associates and the surrounding bushes.

He yawned. "I hate late night guard duty."

The woman stood and took a few steps, her poorly lit face barely noticeable in the dark. Behind her, a man snored louder. The woman flinched and paused. "Something is out there. The crickets are too quiet."

He belched. "You worry too much."

The tiger, a barely visible silhouette, leaped, slashed her neck and mouth. She dropped to the ground with a thump. The man rushed toward his gun. The tiger darted toward him, clawed his neck and mouth. He collapsed with a thud.

Next to him, a human woman with a rifle in hand, jumped up. "What the fuck?"

The tiger slashed her face. She tripped and fell. In the near distance, two men rose, guns aimed. The tiger repeated its attack, and both males ended up on their backs. The other bandits leaped to their feet, blasting. The tiger killed all of them using the same technique.

One of the five women, an unarmed blonde, rose. She asked, "What's going on?"

Next to her, another commented, "It's dark, hard to tell."

The tiger changed into Y Ten. She answered the blonde.

Evers, Yinnie and I walked toward them.

The blonde glanced at me, her body shaking. "What do we do now? The bandits murdered the rest of our group and brought us here." She grabbed one of the rifles.

I said, "Come with us."

The blonde winced. "Where are you going?"

Evers mentioned our goal.

Next to the blonde, a woman with one ear rose to her feet. "I've never heard of Kolo. There are too many thieves. How do we avoid them?" She seized a rifle.

I replied, "You'll see."

The woman with one ear, the other chopped off, scowled. "What will I see?"

I said, "You'll find out soon enough."

She sighed. "My name is Rosa. What's yours?"

I answered and gave her the rest of my group's names.

The blonde announced, "I'm Anna."

My lenses sent neutrinos into both of their minds. The particles returned. Anna Smith, a Bio-Physicist from Nipl, left that town, accompanied by her twelve-year-old daughter, Chloe, when NX military aircraft strafed it. Two days later they boarded a spacecraft, one filled with refugees. It touched down near Fao. Moments after they along with the other refugees stepped off the ship, gunmen robbed several of them. The other refugees scattered in many directions. Soon Anna lost track of her daughter. Then Anna came here, trying to find a safer place. During that time, she showed photographs of Chloe to strangers. All of them told her they hadn't seen the girl.

This information was replaced by Rosa James' background. A Botanist and a Physicist, she was a resident from Nipl, along with her husband, Rex, and their eight-year-old son, Jason. They boarded another spacecraft. After it touched down, gunmen arrived. She lost track of her family when the crowd took off, trying to get away from the gunmen. Moments later, she met Anna, and they came here, wanting to find a secure area. At the same time, she showed photos of her husband and son to strangers, asking them if they had seen them.

I cringed, upset by their plight. To my right, in the near distance, a droning grew louder.

Anna called out, "DX are coming. Run for cover."

Evers frowned. "What are DX?"

Anna exclaimed, "Jets."

I winced. Two triangular aircraft, about eighty feet long, flew over nearby strangler figs, their wing-mounted guns firing. *Zet, zet, zet.*

Everybody ran for cover as bullets and laser beams tore up

adjacent ferns.

Yinnie screamed.

Soon all of us reached banyan roots and went under them.

As the jets went over nearby palmettos, Evers announced, "I hope they don't come back."

Y Ten said, "We'll see."

The droning grew softer. Soon it became louder.

Anna called out, "They're returning."

Yinnie started crying. Evers hugged her.

Zet, zet, zet.

Y Ten fired. "Missed."

Rosa, Anna, Evers, Y Ten and I discharged our weapons.

Evers frowned as the jets flew toward distant wimbas. "The DX are moving too fast. It's difficult to hit them." Soon they returned fire. *Zet, zet.*

Anna called out, "Got one."

While smoke came out of its tail, the aircraft banked to the right.

Rosa asked, "Why is it turning?"

Evers replied, "Unknown."

Y Ten said, "It's headed for a clearing, about half a mile from us."

I said, "Let's go. Before the other DX comes back."

Anna called out, "We have to cross fifty yards of open space to reach more banyan roots."

Y Ten said, "If we head northeast, toward a denser part of the Munt, it will be harder for the DX's bullets and laser beams to hit us."

Anna burst out, "Let's do it." Everybody took off.

I glanced over my shoulder, my adrenaline pumping. Eight feet behind us, laser beams from an oncoming DX hit the dirt.

Rosa yelled, "Run faster."

CHAPTER TWENTY-SIX

After rushing between hundreds of lupunas and dashing over a ridge, one beneath the jungle canopy, our group slowed to walk. I huffed. "We've lost them."

To my left, Rosa scowled. "For a while at least."

Rosa, Anna, Yinnie, Evers, Y Ten and I sat on fallen wimbas. Rosa handed out bananas that she and Anna had picked recently and everybody ate them. Above us, on huicungo branches, several Paxo squeaked.

Anna smiled while pointing at the creatures. "I love watching them hop from branch to branch."

Rosa laughed. "So do I."

Evers sighed. "Rosa and Anna, do you know much about this area?"

Rosa grimaced. "CZ and her followers have set up a camp between Fao and a village called Ho He. The camp is about three miles north of us."

I cringed.

Evers grimaced. "We met CZ." She added details.

Rosa gnashed her teeth.

Anna coughed, a terrified expression on her face.

I asked, "How many followers does CZ have?"

Anna leaned back, an angry expression on her face. "Rosa and I have only seen the camp once, about five weeks ago. Anyway, there are about nineteen."

Frank's face, a hazy image, appeared in my lenses. Beneath it, meaningless print scrolled. *I'm go . . .* within a second this message vanished. I sent a text message to Evers telling her about this event.

My partner's response came out of the lenses' background, pointing out that the same thing happened to her during that time.

I sighed, disappointed that Frank couldn't communicate with us. Our crew trudged on. Y Ten's message, a memo that was identical to Evers, materialized in my lenses.

After hiking between hundreds of wimbas, our group came upon nine Sigos. I winced as they crawled over tiny bones. At the same time, these worms made a puckering noise.

Yinnie stepped backward. "Ew, they stink."

Anna choked. "They're disgusting." We continued. It started raining.

Within the hour, the storm ended. Soon all of us passed a cataract.

Rosa said, "It's a two-hour march to Fao. This is the Taon Waterfall."

Yinnie pointed at it. "It's beautiful."

Anna smiled. "It sure is." We climbed over piled up rocks as mist trickled down our faces. Far away, hidden in fog, vipers hooted.

Rosa grimaced. "Two weeks ago, a viper bit one of my friends. She collapsed eleven minutes later."

Evers frowned. "Did she wake up?"

Rosa's brow tightened. "No. We thought she had passed out."

Y Ten asked in a deadpan tone, "Do you know what killed her?"

Rosa scowled. "We lost our body examiner tools. As a result, figuring out what did was impossible."

According to my lenses, 62 percent of the time, these examiners could determine the cause of death. However, because viruses and bacteria kept evolving, coming up with an accurate diagnosis became more difficult as time passed.

Also, examiner's archives didn't include any of Lasho's creatures or any toxins these snakes used to kill predators or anything that came too close to them.

Minutes later, our group hiked through a huge lupunas' grove. To our left, about eighty yards away, hidden in the jungle, Gaoots screeched.

I cringed while our crew sped up.

Evers blurted, "Shit."

Anna glanced over her shoulder. "Two of them are coming this way. I wish we could run faster."

One of the Gaoots howled.

Rosa looked in that direction. "Three Dwots just attacked them."

Yinnie stuttered, "Yu, yu, yuck."

Evers grabbed her hand.

At dusk, our collective reached a clearing, a spot surrounded by towering huicungos. On many of their branches, foot-long purple snails purred, then snickered.

I pointed at the gastropods. "Are they dangerous?"

Anna gnashed her teeth. "I've never seen those strange looking mollusks before."

Y Ten replied, "According to my latest probe, they're harmless, only eat bark."

Anna frowned while looking at Y Ten. "What is a beautiful woman like you doing here?"

"I'm a UA, designed to help Brin and Evers."

Anna blinked. "You fooled me. Every humanoid robot I've seen has titanium or some other type of metallic skin."

"I'm a prototype."

Rosa exclaimed, "An impressive one."

Anna paused, a doubtful expression on her face. "Y Ten, you have the most beautiful body I've ever seen. That tight outfit shows off her huge breasts and great ass, features that drive a lot of men crazy."

Evers nodded. "That's true." She mentioned Y Ten's previous encounters with men.

Rosa stared at Y Ten. "Really? The men were surprised, didn't have a clue."

Evers replied, "No clue at all."

Rosa shook her head. "Oh, come on. Some men must have known."

Evers said, "Not these."

Rosa paused, her forehead scrunched up.

Not long after dawn, our group reached the edge of a gorge. To our left and right it stretched to the horizon. Y Ten announced, "According to my recent telescope probe, this new chasm, one that opened four days ago, is eighty miles long, half a mile-wide."

I flinched. "We'll have to cross it."

Evers sighed. "I hate this."

Anna grimaced.

Rosa spat, "Son-of-a-bitch."

Yinnie wiped the sweat off her forehead.

Y Ten pointed to the right. "The best option is to take this five-mile long route, a dangerous hike that leads to a narrow gap, one we can use to reach the opposite side of the gorge."

Evers asked, "Y Ten, can you change into a helicopter or an airplane and take us across?"

"There are too many downdrafts. We would crash before I reached the other side."

I sighed while raising my arm. The arrow didn't come out.

Evers scowled. "Brin, why did you raise your arm?"

I answered.

Evers sneered, "More complications."

Anna scowled. "Y Ten can change into a helicopter or an

airplane? I don't believe it."

Evers offered an explanation.

Rosa glared at Evers. "I don't accept that."

Anna shook her head. "It's a tall tale. Y Ten can't change into it."

Y Ten shrugged. We hiked.

All of us came upon a ledge. On our left, sixty feet across the chasm, branches that were sticking out of a cliff shook, pushed by the wind. Above us, a scraping became louder. I looked up, curious and scared, noticed a cave, then pointed at it. "What's inside?"

Y Ten answered stony-faced, "Dwots."

I winced.

Evers announced, "Shit."

Anna called out, "Son-of-a-bitch."

Rosa spat, "I hate them." Our group marched.

Within minutes we came upon a short natural bridge, hiked across it, reached the opposite rim and moved on. Behind us, a droning grew louder. I glanced over my shoulder, flinching.

Evers called out, "Winged Dwots are coming." Everybody ran.

To my right, one bit Rosa's shoulder. She tripped and ended up on her side.

Y Ten, Evers and I fired at the creature, one of six, and grazed its tail. It screeched. *Oowa.* Beyond it, another swooped down and slashed Rosa's neck. As her mouth opened, the creature grabbed her head with its claws and flew away.

On my left, a bigger one slashed Anna's hair with its claws. Ammo struck its wings. *Ooowa.* The predator dropped to the ground. More bullets ripped its throat open. *Ooowa.* Mucus gushed out of the wound. Next to it, a smaller one clawed Y Ten's right arm. Bullets cut the predator in half. It plummeted while Yinnie screamed. The rest took off, flapping hard. Laser beams hit two, and both dropped into the dirt. *Ooooowa.*

Evers, Anna and I rushed over, blasting. The ammo ripped their wings and heads off. All three of us stopped next to their corpses.

Evers grimaced. "Horrible."

Anna wiped tears from her eyes. "Rosa is dead. I hate it."

I flinched. Behind us, flapping grew louder. To my right, Y Ten said, "Let's go. More Dwots are coming."

All of us darted into the jungle, hopped over knee-high vines and rushed between towering lupunas. I glanced over my shoulder. In the near distance, eight winged Dwots, about four feet above the ground, flapped harder. While chills ran up my spine, I yelled, "Run."

CHAPTER TWENTY-SEVEN

Our group darted underneath hundreds of banyan roots. Evers announced, "They've stopped following us."

I blinked, surprised, and we slowed to a walk. Without warning, Anna shot Y Ten in the cheek. She collapsed.

Evers discharged her weapon. Anna fell over, blood gushing out of her temple. Evers announced, "According to my wrist scanner, she's dead."

I cringed. My lenses sent neutrinos into her mind. They returned. "According to my latest probe, Kolo sent Anna to gun us down."

Evers scowled. "Kolo or somebody on his staff improved Anna's contact lenses. As a result, they transmitted false information, data that fooled our first neutrino scans."

My stomach muscles tightened, a horrified response. "Do you have any idea how they fooled them?"

Evers replied, "No. A more in-depth analysis will take time."

To my left, Yinnie, a shocked expression on her face, kept staring at Anna. To my right, the hole on Y Ten's cheek was slowly closing, healing. I asked, "Y Ten, are you going to be all right?"

She didn't answer.

I said, "We can't stay here. The Dwots might be coming."

Evers scowled. "I'll carry Y Ten on my back. Help me."

I did.

After crossing four muddy knee-deep streams, our crew stepped over hundreds of Sigos.

Yinnie burst out, "They're ugly, and they stink."

My stomach churned, reacting to the repulsive odor. "It's

true."

Evers coughed. "They smell like shit."

We passed moldy orchids, flowers with slugs inside them. Ahead, a five-foot-tall teenage boy, a human with white skin, dressed in torn pants and a dirty jacket, stepped out of the darkness.

I asked, surprised, "Who are you?"

He flinched. "Sean." He lapsed into silence, a sad expression on his face.

My lenses sent neutrinos into his cerebral cortex. They returned. He and his mother, Joni, were from Nor. Two mornings ago, after their spacecraft touched down near Ho He, both of them along with eighty refugees aboard their ship fled as a gun battle between gunmen raged on. During the battle, Sean lost track of Joni. Within hours, after leaving this violent area, he slowed to a walk and showed 3D holograms of her to strangers, asking if they had seen her. All of them said they had not. He ended up here, feeling lonely and hungry.

Evers said, "Sean, come with us. We'll try to help you find Joni."

On her back, Y Ten drawled, "I'm healing. The entire process will take five more hours."

I announced, "Five more. That's great."

Y Ten didn't respond.

Sean mumbled, then glanced at all of us, a stunned look on his face. "Who are you?"

I answered.

Sean grimaced.

Yinnie announced, "Sean, you look tired."

"I'm lonely, would love to tag along with you."

Evers said, "Join us." Our group slogged on.

Sean pointed at Y Ten. "There's a hole in your cheek. Why aren't you dead?"

She didn't answer.

Evers replied, "She's a robot."

Jason blinked. "Really?"

Evers remarked, "Yes."

Far away, hidden in the jungle, artillery fired. I winced. "That battle is beyond my wrist scanner's range."

Evers' forehead tightened. "It's beyond mine, too. When Y Ten is fully recovered, it's possible she can tell us who is fighting and why they're doing it."

I said, "It's dusk . . . time to rest for the evening."

The next morning, moments after our group broke camp, we climbed over a hill, one partly covered by Foohs. I reached down, grabbed one and shoved it in my mouth.

Yinnie gagged. "That creature looks disgusting."

Evers seized another. "They do, but they're edible."

Yinnie picked one up, took a bite, and chewed. "It tastes awful."

Evers sighed. "It does."

Y Ten said, "According to my scan, it's full of Vitamin C."

Yinnie exclaimed, "Y Ten, you're getting better. That's great."

Y Ten remarked in a monotone, "Yes."

In front of us, not far beyond a strangler fig, two teenage girls, Qio with mottled blue and white skin, stepped out of the shadows. The tallest, a brunette with huge lips, glared at us. "Why did you come here?"

Evers offered our names and goal.

Y Ten said, "Please identify your selves."

The brunette paused, an irritated expression on her face. "I'm Zesa."

The other, a thin stranger with thick indigo eyebrows, replied, "I'm Marti. We're lost, trying to find my dad."

My lenses sent neutrinos into their hippocampi. The tiny

particles returned. Both girls, sisters, were from North Vewa. Three days ago, their spacecraft, one filled with two hundred refugees, touched down near Ho He. When all the passengers stepped out of the ship, hundreds of refugees rushed forward and surrounded them. While some of the refugees shouted, asking the passengers if they had any food, both girls looked around, trying to locate their father, Bill. Soon both girls started following several twenty-something humans, men and women, wanting to find something to eat. Hours ago, that group deserted them, told the girls that both of them should go out on their own in order to locate a meal.

Y Ten handed both of them Foohs. Marti and Zesa grabbed them, then ate.

Marti bit off a piece. "This tastes horrible. Yuck."

Evers said, "They're edible, won't make you sick."

Further forward, eighty feet behind both girls, a forty-foot-long spacecraft descended, its engine droning.

Y Ten pointed at it. "That ship is going to crash."

Zesa spun around, a shocked expression on her face.

Marti called out, "Oh my god."

Zesa flinched as the ship disappeared behind towering palmettos. In less than a second, it exploded, and orange flames shot upward.

Evers announced, "We need to help any survivors."

Marti asked, "Us?"

Evers replied, "Yes." She, Y Ten and I rushed toward the craft.

CHAPTER TWENTY-EIGHT

Evers, Y Ten, I stepped over scattered chunks. To our right and left, four severed heads, and other sliced off body parts were partly covered by debris.

Yinnie, Sean, Marti, and Zesa arrived.

Yinnie vomited. Evers hugged her.

Marti choked up. "All of them are dead."

I announced, "Marti, Zesa, Sean, and Yinnie, stand in a spot that is eighty yards from the wreckage. You shouldn't have to look at more bodies."

Marti and Yinnie hurried away.

Sean kept staring, a horrified expression on his face.

Zesa glanced down, wincing. "It's . . ."

Evers barked, "Sean, Zesa, do what you are told." Both took off, following Marti and Yinnie.

Y Ten stooped, picked up a crying baby girl and wrapped a blanket around her. "She's not hurt." Our robot partner gave the baby a piece of Fooh, and the infant chewed.

Evers took a deep breath, walked and glanced at the baby. "It's amazing that she is still alive."

Y Ten said in a monotone, "Yes."

Y Ten, Evers and I hiked, looking for other survivors.

Four hours later, when all three of us had searched the entire crash scene, Y Ten said, "Eighty-one died. The baby is the only survivor."

Evers nodded, eyes wide open, a horrified expression on her face. We marched toward the kids.

I exhaled, trying to relax. An email from Tesk materialized in my lenses. According to it, the message's attachment could be placed on a fern or any other plant. Then the flora would change into Y Eleven, the result of base pair manipulation. Knowing we needed more help, I downloaded the attachment onto a bush. Within seconds, the plant turned into a robot, a UA that was similar to Y Ten.

Zesa pointed at the android. "Wow. What is that?"

I answered.

Marti exclaimed, "Amazing."

Evers said, "It's good to have more assistance."

Y Eleven took a step, then fell apart.

Marti's face scrunched up. "What happened?"

Y Ten answered, "My probe indicated that her antigens weren't strong enough to fight off amoebas and viruses. As a result, she disintegrated."

I sighed.

Sean remarked, "Uh oh."

Marti blurted, "I didn't know that amoebas were so dangerous."

Zesa exclaimed, "They sound gross. I hope I don't get any on me."

Yinnie wiped tears off her cheek. "I'm scared."

Zesa said, "So . . ." Then she lapsed into silence, wincing.

Marti glanced at her hand. "There aren't any amoebas on my skin."

Y Ten said, "They're invisible to the naked eye."

Marti looked at her, a shocked expression on the girl's face.

Sean remarked, "Invisible. Interesting."

Marti glanced at him, a disgusted expression on her face.

Y Ten said, "According to my latest probe, eighty-one percent of them are on the ground. Don't touch it. If you don't, there is a seventy-six percent chance that you will remain healthy."

Zesa sighed. "I'm tired of being dirty and cold."

Evers said, "We'll share our sleeping bags with you, Marti, Sean, and Yinnie."

Zesa offered a weak smile. "Thanks."

Yinnie grumbled, "I don't like the Munt, and I miss my dad." Our crew slogged on, headed toward Fao.

Sean remarked, "Evers, I'm glad that you let me join your group."

She offered a thumbs up.

Far away, an indigo Leopard rose above treetops, moving fast. I blenched while pointing at the aircraft. "It's coming this way."

Marti spat, "Watch out."

Everybody darted under a bush while the aircraft's engine droned louder. It zoomed overhead and kept going.

Y Ten murmured, "According to my telescope, the Leopard's scanner didn't notice our heat signatures."

Evers whispered, "I hope you're right. The Leopard went by so fast that my scanner couldn't probe it thoroughly."

Without warning, the aircraft returned. Soon it stopped, hovering eighty feet above us. On its bottom, white lights switched on, illuminating the jungle floor, a sixteen-foot in diameter area that was two feet from us.

Marti asked in a low tone "What can we do?"

I murmured in hers, "Be quiet and don't move."

She blinked, then mumbled in her sister's ear. Her sister cringed but didn't say anything.

Sean hunkered down, trembling.

Yinnie raised her shaky hand and wiped the sweat off her chin.

CHAPTER TWENTY-NINE

The aircraft moved toward us, several inches, its engine humming. My adrenaline pumped faster. Without warning, the Leopard flew away slowly, its light illuminating a nearby fern, a plant with a six-inch long worm on it. The white light turned red. The aircraft descended until it was seven feet above the ground.

On its bottom, a hatched opened. A helmeted soldier in a taupe uniform jumped out of the hatch, landed in the dirt, walked toward the fern and reached it. Suddenly, the soldier halted, then turned in a full circle. On the trooper's ebony face mask, four horizontal blue stripes flickered, indicating that his or her motion detector was examining the adjacent area.

My heart started pounding, a terrified response. Although Evers clenched her teeth, she didn't say anything.

Marti placed both hands over her eyes. Zesa flinched.

Y Ten kept staring at the soldier, a blank expression on her face.

Yinnie hugged Evers, a terrified look on the girl's face.

In Evers' arms, the baby was sleeping, quiet.

The soldier leaped upward into the hatch. It hummed shut. The Leopard rose, then flew away.

I exhaled, relieved. "Why didn't the soldier's detector notice us?"

Y Ten replied, "Because my anatomy sensor probe manipulated its scans."

Evers said, "Great. How does your probe work?"

"It scrambles the detector's electrons and replaces them with other electrons, particles indicating that we're ferns."

I blinked, amazed. "Is this a new invention?"

"Yes, I created it two hours ago."

Zesa remarked, "It's a cool invention."

Sean added, "Yes, cool."

Y Ten said, "I should have field-tested it first, but there wasn't enough time."

Chills ran across my spine, a mortified response. "We were lucky that it worked."

Marti complained, "This part of the jungle is dark, creepy."

Y Ten announced, "We should move on."

When our group passed thousands of dimly lit mushrooms, ones with maggots on them, Yinnie pointed at the tiny creatures. "They're gross, and they smell like poop."

I nodded while noticing a thrumming. "What's making that sound?"

Evers replied, "It's coming from somewhere nearby, underground."

Y Ten remarked, "Fascinating. It's getting louder."

My adrenaline pumped. "Y Ten, can you tell what it is?"

"No. Rose quartz and silica, sediment in the ground is blocking my telescope's evaluations. My telescope isn't designed to probe anything that's underground."

Evers grimaced. "Is it the start of an earthquake?"

Y Ten answered, "Unknown."

Marti blurted, "It's a creepy noise."

Zesa remarked, "Totally creepy."

Ahead, in the near distance, an egg-shaped vehicle, twenty feet long, one with a giant drill bit on its front, came out of the ground. As dirt fell off the machine, its bottom-mounted articulated metal tracks moved faster.

Evers remarked, "It's loud. What the hell is it?"

Y Ten replied, "It resembles a tank."

Zesa announced, "It looks weird."

Marti exclaimed, "It sure does."

Although Yinnie blinked, she didn't say anything. Soon it

came toward us.

Y Ten darted to the right. The machine passed her. Suddenly, it rose. A cannon popped out of its left side and fired.

I yelled, "Look out."

Everybody dove to the ground. Rockets missed us, struck nearby mushrooms and blew up. While dirt rained down on our crew, Evers, Y Ten and I discharged our weapons. The bullets ricocheted off the machine.

Evers announced, "Shit."

Next to the cannon, weapons whirred.

Bullets grazed my sleeve. I blenched. The left side of the vehicle exploded, and it crashed to the ground.

Evers asked, "What happened?"

Y Ten answered, "Several of my S Eight bullets penetrated the craft's skin and detonated."

Evers exclaimed, "Amazing. I've never heard of S Eights."

Y Ten said, "I invented them forty minutes ago."

I said, "Spectacular."

Zesa exclaimed, "Cool. Y Ten is smart."

On the left side of the machine, a hatch popped open. A five-foot-tall Qio woman in a green jumpsuit, her neck partly covered in blood, climbed out, took a few steps, barely balanced and keeled over. Y Ten stepped inside the machine, her arm raised.

Evers asked, "Shouldn't she be more cautious?"

My mind raced, trying to figure out what to do next. "Yes."

Inside the machine, gunfire rang out.

Evers and I flinched.

Y Ten stepped out of the attack craft, holding a limp Qio man's arm. She tossed his body to the ground. "I'm quicker on the draw than he was."

I blinked, surprised and impressed. "Can we use this to reach our destination?"

Y Ten said, "The fuel tank is half empty. Climb aboard. We'll find out how far it will carry us soon."

Evers scowled. "Do you know how to operate it?"

"I'm a quick learner."

Evers groaned. "I don't like the idea, but will take a chance." Everybody climbed inside. On both sides and the back of the compartment, seats came out of the walls. We sat in them.

Sean blurted, "What an interesting machine."

Marti sneered, "It's cramped."

Zesa sighed. "I'm afraid."

Evers said, "All of us are."

Yinnie cringed. "It smells funny in here."

In front of me, Y Ten plopped down in a seat and waved both hands over motion sensitive screens. The engine started.

CHAPTER THIRTY

I said, "The motor is noisy."
Y Ten announced, "Affirmative." The craft jerked to the right, then the front of it dropped. A grinding sound grew louder. On screens, coordinates on eight maps enlarged.

Yinnie complained, "This room is too small."

Evers asked, "What is on the maps?"

Y Ten replied, "The crust beneath Fao and the surrounding area."

All eight vanished and were replaced by more.

I asked, "Additional maps?"

Y Ten answered, "Affirmative. More will appear when we get closer to our destination. This vehicle, one called a Burrower Eleven, probes Lasho's surrounding crust, figures out where the softer sediment is and heads in that direction. Cutting through boulders is impossible. Traveling through the bottom of lakes is tough and going through mud burns up a lot more tritium, the burrower's fuel."

I blinked, surprised by the machine's capabilities. "Y Ten, does Burrower Eleven fly?"

"Yes. Its maximum altitude is fifteen feet."

Sean remarked, "Fascinating."

I sighed, realizing that using such a mode of travel might be pointless since trees were always in the way.

Evers scowled. "Operating the burrower sounds difficult."

Y Ten said, "My bio-circuits were designed to solve complex problems."

Evers grimaced. "Okay, but I don't like being underground."

Y Ten asked, "Do you like being shot at or being attacked by Dwots or other creatures?"

Evers snapped, "Of course not."

Y Ten said, "Then relax. We're going to run out of fuel long before we reach Fao."

Evers sat back, a frustrated expression on her face. "If you say so."

Marti exclaimed, "The ceiling is low. I don't like it."

I blinked, annoyed, not sure what to say.

Zesa blurted, "Marti is right, too low."

Sean announced, "It's a well-designed machine."

Zesa complained, "Sean, you're such a geek."

Marti laughed. "Zesa, you're a geek, too."

She snapped, "Am not."

Marti sneered, "Yes, you are. Geek, geek. Marti is a geek."

"Stop giving me a hard time."

"Admit it. You've spent years studying polees."

"Get it right. They're called polypodiopsida."

"I knew it. I'll bet you know a lot about lepos."

"The correct term is Leptosporangiate. You forgot to mention eusporangiate ferns."

Marti giggled. "Can you hear yourself? Only nerds and geeks talk like that."

Zesa sighed. "This is embarrassing. I can't help myself. I like ferns, bromeliads, and some poisonous plants."

Yinnie burst out, "This machine makes a lot of racket."

I said, "True." A whining became louder.

Yinnie asked, "What's making that yucky sound?"

Y Ten answered, "We're traveling through granite. It's denser than sedimentary. As a result, the craft's hull makes a lot more noise because the rock rubs against it with a greater force than sedimentary does."

Zesa wiped the sweat off her forehead. "The air is stuffy."

Evers sucked in air through clenched teeth but didn't say anything.

Yinnie pouted. "I'm hungry."

Evers handed her mushroom chunks.

Yinnie ate some, then opened both eyes wider. "They taste yucky."

Evers scowled. "They're edible. That's the most important part."

Marti leaned forward. "I'm hungry, too."

Yinnie handed her a few chunks. Marti shoved them into her mouth. "They taste like dirt."

Zesa sniffed. "Marti, give me some."

She did.

Zesa winced. "They look disgusting." She tossed chunks into her mouth and made an ugly face. "I hope I don't throw up."

Sean called out, "Y Ten, I've never seen controls like those."

"I reprogrammed them a few seconds ago because eight were poorly thought out."

Sean asked "How many computer codes do you know?"

"Eighty."

Sean exclaimed, "Eighty. That's great. My teacher, a smart Qio, knew sixteen. I thought she was a genius."

Zesa shook her head. "Sean, you talk too much . . . gets on my nerves."

Marti glanced at the floor, a sad expression on her face. "I miss my dad."

Sean winced, then looked at her. "I miss my mom."

Within forty minutes, the front of the burrower rose. Much to my surprise, it jerked forward and stopped. Y Ten said, "It's out of fuel." On the right side of the compartment, the hatch whirred open. Everybody stepped out, then turned left and hiked past strangler figs.

Yinnie fidgeted. "I don't like the jungle. It's too hot."

I said, "We don't like it either."

Soon our group came upon six-foot-long leaves, then pushed them aside. In front of us, Y Ten reached down and touched sepia mold, a four-inch by four-inch growth that partly covered her left wrist.

Evers glanced at the mold, a shocked expression on her face. "Can you get rid of it?"

"My antigens are working on it. This species is called ucor mucedo."

Evers scowled. "Will yours succeed?"

"Time will tell. Ucor's genome keeps evolving. My antigens have to do that, too, or the mold will destroy my left wrist."

I cringed.

Sean remarked, "I've read about mushrooms for years. Many can be used to destroy mold."

Zesa blurted, "Sean, you read too much, need to socialize more."

Evers paused, a concerned expression on her face.

Y Ten asked, "Which species destroy mold?"

Sean hesitated with his brow tight.

Evers grimaced. "Are we going to get sick?"

Y Ten replied, "Detective Evers, good question. Once again, time will tell. Six out of forty of my bio-circuits are running quantum computer models, trying to predict what the Ucor's DNA will do to a human or a Qio's skin, eyes, nose, ears and the rest of their body."

Evers' brow tightened. "When will prediction results be available?"

Zesa remarked, "Sean doesn't know which mushrooms destroy mold." She laughed.

He glared at her.

Marti announced, "Zesa is right, you don't know which ones destroy it."

Sean glowered but didn't say anything.

Evers remarked, "Zesa, Marti, quit teasing Sean."

Zesa glanced at her hands. "We were just kidding."

Evers said, "Like I said, quit doing it."

Zesa grumbled. Marti bit her lip, an angry expression on her face.

Y Ten answered, "Detective Evers, at the current rate, a prediction will be available in four hours."

Sean crouched and grabbed some mushrooms.

Marti asked "Sean, what are you doing?"

He grinned. "You'll see."

Marti chuckled. "You're wasting your time."

Evers blinked. "Is using those six bio-circuits stressful?"

Y Ten said, "I don't know anything about stress."

Evers shrugged, "I know. You're not designed that way."

Y Ten said, "That is correct." Our group came upon a purple kapok. Zesa ripped several branches off.

Feeling curious, I asked, "Why are you tearing those off?"

"The thorns on their branches might kill Dwots."

Evers frowned. "Have you seen them do this?"

"Not long after we reached Lasho, I ripped several limbs off a purple kapok. A week later, I threw them at a Dwot. It screeched and ran away."

Marti laughed. "You probably scared it. Those branches won't do anything."

Zesa blurted, "Shut up."

Marti remarked, "You shut up."

Evers announced, "Stop arguing."

Zesa shook her fist at Marti. "She started it."

Marti glared at Zesa. "Did not."

Evers announced, "Stop."

Zesa glowered while mumbling incoherently.

Marti began staring at her hand, an angry expression on her face.

Sean handed the mushrooms to Y Ten. He said, "These

Amanita Muscaria might destroy the ucor."

She rubbed it against her wrist, a blank expression on our robot colleague's face. Our tribe slogged on.

Marti scoffed, "Y Ten, Sean is wasting your time."

Y Ten kept staring straight ahead.

Marti scowled. "Y Ten, did you hear me?"

She replied in a monotone, "Yes."

Marti asked "Why didn't you answer? That's rude."

"I'm busy."

Marti remarked, "The mold is still there. The mushroom didn't work, won't." She guffawed.

Y Ten kept staring straight ahead, a vacant look in her eyes.

Marti's forehead tightened. "I've never met anybody like you."

Y Ten glanced at her telescope.

Marti, a frustrated look on her face, bit her lip.

Zesa exclaimed, "Marti, you're being ridiculous."

She snapped, "Am not."

Zesa glared at her but didn't say anything.

Within the hour, we came upon a dimly lit lupuna grove. Ahead, a Gaoot rushed out of shadows, coming in this direction.

Yinnie screamed.

I blenched. Without warning, it veered to our left, then darted behind a huge bush.

Evers aimed her wrist in that direction while announcing, "It's gone. Where did the beast go?"

Y Ten remarked, "I don't know. To our right, about eighty yards away, hidden behind a wall of creepers, a faint rustling is getting louder. However, my telescope's screen is filled with meaningless dots, can't tell what is making the noise."

Two Dwots sprinted out from behind the wall, then raced toward us.

Evers shouted, "They're moving fast." She fired at both and missed.

Yinnie screeched.

Zesa tossed branches at them. They squealed, rushed away and vanished into the jungle.

Marti announced, "I don't believe what I just saw."

Zesa bragged, "Told you so. The poisonous branches scared them away."

Marti remarked, "Maybe."

Sean commented, "Zesa, throwing them was a good idea."

"Thanks."

Marti announced, "The Dwots might come back."

Zesa added, "If they do, I'll throw more branches at them."

Marti stomped off and sat on a log, a disgusted expression on her face. She asked, "Y Ten, is the mold gone?"

"Yes."

Marti asked, "Y Ten, are you teasing me?"

She replied in a monotone, "No."

Marti asked, "Why is everybody giving me a hard time?"

I said, "Nobody is giving you a hard time. Relax."

Marti grumbled incoherently, an irritated expression on her face.

Soon our group climbed over a hill that was surrounded by towering bamboo. In front of us, in the near distance, a five-foot-tall Qio woman in a turquoise jumpsuit came toward us. My lenses sent neutrinos into her hippocampus, and they returned. An analysis would be available soon.

She announced, a serious expression on her face, "I am Theresa. Strangers, please tell me about yourselves."

Y Ten mentioned our names and the crew's goal.

Theresa scowled. "There is a camp we call Hope. It's a short walk from here. It's safe, a good place for the girls, the boy, and the baby."

Evers frowned. "Take us there."

I said, "It's important that we find Kolo."

Evers glared at me. "Brin, I'll join you later. I want the girls, Sean, and the baby to be safe."

Y Ten said, "Brin, I'll protect Evers, the girls, Sean, and the baby."

My stomach muscles tightened, an angry reaction. "Finding Kolo is important. I need your help."

Y Ten remarked, "So is protecting them."

I asked, "Evers, what about our mission?"

Her forehead tightened. "I'll join you soon."

I blurted, "But Kolo might destroy all of Lasho."

She glowered. "Like I said, I'll join you soon."

I walked away, teeth clenched, an angry response. Results appeared in my lenses. Theresa, a mother, was from South Imm. Five weeks ago, after tanks attacked South Imm, she, her husband, son and hundreds of other residents rushed out of town. Just before they boarded a spaceship, she lost track of her family. The craft touched down near Fao. Theresa met four women along with two men and they fled because two of the women pointed out that armed bandits would arrive in Fao soon. The next morning, Theresa and her new friends set up Hope.

Within minutes I hiked between towering bromeliads. Ahead, far away, hidden behind hundreds of wimbas and other trees, a thrumming grew louder. I flinched. A police cruiser flew over them, coming in this direction. I exhaled, relieved. As I watched in horror, the craft plummeted.

I darted behind a wimba. The ship crash-landed. *Boooom.* I cringed as carbon nanotube chunks and flames shot past me.

CHAPTER THIRTY-ONE

I stepped out from behind the tree, then turned, walked, and passed debris. In front of me, four bodies were partly covered by dirt along with hull fragments. I blenched. To my right, two human women, both in gray jumpsuits, police uniforms, moaned. I pivoted, then stepped over shattered chairs, and stooped over one of them.

She, a redhead with some blood on her narrow face, asked, "Who are you?"

I winced. "Brin. Why did the cruiser crash?"

She flinched. "My left arm hurts."

I probed it with my wrist scanner. "You pulled a muscle. Fortunately, your arm isn't broken." My lenses sent neutrinos into her hippocampus. They returned. She was Detective Debra Brown, from Teto. Frank had sent her to this location to help me. More information would be available later.

She rose slowly, blinking. Then she glanced over her left shoulder, frowning. "Is anybody else alive?"

I pointed to the right. "Over there." I pulled this colleague up, and both of us walked in that direction while smoke spread, obscuring part of the wreckage. As my adrenaline pumped faster, we reached a human woman, a stranger who was on her back, beneath a large hull chunk. I stooped, then yanked it off. She scowled. "My stomach feels like somebody kicked it."

Debra blinked. "Mary, according to my wrist scanner, it's just bruised." She pulled the police officer to her feet. Mary blanched. "Did anybody else make it?"

I replied, "Unknown," and told her about my status. My lenses sent neutrinos into her hippocampus. They returned. She, Inspector Mary Garn, Detective Brown's colleague, was from Deeb, a village near Roov's north coast.

Garn wiped dirt off her belt. All three of us walked, passed severed arms and legs and came upon a man with a big jaw and a bloody ear. He sat up, then wiped debris off his forehead. "Mary, Brin, Debra, is anybody else alive?"

Debra frowned. "We're still looking."

My lenses sent neutrinos into his hippocampus, and they returned. He, Detective David Orr, Brown's colleague, was from West Ored. More information would be available soon. Our small group hiked.

Within minutes, everybody stopped near the edge of the wreckage. David scowled. "According to my latest wrist scanner probe, everybody else is dead."

Debra grimaced. "I came up with the same results."

The rest of us said the same thing, and we trudged on.

Debra said, "Brin, the three of us haven't received any of your recent messages, need more information."

"I just sent text, data accompanied by 3D holograms, and videos into your lenses."

Mary exclaimed, "The area around the wreckage is complicated, dangerous."

I nodded, teeth clenched.

A Gaoot rushed out from behind a strangler fig, then sliced Mary's head off.

Debra, David and I fired at it. It slashed David's neck. As blood gushed out, I discharged my weapon. The beast screeched, then ripped the right side of Debra's head off with its claw. I cringed while squeezing the trigger. Ammo struck the beast's eye. It squealed, then turned, rushed behind huge wimbas and vanished, hidden by them.

I winced and looked down. David's lower jaw and throat were gone, torn off by the beast. According to my latest scan, this colleague was dead, the result of a massive bleed out. I slogged on, trembling. In my mind's eye, this horrible scenario kept repeating. If only I had been more alert. To my left, hidden beyond distant treetops, ninety-threes discharged. My mind sped up, worried that shells might strike this area. My lenses sent messages to Frank and Tesk, asking both to send back up. They didn't respond.

Suddenly, a hazy Qio man's face, an intercepted stranger's video message, came out of my lenses' background. He said, "Kolo's plan to destroy Lasho is going forward. We'll talk more . . ." His voice became softer and was replaced by static. I winced.

Within the hour, while hiking through a lupunas grove, I halted, scared by a crunching that was coming from my left. I glanced in that direction, but only noticed a huge Paxo, one that was hanging from a branch. The creature changed into Y Ten.

I blinked, surprised. "What are you doing here?"

"Eleven minutes after we reached Hope, forty gunmen, humans and Qio with rapid discharge rifles, arrived. I changed into a Qio, a woman who resembled one of them, sneaked off, then sent a text message, telling you about my horrible encounter with the gunmen. You didn't reply. At that point, I sent one to Frank and Tesk. They didn't respond. I kept going. At the same time, I scanned this area, detected your infrared heat signature and hiked to this location, wanting you to help me find somebody who can help us save Evers and the others."

Chills ran up my spine. "There are only two of us. We'll have to save them later when other detectives arrive." I mentioned the recent crash landing along with the deaths of my colleagues.

"I'm sorry to hear about their passing."

I glanced at my trembling hand, wishing it would stop

shaking. "That makes two of us." Then I paused, trying to calm down. "Did the gunmen notice your transformation?"

"I was standing behind other refugees. According to my telescope's latest evaluation, they didn't."

"Did any of the gunmen look familiar?"

"No."

"Did you have enough time to scan their DNA or minds with your telescope or lenses?"

"No."

I sighed, then took a deep breath, trying to relax, knowing that if I couldn't, reaching Fao was impossible. "According to my latest scanner probe, airborne bacteria, viruses, and solar winds are destroying our messages, ones sent to Frank and Tesk."

"According to my telescope's last analysis, there is a sixty percent chance that your most recent probe is correct."

I nodded, stomach muscles tensed, a worried response.

"That recently intercepted message could have been created to fool you."

"I don't want to take that chance. We need to find Kolo."

"As you wish. Let's go." Both of us trudged on.

Soon we climbed over waist-high banyan roots. Further forward, several feet away, a Gaoot rushed out of the shadows. Y Ten fired at it. I dodged to the left. She dodged to the right. The creature barely missed us. I glanced over my shoulder. The creature halted, spun around and charged. Both of us discharged our weapons.

It squealed. *Eeee.*

We jumped out of its way. It grazed my sleeve. Bullets from Y Ten's weapon struck its legs. *Eeeee.* The Gaoot stumbled and fell. I fired. My tiny gun's ammo ripped its throat open. Blood gushed out, and the beast stopped moving.

Y Ten said, a blank expression on her face, "Another

obstacle."

I blenched while examining my sleeve, hoping the creature's rough hide hadn't torn any flesh off my arm.

Y Ten glanced at me. "Are you severely injured?"

"No. My arm is only bruised. I was lucky." We resumed our journey.

Within minutes it started raining. Suddenly, it turned into a heavy downpour. On my left, Y Ten, a misty silhouette, barely noticeable, shoved aside branches. Far away, thunder boomed. To my right, lightning struck an adjacent palmetto. I blinked. In the opposite direction, a bolt hit a nearby strangler fig. Chills ran up my spine, a nervous response. Another struck dirt, missing Y Ten by inches.

I blurted, "Watch out."

She jumped to the left, and both of us sprinted away.

After passing hundreds of lupunas, we reached banyan roots, walked under them, and turned. Behind us, lightning ignited a bush. Soon rain doused out the flames.

Y Ten said, "I've never seen this much lightning before."

I exhaled, trying to relax. "Neither have I."

Half an hour later, the downpour ended, and both of us tramped on. Y Ten said, "According to my latest telescope evaluation, a tidal wave will hit this area in forty-two minutes."

My adrenaline started pumping. "Is there any high ground nearby?"

"No. The closest is four miles away."

I blenched. "We'll have to climb a huge tree. With any luck, it won't fall over."

"That is the only option available. The largest banyan is a twenty-minute hike from here."

We trekked and went around bushes. Warning text, coming from my wrist scanner, appeared in my lenses. According to it, their thorns were filled with deadly neurotoxins, chemicals that would kill me in twenty minutes. Beneath the text, more of it indicated that a creature, one whose infrared heat signature was hidden by strangler figs, was trailing us. Additional printed information pointed out that the creature's leg had just brushed against a bromeliad. But the only sound it made wasn't loud enough to ID this species. As chills ran across my spine, I told Y Ten about the creature.

"I know. My telescope is still evaluating its recent photographs."

We jumped over knee-high moss-covered boulders.

She murmured, "A Dwot is following us, is about twenty feet away."

I cringed. To our left, hidden in darkness, a rumbling grew louder. I pointed in that direction. "What is making that sound?"

"The tidal wave."

Chills ran up my spine, a horrified response. At the same time, I pointed at a lupuna. "Although that isn't as big as the banyan, it will have to do."

"Yes." Her fingers turned into claws, and she climbed, me behind her.

CHAPTER THIRTY-TWO

When my partner was halfway up the tree, a tether came out of her back and plummeted twenty feet. I grabbed it, scrambled up and glanced down. Fifteen feet beneath me, the Dwot opened its mouth. My stomach muscles tightened in a frightened response. Within seconds, the wave struck the creature. It squealed. *Woooo*. The water swept it and nearby ferns away.

Above us, a thrumming grew louder. I looked up, wanting to know what made the sound, but only noticed treetops, ones that blocked out the sky.

Y Ten called out, "Three Moon Alteration Spacecraft have arrived."

This type of ship changed a celestial body's surface and its upper crust. As a result, the surface along with the upper crust became more stable.

I blinked, surprised. "Although I've read about them, I haven't seen any."

"That makes two of us."

A whooshing became louder. Above me, a curved wall, about eighty-foot-high, came through the treetops, dropping fast. It went by, missing my leg by inches. My body went cold, a terrified response. I shouted, "It's impossible to get away from the wall unless we climb down and hike toward another destination."

"That is correct."

I looked at the adjacent ground, wanting to know where the wall was going. It struck nearby dirt. As my heart beat faster, a shocked response, the roaring sound of the wave became louder. Suddenly, the wave hit the opposite side of the wall. Some water spilled over its top and rained down on

177

us.

Y Ten shouted, "According to my telescope, other sections of the wall, structures we can't see with the naked eye, are coming down. When they hit the jungle floor, these barriers will stop the rest of the wave."

I blinked, amazed. "Will the tsunami destroy the wall?"

"My quantum computer is analyzing data, hasn't come up with an answer yet."

"Let's head for higher ground. If the wall breaks, both of us will die."

"According to my telescope's probability graph, if the wall breaks, there is a four percent chance that we will reach higher ground."

My jaw muscles tightened, a horrified response. "Let's go." Both of us descended.

We reached the forest floor and hiked through narrow spaces, ones between thorn bushes. To our left, the wall bulged. At the same time, it creaked. I winced. "According to my recent scanner probe, there is a forty percent chance that the wall will hold."

"According to my last telescope evaluation, there is a forty-two percent chance that it will."

My adrenaline pumped harder. "I hate these odds."

"It's time to focus on our goal, not think about failure."

"I can't ignore my fear."

Y Ten shoved a branch aside, yet she didn't say anything.

Within minutes, the creaking grew louder. I noticed a whooshing and glanced over my shoulder, wanting to know what made the sound. Behind us, in the near distance, a wave rushed around the bottom of palmettos, coming this way. I pointed at it, wincing. "Watch out."

"I see it."

I looked ahead as we hiked past wimbas. The wave struck our ankles. She and I fell. It shoved us forward. I stood. It knocked me down. I rose and kept going.

To my right, Y Ten marched, barely balanced. "We can't give up."

CHAPTER THIRTY-THREE

We reached a muddy spot. I glanced over my shoulder. Behind us, the wave, half an inch deep, came in this direction and stopped. I mentioned Sultra.

"If you think I can provide useful advice, tell me what kind is best. However, I don't know which phrases will help anybody who has lost a loved one."

I nodded, acknowledging her comment and exhaled, glad that we hadn't been swept away. "According to the manual, Alteration Spacecraft are operated by Celestial Craft robots, androids that aren't designed to notice sentient life or utility androids."

"According to my latest telescope evaluation, the manual is correct."

"Designing them that way was a stupid idea. Somebody will die." It took six years for eighty IT personnel to build thirty Celestial Craft robots.

"It was and is a stupid idea, and yes, somebody will."

As we passed hundreds of castor bean plants, I pointed at them. "According to my scanner, those are deadly. They shouldn't be anywhere on Lasho."

"Both your points are correct."

Within minutes, both of us sat on a dimly lit hill, and I ate berries. To our right, far beyond the wimbas, a droning grew louder. I flinched. "What's making that nerve-wracking sound?"

"Insects. If they come closer, my telescope can detect their exact species."

CHAPTER THIRTY-FOUR

The droning moved away from us. I said, "They're leaving."

"According to my latest telescope evaluation, that is correct."

"I thought they would attack us." A distant thumping, barely audible, grew louder. "What's making that noise?"

"Unknown. It isn't on my telescope's database."

My neck muscles tensed up, a frightened response. "My lenses just sent neutrinos toward that sound. Unfortunately, whatever is coming is more than a quarter of a mile from here. As a result, they can't ID it. We should hide."

My new partner and I stood, hiked and went under banyan roots and sat in the dirt. Inches from my boot heel, several three-foot-long Sigos hissed. I stomped on two of them. They squealed. *Reeee.*

I looked up. Ahead, not far beyond adjacent Monkshoods, a machine that resembled a kangaroo jumped over a twenty-foot-high wimba, bound for another location. Not wanting the machine operator to notice me, my lenses sent a text message to Y Ten.

Her response scrolled. *Like you, I've never seen anything like it before, and it isn't on my telescope's archive.*

I flinched. An intercepted message, one that was coming from the machine's operator came out of my earplugs. He announced, "This is Hopper Five. Although my latest telescope probe hasn't detected any sentient beings, I'll keep looking. Sigos are noisy, making it difficult to hear any sentient being's footsteps or their conversations. According to eight quantum computer models, there is a four percent chance that any sentient beings . . ."

My lenses sent a text message to Y Ten.

Her response scrolled. *Yes, Hopper Five is too far away, making it impossible to hear everything the operator said.*

To our right, far from us, a thumping became louder. I whispered, "Another hopper is coming."

She murmured, "Yes. It's Hopper Six."

Minutes later, this machine stopped.

I winced. It turned. On both of its sides, laser guns fired, and beams grazed my left arm. Y Ten and I jumped in the opposite direction. We discharged our weapons. Bullets went through the hopper's window and hit the operator. The machine toppled over.

We hiked toward it. A laser beam came out of Y Ten's finger, hit a keypad, and a nearby hatch clicked open. Y Ten climbed inside.

I blinked, surprised. "Why didn't you use a laser beam before?"

"I created this type of weapon eight minutes ago."

I flinched. "Do you know how to pilot this?"

"I will in eight seconds." She pushed the operator's body out. "Enter, before other hoppers arrive."

I raced inside and plopped down on a seat, behind Y Ten. The hatch whirred shut. The hopper rose. Within seconds, it lurched upward. My body jerked in the opposite direction. I complained, "Riding this makes me dizzy." A helmet popped out of my collar and covered my head. A face mask came out of this protective gear.

"Not for long."

I blinked, caught off guard by her comment. Six kept moving, but the jerking stopped. "That's better."

"Antigravity software just switched on. If Six maintains its current speed, four graphs predict that we'll reach Fao in eight hours."

A voice, an intercepted message, came out of my earplugs, "Hopper Six, your recent coordinates indicate you're traveling in the wrong direction."

I asked, "Y Ten, what should we do now?"

"I just sent him a fake message, telling this field coordinator that we're headed for point four, five, eight, the previous operator's coordinates."

"Great. Whom does the coordinator work for?"

"According to screen fourteen, Kolo."

"I didn't know he owned this kind of machine."

"That makes two of us. The information isn't on my databases."

Within minutes, Six landed on the edge of a gorge. Y Ten announced in a monotone, "This barrier is forty miles long, two hundred feet across. According to screen B's warning alert, Six is only designed to jump one hundred sixty feet. In order to go around this obstacle, we'll have to turn left, travel sixteen miles, then go right."

My adrenaline started pumping. "If Six jumps over this, what is the likelihood that it will reach the opposite side?"

"According to five computer software models, twenty-one percent."

I flinched. "Take the shortest route."

"Although that's a bad idea, let's do it."

Chills ran down my spine. Outside the window, the bottom of the chasm whizzed by.

Y Ten announced, "We're not going to make it. Hold on."

CHAPTER THIRTY-FIVE

A roaring grew louder. I asked, "What's making that noise?"

"I just activated Six's jet engines."

I paused, caught off guard. "I didn't know it had any."

"Now you know. Hold on. It's going to be close."

I winced. "Don't remind me."

It landed on the opposite rim with a jolt and kept going. My stomach muscles tightened, a horrified reaction. "I'm glad we made it."

"So am I."

After passing a wimba grove, a male voice came out of a wall-mounted speaker. "HS, this is H Nine. You're at the wrong coordinates, violating protocol."

Y Ten responded, speaking in a lower tone than usual, "I copy. We'll change direction." A laser blast struck the left side of this machine. It lurched in the opposite direction and crashed to the ground. I kicked the hatch open, crawled out, stood, darted away and glanced over my shoulder. Behind me, Y Ten rose to her feet.

Laser blasts grazed my boot. I winced, then glanced over my shoulder. Twenty feet away, guns on another hopper discharged. *Tet, tet, tet.*

I spun around, took off, dashed between wild date palms, and kept going while ammo struck the back of my bulletproof vest.

Behind me, a crunching became louder. I blenched, then glanced over my shoulder as a hopper touched down on adjacent ferns, crushing them. I looked straight ahead, veered to the right and darted between muddy areas. *Tet, tet, tet.*

Ammo struck my pant leg's bulletproof fabric.

In the back of me, something crashed to the ground. I glanced over my shoulder. The hopper had toppled over. I looked straight ahead, jumped over rocks and sprinted through gigantic weeds. Text appeared in my lenses. *This is Y Ten. I'm on your left.*

My lenses responded, thanking her for the update.

After passing a strangler fig grove, I slowed to a walk. Further forward, in the near distance, Y Ten stepped over mushrooms. Both of us continued. My helmet and face mask went back inside my collar. I took a deep breath, gathering my strength, then said, "It amazes me that we escaped. Thanks for your help."

Y Ten gave me a weak salute.

I shrugged, knowing that was the best thank you gesture she would offer.

Two hours later, not long before dusk, we came upon gigantic orchids.

Y Ten pointed at them. "They're booby-trapped. Don't get any closer or they'll explode."

I blenched. My partner and I went around them. To my left, a crunching became louder. I glanced in that direction, wanting to know what made the noise.

A twenty-foot-long sepia machine, one that resembled an alligator, rose out of the dirt. On its nose, six giant drill bits stopped rotating. On its top, a gun fired. Bullets ricocheted off my shoulder pad. I dove to the ground.

Laser beams shot out of Y Ten fingertips and struck the machine's tiny window.

My lenses sent neutrinos into the operator's mind. Some returned. This vehicle was called Digger Nine. Its gun sprayed us with more ammo.

More beams came out of Y Ten's fingertips, then pierced

the window. Y Ten jumped on top of the vehicle, firing. Beams struck the top of the machine. It halted. On its side, a hatch whirred open. My partner jumped onto the ground, then stepped inside Nine. Within seconds, she pushed the operator's body, a Qio female, out. Y Ten announced, "Come inside. Let's go."

I entered and sat behind her, blinking. "Do you know how to operate this?"

"In fourteen seconds I will." The hatch whirred shut. Within seconds, the machine turned left, jerking. Soon it lurched forward.

I sighed. "This is a rough ride."

"Affirmative." In front of her, onscreen coordinates flashed. "We'll be traveling anywhere between fifteen to one hundred feet beneath the ground."

My adrenaline started pumping. "Does this machine cut through granite and other kinds of rock?"

"Sixty percent of the time, it goes between them. Nine percent of the time, it goes around these obstacles."

"How about the rest of the time?"

"It cuts through them."

"That's impressive. Who owns this?"

"According to screen fourteen, Kolo."

"His fleet of machines is spectacular."

"Affirmative."

We went around the fourteenth granite boulder, an obstacle that was eighty feet beneath the forest floor. A male voice came out of a wall-mounted speaker, "DN, this is Field Coordinator Thirteen. You're in sector Orange, the wrong area. Head for sector Pink."

Y Ten spoke, her voice at a lower pitch. "I copy."

I blinked, surprised. "You sound different."

"Seconds ago, I scanned Nine's former operator,

discovered that he spoke in a baritone and imitated his voice."

"Are you going to follow the coordinator's directions?"

"Of course not."

"What if he finds out that you aren't and tells another digger, a hopper or some other type of machine to chase this digger and kill us?"

"I just sent his telescope false coordinates, ones indicating that we're following his orders."

Soon Nine went between tree roots. Outside, a cracking grew louder. I flinched. "What's making that horrible noise?"

"According to screen twenty-four, two of Nine's corkscrews just tore apart a wimba's roots."

I nodded.

"Screen five indicates a machine called a burrower is coming in this direction, will arrive in forty seconds."

I blinked, surprised. "What else does five say?"

"Nothing. Five's database is scrolling. But all the information is useless, only tells me that the surrounding area is composed of sedimentary rock."

Something rammed our left side. I asked, "What hit us?"

"According to screen eight, the burrower did."

My body went cold, a horrified response. "Can it destroy Nine's wall?"

"According to screen eight . . ."

It banged against the same spot, interrupting Y Ten.

I flinched.

Y Ten announced, "If it smashes against that wall six more times, yes."

"We should head for the surface and get out before it destroys this vehicle." My helmet and face mask rose out of my collar and covered my head.

"Good idea."

Nine reached it and halted. The hatch clicked open. I looked outside. To our left, a gray vehicle that resembled a shark came out of the ground. On both of its sides, machine guns discharged. *Fep, fep, fep.* Ammo struck Nine, missing me by inches. My stomach muscles tightened, a shocked response.

On Nine's top, a rocket launcher fired. The projectile hit the gray machine's snout. I blurted, "Direct hit."

"Aff . . ."

A hopper arrived. On both of its sides, laser guns discharged. Beams grazed my helmet. Both of us jumped out, then turned right and darted between rubber trees. Ammo struck my leg's bulletproof fabric. I grimaced. We raced by flowers and kept going while ammo ripped them apart. In front of us, a Gaoot roared. I aimed my tiny gun at it.

Beams, ones coming from somebody else, struck the creature. It howled, darted into the shadows and vanished, hidden by them. Both of us sped up, reached a ten-foot-wide chasm, and jumped over it. As chills ran up my spine, we came upon a cave entrance, then halted.

I asked, "Are there any Dwots inside? It will take a few moments for my wrist scanner to probe this area."

"It will take eight seconds for my telescope to evaluate it."

Not far behind us, voices shouted. I flinched. To our right and left, thick underbrush blocked our way. I winced. "The cave is our only hope." My partner and I sprinted inside.

CHAPTER THIRTY-SIX

A head, Sigos crawled down walls. We passed the poorly lit invertebrates, then hurried to the right, moving down the curved grotto. Hundreds of winged snails dropped from the ceiling, then flew toward us. At the same time, they croaked. Both of us shoved them aside and continued on. Without warning, they sprayed us.

I flinched as my partner and I sprang over dark rocks. To our left, about ninety yards away, outside another entrance, leaves on trees shook. We raced toward them. On our right, a Vablo crawled out of a hole, its jaws open. My partner and I scurried by the creature, went outside and halted next to a tree, one that was at the edge of a cliff.

Eighty feet below us, bamboo swayed in the wind. I glanced to the left, then noticed a cliff, one that was steep, impossible to climb across. I pointed at it. "Impossible." I glanced in the opposite direction and spotted a six-inch-wide ledge. Y Ten started across it, moving slowly, me behind her.

Within seconds, the ledge curved around the cliff. Beneath my boot heel, tiny rocks tumbled off the ledge and dropped eight thousand feet into the jungle. As my adrenaline pumped harder, Y Ten stepped over a huge branch and kept moving. Without warning, a gusting wind pushed me sideways. I flinched but never slowed down. Soon I glanced to the right. Y Ten raised her arm, grabbed a branch and began scaling the cliff, me following her. It cracked, and tiny pieces broke off. I yelled, "Damn."

"Don't panic."

I flinched.

She stepped onto the top of the cliff, grabbed my hand, then pulled me up. As sweat poured down my face, we hiked across a fifteen-foot-wide mountaintop. While the wind howled, both of us started down the peak's other face, a gradual slope. Y Ten said, "According to my telescope, we lost the hopper driver and two gunmen a few minutes ago."

I exhaled, relieved.

As night set in, both of us sat between kapoks, trees with six-inch-long beetles on them. I pulled berries out of a pouch and ate.

Y Ten said, "I'll stand guard while you sleep."

I thanked her. Far away, ninety-threes went off, rumbling. Chills went down my spine, a terrified response.

At dawn, my partner and I departed. Soon we trekked over a ridge. Ahead, in the near distance, a forty-foot-long police cruiser, descended. To our left, a hopper leaped out of the jungle, guns blasting. Laser beams struck the cruiser, and it crash-landed.

Y Ten and I fired at the hopper while it shot at us.

Our ammo struck the operator's window. The machine toppled over. Its hatch opened. The operator, a human male, climbed out and keeled over.

We rushed toward the cruiser, then walked by smoldering chunks. Next to them, four bodies were partly covered by debris. In front of us, two human women in gray jumpsuits, police uniforms, sat up and wiped the blood off their faces. According to my scanner, one was Detective Jane Ard, a policewoman from South Teto. The other was Detective Audrey Green.

To our right, a grinding became louder. I glanced in that direction. In the near distance, a digger burst out of the ground. On its top, rocket launchers clicked. Two of the projectiles hit an area behind Ard and Green, then exploded. Fragments struck both officers, tearing their bodies to shreds.

I flinched. Y Ten and I raced to the left while firing at the machine. Rockets, coming from it, whizzed by us. We dove behind a torn off piece of the downed craft's fuselage as the projectiles blew up. Then both of us sat up while discharging our weapons. Our bullets struck the digger's window.

I asked, "Did you kill the operator?"

"According to my latest telescope evaluation, there is forty-two percent chance that I did."

We stood, then walked slowly toward the vehicle as its engine whirred.

CHAPTER THIRTY-SEVEN

Both of us reached the window. The operator sat up, firing. I ducked, flinching, then squeezed the trigger. Bullets struck the operator's face, and he slumped forward. I glanced to the left, at Y Ten.

She touched three bullet holes on her stomach with a trembling hand.

My body went cold, a horrified response. "Are you going to recover?"

"Affirmative. It will take eight hours. Let's walk toward a more secure location. When we arrive, I must sit and recuperate."

Both of us departed.

Within minutes my partner and I sat close to dimly lit strangler figs, the safest area I could find. Far away, a hopper jumped over treetops, coming in this direction. I winced.

Moments later, it went by us, never slowing down. My stomach muscles tensed up, a terrified response. Soon three more arrived, leaped over a nearby bush, and kept going.

At dusk my sleeping bag covered me. At the same time, it created a holographic bush, a protective facade that surrounded both of us. If a bandit passed by, the only thing they would see with the naked eye was the bush. Would the operator of a hopper or a digger notice us? I wasn't sure. I asked, "Will your alarm wake us up?"

"Not until I recover."

I told her we would use mine.

In the near distance, a rustling became louder. I grimaced.

Moments later, two Qio men with rapid discharge rifles walked by. Without warning, they stopped. The tallest frowned. "Did you hear that humming?"

The other replied, "No."

The tallest shrugged. "It's probably my imagination." Both of them continued on.

I exhaled, relieved. My helmet and face mask went inside my collar.

At dawn, we hiked. It started raining. My helmet and mask rose out of my collar, covered my face and both of us stepped over several Vablos while ants on their backs sprayed mist at our boots. Text appeared in my lenses. *Brin, we . . .* For unknown reasons, it vanished. I told Y Ten about it.

"According to my latest telescope probe, IT personnel are using electrons and microwaves to jam most of Frank's messages."

I blenched. The rain stopped.

After climbing over six hills, we stopped on another. Ahead, not far beyond lupunas, a group of emaciated prisoners, all of them behind a fifteen-foot-high semitransparent carbon nanotube fence, shuffled by a twenty-foot-high tower. Inside the top of the tower, a guard lowered his laser rifle, shot a prisoner, and she collapsed.

I winced. "Why did the guard kill her?"

"My guess is that he did it for pleasure."

"I would like to free the prisoners, but there are twenty-one guards, too many to kill."

"Yes, too many to kill." We resumed our journey.

Two hours later, our small party halted near a clearing. Eighty feet away, behind a fifteen-foot-high semitransparent wall, eleven emaciated prisoners, all dressed in filthy, torn jumpsuits trudged around a guard tower. One of them, a Qio woman prisoner, rushed toward the wall and reached it. At the same time, she began shaking. Within seconds, she took a few steps and fell. My body went cold, a terrified response. "The wall is electrified."

"Affirmative." She pointed at a blockhouse. "Sixteen guards are inside that, too many to kill. Let's move on."

At noon, both of us stopped behind towering ferns, plants that were at the edge of the jungle. Sixty feet away, not far beyond a fifteen-foot-high barbed wire fence that surrounded sixteen one-story buildings, bony prisoners, all dressed in soiled coats and baggy pants milled about. To their left, a guard inside a nearby tower aimed his laser rifle at them.

Y Ten said, "According to my recent telescope evaluation there are eighteen guards, too many to fight."

I clenched my teeth, angry that we couldn't help the men. Forty feet above the camp, a fleet of copper doves, a type of drone I hadn't seen before, flew in this direction. Both of us veered to the right and sprinted into a darker part of the jungle.

In the late afternoon, both of us walked under banyan roots and stopped, hidden by them. In the near distance, not far beyond a fifteen-foot-high semitransparent barrier that surrounded eleven shacks, and two one-story buildings, a group of scrawny human women, all dressed in ragged tunics wandered aimlessly. To their right, a guard inside an adjacent tower fired his rapid discharge rifle, and one of the women toppled over.

I flinched.

Y Ten said, "There are only six guards." She changed into one, a Qio female. "I'm going to kill them, then free the prisoners."

I blinked, surprised by her decision. "Can I lend a hand?"

"After I shoot a guard, I'll open the gate, let you in, and you can help me locate the rest. If any resist, kill them."

My adrenaline started pumping.

CHAPTER THIRTY-EIGHT

The guard, Y Ten's new shape, marched and halted near a sign, one with the word *Helton* on it. Not far beyond the sign, the gate opened. She entered the camp. A six-foot-tall Qio male guard, dressed in a blue uniform, stepped out of a nearby shack and frowned. "Why did you come here?"

"I'm a replacement."

He scowled. "Nobody told me about a replacement."

A laser beam came out of her fingers, struck his forehead, and he keeled over. At the top of the tower, a sentry spun around, fired at Y Ten, and bullets grazed my colleague's leg. Her laser beam struck his chest, and he collapsed.

Another guard rushed out of a building, spraying bullets. Y Ten ducked while ammo struck nearby dirt. A laser beam came out of her fingertips, struck his face, and he fell, trembling. She shot him in the forehead. I sprinted inside, then both us of darted toward the buildings. Four sentries rushed out of them, guns blazing.

Y Ten and I fired. Three of them stumbled and fell. The last raised both hands above his head, surrendering. Eight bony women, all dressed in filthy overalls surrounded him. One yelled, "Asshole!"

Two of them struck his cheek with boards. He screamed, tripped, fell and others kicked him.

I flinched, and we kept going. More women, about twenty, stepped out of a dilapidated building, amazed expressions on their faces. One was Evers. She offered me a weak smile. I rushed toward her and hugged my colleague. Then she pulled back, a pleased expression on her face.

Behind her, Wendy and Nellie offered half-hearted grins.

I flinched because these friends resembled skeletons. Then

I reached into my belt pouch, pulled out berries, the only food I had and handed this small meal to all three. They ate. At the same time, tears ran down their cheeks.

Wendy drawled, "They rarely feed us."

I cringed.

Evers added, "Two mornings ago, a guard told several of us that Kolo will use a particle accelerator to destroy Lasho a few days from now."

Y Ten asked, "Did the guard tell you how Kolo was going to use the accelerator to do this?"

Evers spoke slowly her hands trembling. "No."

I frowned. "Did the guards tell you where the accelerator is?"

Nellie replied, "No."

My stomach muscles tightened a terrified response. "We need to find Kolo and stop him."

Y Ten said, "Let's go. Detective Evers, Wendy, and Nellie, you should stay here and recuperate."

All three agreed.

Both of us rushed away. I blurted, "I wish we could have done more to help Evers and the others."

"That will have to wait."

Within minutes, we found a parked hopper, climbed inside and departed, headed toward Fao.

After traveling through eight groves and two rivers, using Y Ten's telescope to guide us, we stopped near one of many thirty-foot in diameter domes. The hatch clicked open. My partner and I climbed out. She said, "According to my latest evaluation, there are four humans inside this building." We walked through its wall, one made of nanorobots.

I blinked, surprised that we could pass through it. In the near distance, four humans walked across the empty room. I said, "According to my scanner, all of these men are composed of iron particles. Where is Kolo?"

One of the four pointed at me. "Who are you?"

I blinked, surprised that he was speaking to me.

Y Ten said, "Brin, your question is a good one. IT personnel programmed these particles, an attempt to fool anybody who is trying to find him. Unfortunately, every adjacent building's wall is blocking my probes. We must enter each one."

"They're blocking my scanner's probes as well."

Three Qio women rushed inside the building, guns blazing.

While ammo grazed my sleeve, Y Ten and I dove to the ground, blasting. All three bellowed and dropped to the ground, blood gushing out of their necks. Without warning, one raised her hand and fired.

Bullets ricocheted off my bulletproof shoulder pad. At the same time, beams, all coming from Y Ten, struck the Qio woman's eye. She hollered and collapsed. Both of us darted out of the building, then rushed toward another. But its wall wouldn't move apart. My partner and I fired at it, tearing off chunks. Within minutes we created a hole. Both of us rushed inside and noticed the room was empty.

I blinked, caught off guard. "Kolo or somebody fooled us."

"These domes walls were and are blocking our scans."

I blurted, "We'll have to break into each building one at a time."

"Affirmative."

To our right, two police cruisers descended. One crash-landed into a spot between domes. I blenched. "Nobody can survive that."

"According to my latest probe, that is correct."

The other touched down, its hatch open. Three men along with three women, all in camouflaged gray police jumpsuits, rushed out, coming this way. The tallest, a human male said,

"I'm Detective Harris."

I mentioned my name.

He nodded. "Everybody aboard knows about you, Y Ten and Evers. Let's find Kolo."

I talked about the garbled messages, all from Tesk and Frank.

Harris said, "Understood. That's why we couldn't tell you our team was coming. I have new equipment for you. Put it on your sleeve." He gave me a ring. I put it on.

To our left, eighty yards away, about twenty men in sepia camouflaged uniforms darted out from behind a dome, blasting.

Laser beams struck Harris's pant leg. He blenched. Everybody in our group returned fire as we rushed behind a nearby dome. On our right, a digger came out of the ground. On its top, a rocket launcher clicked. The projectile hit a detective and blew up, tearing her to pieces.

My body went cold, a mortified response. A grenade landed next to the digger, then exploded, destroying the front of it. Inside the machine, the operator discharged his rifle. Ammo struck a male detective's bulletproof vest.

Beams hit the operator, and she collapsed.

A half an inch in diameter shield, a new invention, came out of every detective's ring. In less than a second, all of these protective devices expanded until they were six feet in diameter. At the same time, the detectives walked toward the men in camouflaged uniforms while ammo and laser beams ricocheted off the shields.

As my adrenaline began pumping, a tiny mirror popped out of the ring, making it possible for me to glance around the dome without being hit by ammo or beams. "I hope those shields work."

Y Ten said, "They're made of carbon nanotubes, material that bullets and beams can't penetrate."

Above us, a hopper rushed in this direction. We fired at it. The machine hit the ground and toppled over. Its hatch opened. The operator stepped out, teetering and dropped to the ground.

In the mirror, the men in camouflaged uniforms retreated and sprinted behind a dome. All the detectives rushed toward them. Y Ten and I took off, following our colleagues. Information appeared in my lenses. Detective Harris, a muscular human male, and Lieutenant Oppot, a gaunt Qio woman, were leading this team.

CHAPTER THIRTY-NINE

A head, Harris announced, "They're hiding inside the domes." He raised two of his fingers, issuing a command. Half the detectives, led by him, sprinted toward a blue dome. The rest, following Oppot, darted toward a red dome.

Harris's group hurried inside the blue one, and vanished, hidden by its wall.

I cringed. "Harris and his team aren't firing their weapons. Are they dead or does the wall cover up their voices, their messages or the sound of their weapons?"

Y Ten replied, "Good question. Unfortunately, my telescope can't evaluate any noise or movement that is behind the wall."

To our right, Oppot's team kicked the red dome, trying to break in. Soon they blasted a hole in it and bolted inside while discharging their weapons.

On our left, Harris's group rushed out of the blue dome. He glowered. "Brin, there's nobody inside."

I nodded, then told him about our inability to keep in contact with him, hear his weapons fire or keep track of their movement when his team was inside the dome.

He scowled. "That's a problem. However, we'll have to update our scanners and lenses another time." He along with his group spun around, then ran toward a yellow dome.

After searching fourteen more domes, unable to find the men in camouflaged uniforms, Oppot barked, "They're close by. Keep looking."

Y Ten and I dashed inside a turquoise dome. Near the middle of it, a six-foot-tall Qio male in a camouflaged uniform rushed inside a hole that was on the floor. Much to my surprise, the hole closed in less than a second. Unfortunately, there weren't any seams around this exit, making it impossible to find it.

My lenses' receive field was blank. Oppot hadn't contacted me in the last few seconds. I told Y Ten about this.

"I'm having the same problem." I sent an email message to Oppot. Nobody replied. I bit my lip, disappointed, then I ran outside and told the others about the hole.

Oppot's team hurried inside the turquoise dome. I pointed at the spot where the exit had been located.

Oppot scowled. "There isn't any sign of it. You made a mistake."

I blurted, "No. It's there."

Y Ten fired beams at the area that I was pointing at. Although they ripped pieces of the floor off, there wasn't any sign of an exit.

I rubbed my face, disappointed.

Oppot barked, "You screwed up." Her team sprinted away.

I bit my lip, upset with her attitude. Y Ten and I discharged our weapons, tearing more fragments off. I said, "We're not getting anywhere, but it's important not to give up." We blasted.

Within fifty seconds, after cutting deeper, I noticed part of the hole. We resumed our efforts until the hole was big enough to enter. Then I smiled, pleased by our efforts. "I'm going to tell Oppot about this. You stay here, watch the hole."

"Good idea."

I ran outside, noticed that the other detectives had departed, then bit my lip, frustrated. To our left, in the far distance, hidden behind other domes, they fired.

I rushed toward them. Behind me, gunshots, a barely audible noise, one coming from inside the turquoise dome, rang out. I winced, then spun around, retraced my steps and re-entered the building.

Ahead, Y Ten said, "A few seconds ago, after you left, a five-foot-eight-inch-tall Qio woman in a camouflaged jumpsuit rushed out of the hole, blasting. I fired, and she ran back inside. My telescope can't evaluate whatever is inside the exit because the floor and the surrounding area are composed of carbon nanotubes and other carbon-based materials. Entering the hole alone is a bad idea."

I flinched. "Shoot into it for eight seconds, then I'll enter."

"Although that's a dangerous plan, proceed." She discharged her weapon.

I rushed inside, gun blazing.

CHAPTER FORTY

In front of me, on a poorly lit seven-foot in diameter tunnel wall, chunks fell off. I walked slowly, my boot heels crunching fragments, creating noise that made it impossible to catch the men and women in uniforms by surprise. Y Ten's voice came out of my earplugs. "I'm behind you, several feet away."

I nodded while gloves came out of my sleeves and covered both hands. The tunnel curved to the right. I went in that direction, advancing slowly. Text, a new message from Oppot, appeared in my lenses. According to it, if I downloaded molecules, they would expand, creating a protective shield. Far away, a whooshing grew louder. As I watched, horrified, a wall of water rushed in this direction and shoved me backward. Soon my helmet's pump ejected the water. As my heart started pounding, a terrified response, the headgear pumped air in, and I took a deep breath.

A piton shot out of my glove and went into the wall. I grabbed the piton, shoved myself forward while another came out of the glove and went into another part of the wall. As the water shoved me backward, I seized the spike and moved forward. The water heated up. I winced because it started hurting my skin.

Y Ten's voice came out of earplugs. "At this rate, you will be boiled alive soon."

I grimaced.

To my left, she raised her right hand. It turned into a drill. My colleague placed it against the ceiling and bored. Within seconds, the drill bit created a hole. As I clenched my teeth, trying to cope with pain, she grabbed my left hand, yanked me toward her, and pushed me upward into the hole. I climbed, entered a dome, then turned, grabbed her hand and pulled my partner out of the steaming water.

"If you stayed in that tunnel for eighteen more seconds, you would have perished, scalded to death."

I nodded, trembling. "My tiny gun doesn't work."

"I just updated your DNA. As a result, it used part of your skeleton to create a new type of handgun, one that fires molecular size smart bullets. Look at the back of your hand, and you will see the Molecule Shooter. It's an eighth of an inch long, the same color as your skin."

I glanced down, then barely noticed it. The trigger, a mechanism activated by thought appeared in my lenses. Above it, the weapon's scope enlarged. "Learning how to use the Shooter will take time."

Behind her, a Qio woman in a camouflaged jumpsuit rushed through the wall, her gun blazing.

As laser beams struck my partner's sleeve, both of us dove to the floor while discharging our weapons.

A tiny shield popped out of my partner's hand. This protective gear expanded until it was six feet in diameter, protecting my colleague. Smart ammo and laser beams ricocheted off it.

I squeezed the Shooter's trigger. The Qio woman collapsed. I glanced to the right. A human in a camouflaged jumpsuit darted through the wall, blasting. *Ket, ket, ket.* As chills ran up my spine, ammo from his weapon ripped pieces of fabric off my sleeve.

He raised his six-foot in diameter shield. Then he lowered it. Bullets from our weapons struck his forehead, and he keeled over. A Qio woman in a camouflaged uniform sprinted through the wall, spraying bullets. They struck my helmet, tearing off pieces. Without warning, she spun around and dashed through the wall.

Y Ten said, "It's hard to tell why she left. Let's search for

Kolo."

I nodded. Both us did an about-face, ran toward the opposite wall, went through it, reached open space and entered a purple dome. Without warning, my skin became hotter. "I feel like I'm on fire."

"Particles in the dome's wall were designed to burn off your skin. It will take several seconds for my particle neutralizer to counteract this effect."

I stopped, flinching, unable to concentrate enough to discharge or aim my weapon.

CHAPTER FORTY-ONE

The burning sensation subsided. I exhaled, relieved. Both of us took off. I asked, "Will going through this destroy my skin?"

"It's hard to tell until you pass through it."

I clenched my teeth feeling horrified, and when I went through the wall, and my skin became hotter. "Not again."

"It should cool off soon."

I shuddered. "In two minutes?"

"Wait and see."

The burning sensation went away. "I'm glad that's over with."

"According to my telescope evaluation, we can't walk through the next dome's wall." My partner and I discharged our weapons. The building itself blew up. The blast knocked us backward, and we ended up on our sides. As I winced, both of us rose to our feet. I asked, "Why didn't your telescope warn us about the explosive dome?"

"According to my computer model A, somebody, I'm not sure who, keeps changing some of the dome's wall composition every few seconds."

My body went cold, a shocked reaction. "How many walls have changed?"

"Forty-nine."

"Can the model describe the changes?"

"The walls have become harder. In order to enter any domes, we must destroy their walls."

"Will any of the domes explode?"

"There is a twenty percent chance that any of them will."

My mind sped up, trying to figure out what to do next. "Zero percent would be better."

"Affirmative."

"Is Kolo inside any of them?"

"According to model D, we won't know until we enter each one."

I cringed. "My scanner can't detect these changes."

"In the last few seconds, forty algorithms have updated my telescope. As a result, it can detect them. However, the walls themselves keep changing. Unfortunately, I don't know if more updates will make it possible for my telescope to figure out if the walls have become even harder."

My stomach muscles tensed up in a terrified response. "When will you know?"

"Unknown."

My jaw muscles tightened, an angry response. Without warning, object programming, meaningless computer code, scrolled through my lenses.

Yes.eval.

I asked, "Is somebody trying to jam my lenses?"

"Affirmative. Be alert. According to model G, it's going to get worse."

More code scrolled down until it filled up my lenses. I exhaled, trying to relax. We darted to the left, bound for a tan dome. As I watched in horror, all of the domes jerked to the right, about five feet. Soon each one returned to its original position. I flinched. Within seconds, eight went around two in a clockwise direction. Soon all eight halted and moved around both, advancing counterclockwise. At the same time, darts flew out of some of their walls and bounced off my helmet. I cringed. Suddenly, yellow gas spewed out of others.

I coughed, reacting to the fumes. While my helmet's blower flushed them out, hawk-like drones swooped down on us, their beak-mounted guns blasting. In a millisecond, the ammo ripped the fabric off my shoulder pads. We returned fire, and the intruders flew away.

All around us, eight domes flattened, revealing Oppot and

her colleagues. Laser beams came out of the floor, vaporizing her along with every member of the policewoman's team. I blenched. Nine small rectangular buildings popped out of the same area and expanded. We jumped on top of one, not wanting to be crushed. To our right and left, tiny holes on the rooftop enlarged. At the bottom of the twenty-feet-deep holes, spikes lurched upward. As chills went down my spine in a nervous response, we took off, bound for a grassy area, an open space beyond the buildings.

A droning became louder until it was deafening. I clenched my teeth, wishing the painful noise would stop. Text appeared in lenses. *Sound Reduction will begin in three seconds.* I exhaled, glad that this software would kick in soon. The droning was replaced by a soft clicking that was barely noticeable.

To my right, Y Ten said, "The obstacles keep changing."

I nodded, teeth clenched. Ahead, a bomb went off. Shrapnel hit my face mask and suit. Several pieces dropped off the mask. Remaining fragments partly blocked my view. I dove to the ground, wanting to avoid another blast. The ring on my sleeve expanded until it was three feet in diameter. Ammo bounced off it. At the same time, I glanced down, worried that other pieces might have ripped holes in my suit. On my leg, three fragments expanded. I reached out, yanked two out, threw them away, grabbed the other and tossed it. Within seconds, the suit's fabric became thicker, offering better protection.

To my right, Y Ten crouched, then glanced at me. "Are you injured?"

"No." I sprang to my feet. Then we rushed toward the grass-covered area. Further forward, a fence popped out of the ground. My jaw muscles tightened, an angry response. Both of us jumped over the five-foot-high barrier and reached the grass. It vanished and was replaced by the jungle.

"The open space was a hologram, an illusion designed to fool us."

I blinked. "It fooled me." Not far beyond towering ferns, most partly hidden in the shadows, four men in camouflaged jumpsuits discharged their rifles.

I hunched down while placing the shield in front of me. Ammo struck it, making a ting noise. As my heart started pounding, a terrified response, I glanced to the right. Y Ten raised her rectangular shield. I hadn't seen the equipment before.

I looked at the men. A grenade rolled across nearby dirt. It detonated. Fragments struck my shield, then knocked me backward, about half an inch. I leaned forward, not wanting to fall. At the same time, my mind started racing, trying to anticipate their next move.

To my right, beyond my peripheral vision, a whooshing grew louder. I glanced in that direction, wanting to know what made the noise as flames came out of Y Ten's hand. I looked at our attackers while a stream of fire, coming from Y Ten, struck them.

Two collapsed, screaming, "Ieeeee."

One yelled, "Help." The others did an about-face, ran off and disappeared into the jungle.

My stomach tensed up, a nervous reaction. "Y Ten, your flamethrower is great. Why didn't you use it before?"

"I finished constructing it moments ago."

"Outstanding. Tell me how you created it later. Let's find Kolo."

"As you wish."

CHAPTER FORTY-TWO

Within minutes, at dusk, I sat. "It's time to bed down for the night."

"I'll stand guard while you sleep."

I yanked berries out of a pouch-mounted sleeve and chewed. "How did you create the new flamethrower?"

"It took a great deal of time and effort. I just exported a new computer code, two thousand pages, into your lenses. The code points out how my circuits heat up nearby oxygen. When it ignites my hand's fan switches on, then blows the flames at an assailant."

"Interesting. There aren't many berries left."

Y Ten reached down, seized beetles and gave them to me. "This species is edible, full of protein."

My stomach muscles tensed up, an uncomfortable reaction. "Okay." I ate them.

Far away, a faint rustling, barely audible, grew louder. I flinched. "What's making that noise?"

"Two Paxos."

I exhaled, relieved.

At dawn, we slogged on and passed towering strangler figs, trees that blocked most of the sky. In front of us, several Vablo crawled over moss-covered dirt.

Y Ten said, "According to my telescope, a Gaoot is sixty yards from this spot, coming in this direction."

I cringed.

"I just finished creating a Plant DNA Transformation Tool, one that tells us more about Fao."

"Impressive." Text from her appeared in my lenses. According to it, in many cases, if it wasn't raining, PDNAT could transmit electrons to any bush that was five miles away or less. When these particles reached this flora, its genome changed. As a result, the bush could scan 20 percent of the adjacent plants, buildings, machines, and animals if they were within a hundred-yard radius, save that information and send it back to Y Ten's telescope. Unfortunately, her telescope's maximum range in terms of receiving this information was five miles.

It started raining. I sighed. "Hiking through this mud will take a long time."

"Affirmative. By the way, the rain reduces my Transformation Tool's ability to scan effectively by thirty percent. At any rate, the TT indicates that there are thirty-five small wood buildings in Fao."

"Is the tool better than your telescope in terms of transmitting electrons to any bush that is five miles away or less?"

"Fifty-one percent better."

I cocked my head to one side, impressed. "How many residents are there in Fao?"

"Three. All are men. Unfortunately, no more information is available."

"That isn't much to go on. It will have to do."

A Ulo came out from behind a wimba, swooped down and bit Y Ten's hand off. I fired at the reptile, wincing. It screeched. *Yeeeta.* It lunged at me, beak open and knocked me sideways. Beams from Y Ten struck its neck. *Yeeeta.* It turned and flew away.

I asked, "Will your hand grow back?"

She replied, a blank expression on her face. "In four hours, maybe more."

"Can you update your body's ability to heal faster?"

"Unfortunately, thirty minutes ago airborne protozoa and viruses started attacking my bio-circuits. In the beginning, the bio-circuits destroyed them. However, somehow the organisms evolved so much that they couldn't destroy all of them. As a result, the circuit's ability to heal any wounds or replace body parts slowed down.

"Also, the bio-circuit's demise made it possible for the Ulo to attack us without being noticed."

I winced. "Airborne protozoa? I've never heard those."

"This part of the Munt, an area that within an eight-mile radius of us, is filled with them. They jump from branch to branch or ride air currents."

My body went cold, a horrified response. "Can your bio-circuits repair themselves completely?"

"Maybe. Time will tell."

I bit my lip, scared.

In the afternoon, after climbing over three ridges, all partly covered by towering mushrooms, I gagged. "These fungi stink."

"Affirmative."

"Your hand has grown back. It took just as long as you mentioned."

She offered a mild salute.

Ahead, several purple butterflies came to rest on a palmetto trunk. On our right, beyond my peripheral vision, a soft crunching grew louder. I blinked, worried, then glanced in that direction. Eight human males in dirty tunics stepped out of bushes, their rifles aimed at my partner and me.

The tallest barked, "Come with us." He rushed toward me, the butt of his gun raised, then hit my shoulder with it. I blenched as pain shot through it. My lenses sent neutrinos into his mind. They returned. His name was Pat Ma. He, a refugee from Oro, had reached Lasho five months ago. Two days later he stabbed two refugees, took their money and hiked toward Last Chance. More information would be available in the near future.

A message from Y Ten scrolled through my lenses. *There are too many of these hoodlums. Although we could kill a few, the others would gun us down. We'll have to go with them.*

I bit my lip, angry that she was right. All of us got a move on.

After trudging through a swamp's knee-deep water for a couple of hours, our group came upon a muddy bank, went around towering ferns and halted near sixteen one-story gray buildings, all of them surrounded by eighteen ten-feet high poles. Next to one of the buildings, five men, some dressed in filthy tunics, others in soiled jumpsuits, strangers who resembled walking corpses, began staring at us. I whispered in Y Ten's ear, "These prisoners haven't eaten in a long time."

"That's my guess."

One of the men rushed in this direction. When he was between two poles, electrical sparks shot out of them, struck him, and he fell.

I winced. A guard in a sepia uniform rushed out of an umber building and pointed at two men. He announced, "Bury him next to your garden." Both men shuffled toward the body, grabbed it, dragged the corpse about thirty feet, placed it on the ground, picked up shovels and started digging.

Behind us, one of the men in dirty tunics shouted, "Go inside." He kicked the back of my leg. I clenched my teeth, angry. My partner and I walked between poles and entered one of the gray buildings. A text message from Y Ten appeared in my lenses. *Reaching Fao will take more time.*

Both of us sat on a dirty bunk, one with a urine odor. I cringed.

An emaciated human male with sunken cheeks glanced at me. "All of us are going to die. There is no escape."

Chills ran up my spine, a mortified response.

A bony human male with broken teeth walked up to me. "Do you have any food?"

I gave him several berries. He shoved them in his mouth.

A gaunt Qio with sores on his chin, turned toward me. "Do you have anymore?"

I shook my head.

He stuttered, "Ba, ba, but . . ." Much to my surprise, he turned and hobbled away.

Y Ten whispered in my ear, "According to my latest telescope evaluation although the men who brought us here have departed, there are too many guards. We can't kill them all. Let's break out another time."

I rubbed my jaw, feeling helpless.

The next morning, a distant thrumming became louder. I looked through a window. Outside, beyond the poles, a Johnson tank went by, flames coming out of its turret. The flames struck adjacent wimbas and the trees caught on fire. Within seconds, the armored vehicle stopped.

In my lenses, my partner's message scrolled. *The Johnson operator is destroying the trees. He wants to make it harder for anybody or any creature to sneak up on this prison camp, one called Reput.*

I sighed, knowing that killing the operator and its crew would be tough. I sent Y Ten a text message, one mentioning this topic.

She replied, her note acknowledging that she agreed with me.

I flexed my aching shoulder, hoping it wasn't broken.

My partner's message scrolled. *Do you see that man with huge ears? He is on your left, sitting at a table.*

My lenses responded, indicating that I noticed him.

He is a spy named Zeek. Every few days he leaves a handwritten note in the dirt, a few feet from this building. A guard finds it several minutes after Zeek leaves. So far, the guards have executed three men, prisoners who said they were planning to escape.

I sent a response memo, one acknowledging hers.

Another came out of my lenses' indigo background. *According to my latest Transformation Tool probe, forty minutes ago, a gun battle between refugees and twenty of Kolo's men started. The conflict is taking place in gullies, ones that are just a few feet outside of Fao. Fao is two miles from here.*

An hour before the battle started, Kolo's men kidnapped two girls, a refugee mother's daughters. One of Kolo's men told them that if the refugees leave, they would release the girls. The refugees complained and said they should let go of them immediately. Two refugees fired and everybody else joined in.

I winced, and responded, acknowledging that I had received her message.

Not long after midnight while everybody was asleep, Y Ten climbed out of her bed and took a few steps, never making a sound. Her right hand changed into a knife. She placed the other hand over Zeek's mouth, stabbed his forehead and blood trickled out. As he tried to scream, she pressed harder, muffling the noise. His body went limp. My partner removed her left hand. The other changed into its prior shape. She returned to her bunk, moving silently and lay down.

At sunup, two guards entered the room and noticed the body. The tallest asked, "Who killed Zeek?"

A prisoner replied, "I don't know."

Others called out, repeating the same answer.

The shorter guard announced, "Everybody, go outside."

In front of us, both guards yanked out their pistols. The tallest asked, "Who killed Zeek?"

A frail prisoner responded in a shaky voice, "Not me."

The shortest guard shot a prisoner. He screamed and

dropped to the ground.

The guard's comrade yelled, "Answer my question, or we'll shoot somebody else."

Y Ten announced, "It was me."

The shortest guard pivoted and shot her. She fell.

I winced.

Another pointed at the crowd. "Two prisoners will bury the corpses in the morning. If any of you rebel, you'll end up like these two idiots."

Several prisoners gasped in horror.

That guard yelled, "Everybody return to your bunks."

The crowd dispersed.

Not long after sundown, I heard gunshots and sat up in my bunk, my adrenaline pumping.

Another prisoner, their face barely visible in dim light, peeked out the window, then blurted, "It sounds like a gunfight has broken out in the sentry's bungalow."

Another asked in a hoarse voice, "Eric, who is shooting?"

He coughed. "I can't tell. It's dark, hard to see what is going on."

I walked toward the window, squinting. Outside, a poorly lit six-foot-tall humanoid silhouette, barely noticeable, walked toward us.

Eric cleared his throat. "Somebody is headed this way."

Hoarse voice asked, "Who is it?"

Eric sniffed. "I can't see their face."

Hoarse voice announced, "It's probably a sentry, coming to kill us."

Eric sneezed. "Probably." He turned and shuffled away.

The door opened. The six-foot-tall guard, their face hidden in shadows, entered and said, "Brin, let's go."

I blinked, surprised, headed for the door, and left the building, following this stranger. I asked, "Why are you helping me?"

"It's me, Y Ten."

"Amazing. I thought you were dead."

She veered to the right while shooting at a pole.

I asked, "Why did you do that?"

She whispered, "It shuts off one section of the electric fence."

We hiked between poles and continued, bound for the tank. I spoke in a hushed tone. "What about the prisoners?"

She murmured, "We might be able to help them."

On top of the Johnson, a hatch opened. The driver stuck his head out. He asked, "Why did you come out here?"

Y Ten replied, "Good question." She shot the driver in the mouth, slicing part of his head off. The driver slumped forward. My partner hopped on the vehicle, grabbed the body, yanked it out, tossed it to the ground, and jumped inside the tank.

I walked toward my partner, wondering what she was doing.

T Ten climbed halfway out of the hatch. "I just killed the entire crew."

I said, "Good work." Behind me, somebody hollered. I glanced over my shoulder, trying to find out who it was. Two guards darted out of a building, guns blazing.

I rushed toward the Johnson as ammo struck nearby dirt, barely missing my ankles.

Y Ten ducked inside the tank. On its front, a hatch popped open. I jumped inside. The hatch closed and I stepped over two corpses. The turret fired.

Y Ten said, "My recent shots destroyed every guardhouse and the tower."

I blurted, "Great." The hatch whirred open.

Y Ten said, "Get rid of the bodies."

I pushed them out, and it closed, whirring.

Y Ten said, "Let's head for Fao." The Johnson veered to the left, jerked forward, and knocked down palmettos.

"This vehicle is noisy. Bandits will notice it."

"I just switched on the cloaking shield. Now the Johnson is invisible."

"Great."

CHAPTER FORTY-THREE

After knocking down thousands of poorly illuminated bamboo plants, all of them beneath the jungle canopy, the Johnson started across an eighty-foot-wide muddy river. Soon the water rose and covered the tank's body. A floating log banged against its left side. The Johnson lurched in the opposite direction. Without warning, the engine stalled.

I exclaimed, "We're stuck."

Y Ten replied in a monotone, "Not yet." The engine roared to life.

"Great."

It stalled.

I cringed. "Shit."

"You worry too much."

I winced. Another log struck the left side, and that part of the machine rose. I announced, my adrenaline pumping, "It's going to tip over."

She spoke, a blank expression on her face. "Maybe."

The engine started. The Johnson jerked forward. A crunching grew louder. Within seconds, the left side dropped.

As chills ran down my spine, I asked, "Are the tracks coming off?"

"There is a forty percent chance that they will."

"Shit."

The tank went over piled up rocks and kept going while a grinding sound became louder. I flinched. "What's making that noise?"

"Rocks are caught in the treads."

"Will they destroy the treads?"

"There is fifty-two percent chance that they will."

I clenched my teeth, frightened and angry. The front of the

Johnson rose. At the same time, it pushed aside a boulder. In a millisecond it reached the muddy shore, lurched forward and entered a fifty-foot-high, two-hundred-foot in diameter web.

I blurted, "There are hundreds of Dwots in this."

"Affirmative. Do you see your machine gun's trigger? It's a blue motion activation screen."

As my heart started pounding, a nervous reaction, I said, "Yes."

"Fire when ready."

Eight of them climbed onto the tank, spitting venom. All four of the Johnson's tiny windows clicked shut. On a sound-imaging screen, all eight crawled in several directions, their jaws twitching. I blenched while squeezing the trigger. Smart ammo tore several to shreds. Others squealed. *Eeeee.*

Flames came out of the barrel. A huge section of the web caught on fire. Other Dwots rushed toward us, spitting. Fire engulfed them.

I yelled, "Direct hit."

She responded in a monotone, "It's not over yet."

"Can the Dwots notice us?"

"According to computer model G, they detect the Johnson's electrical field."

CHAPTER FORTY-FOUR

Venom began leaking through narrow spaces, all between threes windows and their frames. I leaned back in my seat as the orange substance, one with a vomit-like smell, ended up on my pant leg. While my eyes watered, responding to the stench, I waved my hand over a motion activation screen. More bullets missed seven Dwots. In less than a second, the ammo returned and cut the arachnids half. Others screeched. *Eeeee.*

The Johnson entered a cloud of smoke. On the partly shrouded barrel and beneath it, more of the creatures, all on fire, collapsed. Others rushed in this direction, spitting. Ammo struck them. *Eeee.* They crawled several yards and fell.

Within moments, the smoke cleared. Ahead, to the left and right, most of the web was burned away. Dwot corpses covered just about every inch of the ground. The tank rolled over them. At the same time, a crunching became louder. Soon it reached knee-high grass, a spot beyond the web and went between towering wimbas. Y Ten said, "According to gauge fourteen we're low on fuel, will run out of it soon."

I cringed. "Trouble."

"Affirmative." She reverted into her original shape, a woman.

After knocking down small lupunas, the Johnson reached a four-foot-high wall of creepers and stopped. Y Ten said, "All the fuel is gone. As a result, the cloaking device shut off."

Chills ran up my spine, a worried response. Both of us climbed out and stepped over four Dwot corpses. One raised its leg while spitting venom. The lethal substance hit Y Ten's right hand. She jerked, and sat, her back against the turret.

I blenched as bullets from my weapon struck the creature. It fell.

I turned toward my partner while asking, "How bad is it?"

"I'm not going to recover." Her eyes closed.

I grabbed my partner's arm and shook it. "Get up. I need your help." While my mind kicked into overdrive, trying to figure out how to assist her, my colleague slumped forward. According to my scanner, the venom had shorted out all of her bio-circuits.

I rose to my feet, hands trembling, shocked by my colleague's passing, then turned, climbed off the Johnson and trudged on. Ahead, far away, a bomb went off. I flinched.

Within two hours I came upon a hill, in a stooped position, trying to avoid enemy fire. On this side, Supervisor Frank, and a small group of detectives, all dressed in camouflaged amber jumpsuits, all of them on their stomachs, Tactical Purpose Armaments, in hand, were speaking to each other. Frank blurted, "Fire at will." All of their guns went off. In the near distance, the side and front of a small green-house, one of eight, exploded.

To the right and left of the detectives, Tira and her colleagues, all of them on their stomachs, fired their rapid discharge rifles.

Frank looked at me, a surprised expression on his face. "Brin, you didn't respond to Tesk or my messages. We thought you were dead."

I blinked, surprised by the comment, then dove to the ground as bullets whizzed past my shoulder. "How long have you been here?"

"About forty minutes." Ammo struck the top of the hill, inches from our heads.

I blenched.

He asked, "What happened to Y Ten and Evers?"

I answered.

He grimaced. "That's too bad. At any rate, we're pinned down. Eight minutes ago, three refugees rushed over this hill, trying to defeat our attackers. Laser beams struck them, killed all three."

My stomach muscles tensed up, a terrified response.

Two detectives tossed smart grenades. They flew toward a yellow house. Without warning, the explosive devices plummeted, hit the ground and went off.

I said, "Somebody is jamming the grenade's guidance system."

"Yes. We can't hit that yellow house." Laser beams came out of it, struck the top of this hill, a spot that was close to us and cut a two-foot deep groove in it.

I announced, "At this rate, there won't be any hill left in a few minutes."

"Correct."

I exclaimed, "Provide covering fire. I'm going to rush that yellow house."

Frank glowered. "Is that a good idea?"

"We'll see." I jumped up, darted over the hill, my adrenaline pumping. A beam sliced fabric off part of my sleeve. I veered to the right while another grazed my leg, reached a shallow hole and hopped inside. A beam struck the top of my helmet, tearing off chunks. To my right, in another hole, a Qio woman refugee fired her rifle. A beam struck her shoulder, tearing it off. She screamed, then collapsed.

I winced. A tiny rocket hit the side of the yellow house and bounced off.

Frank's message appeared in my lenses. *A few minutes ago, that house was made of wood and concrete. However, for unknown reasons, the wood changed into carbon nanotubes. As a result, our bombs won't damage it.*

I nodded while sending him a text response. To my left, a

crunching grew louder. I glanced in that direction as a hopper rushed toward me. On its top, a machine gun sprayed bullets. Ammo struck the top of my helmet, ripping pieces off.

A gravitational wave, sent by a detective's weapon, struck one of its legs. The hopper fell over. Its hatch opened. The operator crawled out. Ammo struck his chest. He bellowed, "Help" and dropped.

I looked straight ahead. Flames went through both of the yellow house's windows. On its left side, four humanoid silhouettes, all covered by burning liquid, stumbled out and fell.

CHAPTER FORTY-FIVE

All the detectives, every refugee and I dashed toward the houses and went around one. In front of us, a hooded figure raced out of a brown shack, moving toward a sienna building.

I shot at the figure. He or she sprinted behind a green one-story dwelling. My lenses sent neutrinos into the stranger's mind. Several of us rushed inside the yellow house. Near the middle of it, a six-foot-three-inch tall human with eyeglasses, a man who was standing next to a six-inch long particle accelerator, equipment that was on a table, fired at us. Bullets struck his chest. Blood gushed out. He yelled, "You . . ." took a few steps and collapsed.

To my right, Tira raised her fist. "We just killed Kolo."

Several refugees cheered, "Death to the tyrant."

A detective reached the accelerator, then demolished it with his rifle. The detective announced, "If we arrived twenty minutes later, Lasho would have crashed into Cirok because the accelerator had sent enough protons into Cirok's atmosphere."

I asked, "What do the protons do?"

"They collapse the space between both celestial bodies and gravitational pull yanks Lasho toward Cirok with such great force that it smashes into the planet."

I winced. The neutrinos returned. According to them, the hooded figure was CZ. Four seconds ago, she had rushed inside a sienna building, boarded a twenty-foot-long space vessel. Then it took off, bound for parts unknown. Her goal was to build another particle accelerator and use it to destroy Lasho or another moon.

Tira frowned. "There are two death camps nearby. It's time

to kill their guards and free the prisoners."

I said, "Tira, I'm glad that you and your friends survived."

She grinned. "We don't give up."

I nodded.

She glowered. "You lucky son-of-a-bitch, I didn't think you would make it."

I offered a quick smile. Everybody dashed off.

After rushing through a wimba grove, our group halted behind a ten-foot-high wall of creepers. I and everybody else pushed the plants aside about half an inch. I looked straight ahead and noticed six dilapidated one-story tan buildings, a two-story sepia one and a thirty-foot-high tower, structures that were surrounded by thirty-six-foot-high poles.

Tira said, "If a prisoner rushes between the poles, wanting to escape, bolts come out, strike them, and they die."

I blenched. On top of a pole, a sign read. *Noho Camp. Work is sacred.* At the bottom of the tower, Raya, dressed in a gray uniform, aimed her rifle at a woman, fired and the prisoner keeled over.

I flinched.

Tira whispered in my ear, "I hate Raya."

I exhaled, trying to calm down.

Nellie, along with another girl and Wendy stepped out of a tan building. Nellie pointed at the woman's corpse and started bawling.

Raya aimed her weapon at Nellie. It went off. Bullets struck the ground near Nellie's feet. She jumped backward, a horrified expression on her face.

My lenses sent neutrinos into the girl's mind. The particles returned. Her name was Mindy.

I blinked, surprised.

Wendy gnashed her teeth.

Inside the tower, near its top, Ilia, dressed in a gray

jumpsuit, yelled, "Shoot Mindy. That girl is a fucking pain in the butt."

Mindy glared at Ilia.

Behind all three girls, a Qio with big eyes, a stranger in a filthy dress, stepped out of the building. Ilia fired. The big-eyed lass screamed, took a few steps and keeled over.

Mindy rushed toward her, then stooped and touched the girl's wrist. "Nola is dead."

Ilia chuckled. "Too bad."

Mindy blenched, then glanced at Ilia. Ilia's weapon discharged. Ammo struck dirt, inches from Nola's body.

Mindy, a horrified expression on her face, winced. Ilia laughed.

Tira murmured in my ear, "Watching this makes me sick."

I swallowed, shocked by Ilia's cruelty.

Vin and a human male, both dressed the same way as Raya, rushed out of the sepia building, their rifles aimed at the girls. Vin asked, "Ilia, do you need our help?"

She announced, "Tell all the prisoners to come outside."

Vin along with his colleagues marched away while barking out orders.

CHAPTER FORTY-SIX

All of the prisoners, about a hundred men, women and children, bony figures in filthy clothes, stopped in front of Raya and eight sentries.

Raya announced, "It's time for another inspection."

All the prisoners pulled tiny objects out of their pockets and tossed them to the ground.

Vin walked up to an old woman. He asked "You like wasting our time, don't you?"

She shook her head, her lips trembling.

Vin snarled, "Don't lie to me. I know what you're thinking." He shot her in the mouth, and she keeled over. Behind her other prisoners gasped in horror. Two women screamed.

Tira whispered in my ear, "I hate watching this."

I nodded, teeth clenched.

Vin and two other guards pushed aside other prisoners, then walked between them, their rifles aimed at the inmates, and kept going. Two women shuddered while others sobbed.

A sentry laughed and placed his barrel against a girl's neck. "Don't be afraid. Like every guard here I'm just doing my duty." He chortled.

As she quivered, he strolled away, then announced, "Make sure you've removed everything from your pockets."

In front of him, a boy flinched. The sentry blurted, "I don't like that look on your face." Tears rolled down the kid's face. He shoved the boy to the ground. A girl stooped over the young man. The sentry moved on. All around the jailer, prisoners stepped away, mortified expressions on their faces.

The sentry laughed and slapped an old man's cheek. The decrepit male dropped his cane. The jailer kicked a girl's leg.

She fell, then started crying. The sentry marched on. At the same time, he barked, "All of you are worthless turds. You're lucky I don't shoot you in the neck. Tomorrow, I will." He chuckled, then turned and marched toward Raya. In front of him, prisoners retreated, creating a path.

My stomach muscles tightened with an angry response.

Tira murmured in my ear, "We should attack now."

Frank whispered, "Let's wait a few minutes."

Tira glared at him. "Why?"

He replied in a low tone, "Because the guards are too close to the prisoners."

She grumbled incoherently, an angry expression on her face.

Within minutes, this sentry and the others stopped next to Raya, then pivoted and began staring at the prisoners.

Raya called out, "Inspection is finished. We'll conduct another tomorrow." She and one of her colleagues strutted toward the sepia building. Sixteen guards marched out of it, saluted her, and all of them entered.

I said, "Let's attack."

Tira blurted, "Good idea."

Frank added, "I agree." Everybody pushed the creepers aside, started firing and rushed forward.

Bullets destroyed two poles. A gravitational wave struck Ilia. She slumped forward and fell out of the tower. Eight guards darted out of the sepia building, spraying bullets.

To my right, beyond my peripheral vision, somebody howled in pain. I flinched.

Two guards stumbled. The rest kept blasting. Without warning, three tripped. The others spun around. A smart grenade crashed through the sepia building's window. The device exploded, and the front of the structure flew apart. I flinched as pieces of the roof and wall rained down on us.

Inside the back of the partly destroyed property, several guards coughed. Others fired at us.

Ammo struck them. To my right, Frank announced, "All of the sentries are dead. Let's help the prisoners." All of us turned and walked toward the other buildings. Several refugees stumbled out of them, stunned expressions on many of their haggard faces.

Two detectives announced, "The prisoners are hungry. Let's feed them." Both sprinted inside the sepia building.

A bony Qio woman with gray hair walked in my direction, then hugged me. At the same time, she wept.

I blinked, surprised by her act.

Both detectives hurried out of the sepia building, large bags in hand. Soon both reached inside, yanked out bread and gave them to refugees. Two skeletal refugees, women with gray hair, grasped the food with trembling hands.

I exhaled, relieved that the gaunt prisoners wouldn't starve to death.

Tira announced, "It's hard to believe that anybody could treat people like this."

Frank asked, "What sick mind dreamed this up?"

In the far distance, a thumping grew louder.

Frank asked, "What's that sound?"

Tira replied, "Hoppers are coming."

I blenched.

Mindy blinked. "What is a hopper?"

I answered.

Frank scowled. "I don't believe that such a machine exists."

Tira frowned. "Frank, you better have your weapons ready."

A detective glowered. "It's probably just an animal searching for food."

Tira exclaimed, "Shit, if you ignore me many of us will die."

The detective scoffed, "You worry too much."

My stomach muscles tightened, a shocked response. "Detective . . ."

Three hoppers leaped out of the jungle, coming this way. Mindy screamed.

To my right, Frank shouted, "Fire at will."

On his left, a laser beam struck a detective's helmet, tearing her head off.

My body went cold, a terrified response.

Ammo struck two hoppers. Both toppled over as their weapons were firing. Their hatches popped open. One operator jumped out, blasting. A smart grenade landed next to her. It exploded, and her body disintegrated.

Ammo struck the other hopper, then bounced off. A smart grenade broke through one of the machine's windows and blew up. A severed arm flew out.

Tira shouted, "Direct hit."

Another grenade went through the other hopper's biggest window, one used by the operator. The weapon detonated, and flames poured out.

Tira yelled, "Die you bastards."

Frank announced, "All the hoppers are down, and their drivers are dead."

Two more hoppers arrived, guns blazing. Ammo grazed my left shoulder. I flinched, then ducked.

One of Tira's friends screamed, "I'm hit."

Frank glanced at me, a shocked expression on his face. "I just called for backup."

I bit my lip, horrified. "Will they arrive soon?"

Frank blinked. "Unknown."

To his right, the other two detective's heads and upper torsos were gone, sliced off by laser beams. My stomach tightened, a shocked response. I squeezed the trigger. Bullets struck one hopper's legs. The machine lurched backward and keeled over. The operator climbed out of its left side, discharging their weapon. A grenade hit the adjacent dirt, blew up and the operator's severed arms, and other body parts flew in several directions.

One of Tira's friends hollered, "Wow."

I glanced to the right. A laser beam tore the left side of Frank's helmet off. He bellowed, "Medic."

As my adrenaline pumped harder, I yanked a bandage out of my pocket and placed it on his bloody ear.

Ahead, beyond my peripheral vision, a thumping became louder. I looked in that direction while a hopper's foot stomped nearby dirt. I fired at the machine's leg, then jumped to the left. The hopper fell and crashed to the ground, inches from my foot. Its hatch popped open. The operator's weapon chattered. *Ep, ep, ep.* Ammo struck my right sleeve, one made of bulletproof fabric. I blinked while squeezing the trigger. A laser blast ripped the operator's cheek off. She hollered, then keeled over.

I glanced to the left, my heart pounding, a mortified response. Next to a fallen hopper, a digger came out of the dirt. On its top, a ninety-three discharged. *Nup, nup, nup.* A mortar shell hit nearby dirt, and sediment rained down on all of us. I ducked, flinching.

A grenade landed on the ninety-three's barrel, exploded, and haze swept over the machine.

To my right, Tira announced, "Stop shooting until the smoke clears." A thrumming grew louder.

I glanced to the left, teeth clenched, but only noticed palmettos. "What's making that noise?"

Tira replied, "When the smoke clears, we'll know."

I looked in the opposite direction while the haze dissipated, revealing dead machine operators. Two ten-foot-long hornets flew over strangler figs, coming this way.

One of Tira's friends called out, "They're repulsive."

Everybody fired at them. Both gigantic insects rose about twenty feet, their wings flapping hard. Six more hornets, four feet longer than the first ones, arrived. One swooped down, grasped a digger operator's corpse with its pinchers, and took off.

Tira shouted, "These insects smell like death." Three of them spit yellow mucus.

Some of it landed on Frank's right shoulder. He blurted, "This liquid is eating a hole in my uniform." He yanked the outfit off, a panicked expression on his face.

As the stench became stronger, I glanced down at my boot. On it, yellow mucus started dissolving the footwear's outer layer. I shoved my boot into the dirt and yanked it out. Most of the gooey substance was gone. I looked up while one of the hornets flew toward me. I winced, then dodged to the left, blasting. Bullets struck its eye. The insect screeched. *Oooona.* Suddenly, it turned and took off. Beneath it, another one reached down with its pincher, grabbed a severed head, then rose and flew away.

Behind it, ammo struck one's thorax, tore the insect in half and each body part plummeted.

Tira hollered, "Kicked your ass."

The other hornets shot upward and departed.

CHAPTER FORTY-SEVEN

With an exhausted expression on her face, Tira announced, "All the hoppers and the burrower are destroyed. Every machine operator is dead."

Sylvia exclaimed, "Awesome."

Wendy choked up. "I don't think I can take any more of this."

Nellie exhaled while looking at her trembling hands.

Tira announced, "Let's head for Noen, the other concentration camp. A lot of my friends are there."

Frank scowled. "Yes."

I glanced at him. "Can you make it?"

"Yes. The nanorobots sutured the wound and applied pluripotent cells to it."

I blinked, worried.

Nellie asked, a frightened expression on her face, "Can we go with you?"

Tira replied, "It's too dangerous. Stay here until we're finished. We'll come back for you."

Mindy asked, "Will you really come back?"

I answered, "We promise."

Sylvia glowered.

Harris grimaced. "Frank, are all of the other detectives dead?"

He sighed. "Yes."

Harris winced. "I hate it."

Frank, Harris, Sylvia, and Tira along with all her friends and I took off.

After our group slogged over three dimly lit hills, all of them beneath the jungle canopy, we came upon droppings.

Tira glanced at them. "Gaoots are nearby. Fuck." Everybody advanced, their weapons aimed in many directions.

One of Tira's friends, a stocky Qio woman named Silvia, whispered, "It's too quiet. Watch out." To our left, Foohs hissed as they crawled over fallen leaves. Far away, a Ulo, flying to our right, glided between wimbas and vanished in the darkness.

Chills ran down my spine. On my left, a faint rustling grew louder.

Tira announced, "Gaoot, I can hear you. Go away."

Harris glared at her. "Why did you say that?"

She glowered. "Most of the time, if they can't sneak up on you, they leave."

Harris snapped, "I don't believe you."

Tira sneered. "How many times have you traveled through the Munt?"

"This is my first time."

Tira shook her head. "A newbie."

Frank said, "Harris, pay attention. Stop arguing."

"Yes, sir."

Our crew tramped on while faint chirping became louder.

Harris glanced to the right and left. "What bird is making that sound?"

Sylvia replied, "A Kwa."

Harris asked, a surprised expression on his face, "A spider?"

Sylvia murmured, "Yes. Its bite is fatal."

Harris shrugged. "It sounds like a bird."

A three-inch long arachnid rushed out of a bush. Harris fired. A laser blast ripped the Kwa's thorax to pieces.

Tira exclaimed, "Die, you bastard."

Harris complained, "If we make too much noise Kolo's troops will hear us."

Sylvia blurted, "If they come, I'll shoot their balls off."

Tira said, "Sylvia, Harris is right."

Sylvia grumbled. Our group went between Dead Man's bells

Tira pointed at them, then whispered, "Be careful, those flowers are poisonous."

Harris asked, "How would you know?"

She replied in a low tone, "I studied them for several weeks." We trekked while sweat poured down our faces.

Harris whispered, "I hate this heat."

I nodded. We passed a fifteen-foot-high Dwot web. Inside it, to our left, fourteen of them crawled several inches, then halted.

Tira mumbled, "If we stop, they'll attack."

Harris glared at her but didn't say anything.

Frank coughed. Our tribe reached a dried-up streambed and marched on. Behind us, a hissing grew louder. I glanced over my shoulder. In the near distance, four Dwots rushed toward us. Without warning, they halted, their jaws twitching. My adrenaline started pumping.

Tira remarked, her voice barely audible, "Keep going. Don't shoot them. If you do, they'll attack."

I looked straight ahead, and we slogged on. Soon our crew passed more Gaoot droppings.

Sylvia commented in an undertone, "Don't slow down. The Gaoot is surprised, won't strike because we caught it off guard."

Harris sighed. "I feel like a sitting duck."

Sylvia muttered, "Keep your voice down, or one of Kolo's assassins might hear you."

Harris bit his lip.

At dusk, our group set up camp. Frank and Harris started chewing flat rectangular pieces of compressed vegetables.

Tira glared at them. "Those look odd."

Frank shrugged. "Are you hungry?"

Sylvia glowered. "Tira and all of us are."

Frank gave both of them along with their friends several pieces.

Sylvia gulped one down. "Tastes good."

Far away, a cackling became louder.

I flinched. "What's making that noise?"

Sylvia replied, "A Paxo."

Harris grabbed his rifle.

I said, "Harris, relax, Paxos are harmless."

He glanced at me, a frustrated on his face. "Are you sure?"

"I am."

When the stars came out, compressed sleeping bags came out of our sleeves, expanded and wrapped around us. At the same time, the bags projected 3D holograms of grass, ones designed to camouflage us.

Tira blurted, "I wish I had one of those."

I switched off my hologram and said, "I'll stand watch until midnight. Use my sleeping bag until then."

Tira grinned.

Sylvia and the other refugees glared at me.

I said, "Sorry, but there aren't enough bags for all of you."

All of them scowled, wrapped blankets around themselves, and lay down.

Two hours before midnight, two dimly lit humanoid silhouettes hiked out of the darkness. I winced and raised my arm, ready to fire. "Who are you?"

Evers whispered, "It's me and another detective."

I blinked, surprised. "It's good to see you. Where have you been?"

Tira jumped up, her rifle aimed. "Who are they?"

I blurted, "Colleagues."

Tira blurted, "Fuck, they scared me to death." She lay down.

Evers continued, "Hours later, after you and Y Ten left, I went on a hike, wanting to locate food. When I was about eighty yards from Helton, coming back, I noticed about nine Qio men with rifles. One shouted at Nellie, told her to shut up or he would kill her. I fled, hoping to find you and Y Ten."

I nodded while pointing at the detective. "Where and when did you meet him?"

"One evening ago, when I was four miles south of here."

"Interesting. Tell me more."

"I came upon a crashed police cruiser, then searched it. Everybody I saw was dead. Within minutes, Detective Luc stepped out of the underbrush, his rifle aimed at me and told me to ID myself. I did."

"How did you find us?"

"When both of us were closer to this location, my wrist scanner detected yours."

I exhaled, relieved. "I'm glad you're alive." We hugged and stepped back.

Evers asked, "Where is Y Ten?"

I answered.

She flinched. "That's horrible. I miss her."

"So do I." A gruesome memory of Y Ten telling me she wasn't going to recover popped into my head and vanished.

Evers frowned. "Judging by that look on your face, something is bothering you. Are you thinking about Sultra?"

"No, Y Ten."

"If I can help, let me know."

I sighed and thanked her.

Near dawn, our collective slogged on and went between towering vines. Close by, a rustling became louder.

Tira cupped both hands around her mouth and called out, "Caw, caw."

I asked, "Why . . ."

Sylvia whispered in my ear, "Be quiet."

I shook my head, irritated. To our right, a Gaoot rushed out of the plants. Tira sprayed bullets. They struck the creature. It bellowed. *Owak, owak.* Without warning, it rushed at Evers. The entire group blasted. Laser beams and ammo ripped its chest open, then the beast collapsed.

Evers' jaw muscles tightened. "Tira, why did you make that odd sound?"

"I was imitating a Dwot. The Gaoot thought the spider was attacking it."

I said, "Impressive."

Harris pointed at Tira. "It could have killed us. You should have warned everybody before you made the sound."

Tira shook her head. "There wasn't enough time."

Harris glowered. "That's a flimsy excuse."

Tira shook her fist. "Fuck off."

Frank said, "We must focus on reaching the next camp, not argue."

Harris grumbled. Everybody departed. Ryan Harris' resume appeared in my lenses. He was from Zy. After this officer received a Bachelor's degree in Police Science from Streiss University, he enrolled in the Zy Police Academy. Two days ago, he was sent to Lasho to help Frank. Although Harris received straight A's while at ZPA, his instructors pointed out that he argued with his classmates far too often. At other times, he lectured many students, told them they weren't paying close attention to their duties. Many students complained and said he was too uptight. The resume vanished.

My lenses sent neutrinos into Tira Gann's mind. They returned. She, a college graduate with a Bachelors in Botany and a Master's degree in Microorganisms, had taught at Ceas College. Eight months ago, after her mother, father and sister, Nipl residents, were slaughtered by Nan's troops, she took off, boarded a spacecraft, and ended up in Last Chance. At that point, she met a small group of refugees. They began searching for food, discovered Blo and stayed because its residents gave them food and shelter. Her resume vanished.

My lenses sent neutrinos into Sylvia's cerebral cortex. They returned. Her name was Sylvia Jenkins. She, a college graduate with a Bachelors in Zoology, a Masters in Biology, and a Doctorate in Botany, had taught at Fara University. A year after receiving her Doctorate she took an online course in entomology. Four months ago, when her husband and two daughters, Dored residents, were gunned down by Nan's troops, she fled, boarded a spaceship, and ended up in Neib. Within hours, she met a small group of refugees. They began searching for something to eat, came upon Blo and remained there since its residents gave them food, shelter, and companionship. Her resume disappeared.

Our group came upon a lake. A tiny boat popped out of Harris' sleeve and expanded. Everybody shoved the craft into the water, climbed aboard while its engine started. Tira said, "I've never seen anything like this vessel before."

As it moved away from shore and sped up, Harris announced, "This equipment was invented years ago."

Tira exclaimed, "Wow."

Harris shrugged. To our left, in the far distance, two Gaoots, their heads above waves, swam toward us.

Tira fired. Both creatures veered away, moving toward shore. She exclaimed, "Got you, assholes."

Evers announced, "I'm glad that you scared them off."

Tira laughed. "So am I. I hate them. One slaughtered a friend."

Ahead, a Ulo came toward our tribe, flapping hard. Tira sprayed it with ammo. The creature squawked. *Ot, ot, ot.* Soon it flew to the left, bound for distant kapoks. She laughed. "Got you, asshole."

I exhaled, relieved, then glanced to the right. In front of our group, in the near distance, bushes on a small island shook. Our craft steered to the left and went around it.

Sylvia pointed at its shore. "Do you see those Dwots?"

Evers replied, "No."

I squinted, trying to find them.

Sylvia announced, "They hiding under bushes. If you look closer, you'll notice their legs."

Evers commented, "Now I see them."

Tira aimed her rifle.

Sylvia remarked, "Save your ammo."

Tira scowled. "Okay, but I hate them."

Sylvia added, "So do I, but if we run out of bullets, we're up shit creek."

Tira spat, "Okay." Our boat sped up, leaving the island behind. In front of us, a flock of red canaries rose and zoomed over our heads.

Evers glanced up at them, a surprised expression on her face. "What are those called?"

Tira smiled. "Lowtas."

Evers blinked, a worried expression on her face. "Are they dangerous?"

Sylvia laughed. "No. All they do is sing beautiful songs and eat."

Evers grinned. "What a relief." She handed out berries.

Tira ate some. "They taste good."

Within minutes, our crew reached the shore and stepped on it. In the near distance, tiny crabs scurried about. Evers glanced at them. "Are they edible?"

Sylvia shook her head. "No. If you take one bite, your stomach hurts. Then you vomit blood, pass out and die."

Evers' jaw muscles tightened. "Yow."

Harris frowned. "Sylvia, how do you know this?"

This new friend sighed. "You're a pain in the butt. Anyway, a few weeks ago, a friend of mine ate one. Soon she started complaining, said her stomach hurt. Within minutes she threw up blood and dropped to the ground. I walked, then stooped over her and asked what was wrong. She didn't answer. This former buddy of mine never woke up."

Harris winced. "Okay."

Tira scowled. "Harris, I wish you'd knock off your bullshit attitude."

He glared at her. "That's the way I am. Better get used to it."

Frank said, "Stop arguing."

Tira blurted, "He started it."

Frank sighed.

Tira grumbled. The boat shrank until it was as big as a seed. Harris grabbed it, and our crew slogged on.

After entering the jungle, we passed towering creepers. Ahead, far away, bombs went off. Tira announced, "Shit, ninety-threes."

Evers blurted, "Yow."

I winced. Our group kept going.

Soon all of us reached a dried-up stream bed and trudged on. To our left, about sixty yards away, a hopper jumped over towering wimbas, moving toward distant palmettos.

Evers exhaled. "I despise those machines."

Sylvia announced, "That makes two of us."

As we hiked by flowers, Sylvia pointed at them. "Be

careful. Those are Deadly nightshades. They're poisonous."

Harris glowered. "Did you make that up?"

She glared at him. "No. I studied them for weeks."

Harris frowned but didn't say anything. Our group slowed down.

Tira said, "I hate this area. It's too hot." She wiped the sweat off her cheek. A laser beam struck my bulletproof shoulder pad, an inch from my neck. Everybody dove to the ground.

Frank asked softly, "Can anybody see the shooter?"

Harris pointed at a strangler fig, then muttered, "There."

Frank whispered, "I don't see them."

Sylvia murmured, "Look between those two large sepia leaves."

Frank remarked, his voice barely audible, "I see them."

A bullet missed Harris's cheek. He blinked.

Tira crawled away and vanished, hidden by underbrush.

Frank's message scrolled through my lenses. *Where is she going?*

My lenses responded, its text pointing out that I didn't know. In the near distance, hidden in the darkness, somebody screamed. I winced. Had a stranger killed Tira?

I placed my hand in front of Evers' face, then drew two circles. *Who yelled?* She drew a square, responding. *Unknown.*

In front of us, somebody's hands, the only part of them that was visible, came out of vines, then pushed them aside, revealing Tira. She raised a Qio woman's severed head and tossed it to the ground. "I threw my knife at her neck. She fell, and I sliced this body part off." She laughed. "I enjoyed slaughtering this sniper. I want to kill more."

I glanced to the right. Evers blinked, a mortified expression on her face.

I looked straight ahead, my mind racing, wondering what would happen next.

Tira added, "Thieves have murdered three of my friends.

This is one of those thieves." She dropped it.

Evers asked, "Won't one of them find this severed head and come after us?"

Tira pointed down.

Evers asked, "What are you looking at?"

Tira replied, "Come over here. Leaves are blocking your view."

Evers and I walked, then glanced down as a group of cockroaches started eating the hacked off body part. Both of us cringed.

Tira snarled, "In about twenty minutes, it will be gone, devoured by these insects."

Our crew trekked.

Minutes later, further forward, not far beyond huicungo trees, hidden in the shadows, men and a woman laughed.

Sylvia whispered in my ear, "That's CZ and her gang. I recognize her laugh."

A bullet struck Frank's elbow, tearing off the bulletproof fabric.

I flinched. Everybody dove to the ground, discharging his or her weapons. A laser beam struck Evers' helmet, ripping off chunks.

Tira blurted, "Fuckers."

A smart grenade landed near my foot. I grabbed the device and tossed it. It blew up, destroying huicungos. Another plopped down near Frank's leg. He seized the explosive and flung it. It detonated, obliterating more trees. Tira and Sylvia rushed forward, blasting.

As my adrenaline pumped harder, Harris, Frank and everybody else followed them.

Harris cursed, "Damn it."

A missile shot out of Frank's shoulder-mounted launcher. In the near distance, hidden beyond towering vines, the projectile exploded, and orange flames shot upward.

CHAPTER FORTY-EIGHT

Harris, Frank, and the others including me sprinted around towering bushes and halted next to Tira and Sylvia.

Tira, an angry expression on her face, pointed at three corpses. "These are Nate, Yig and Mel, CZ's men. Months ago, Nate told a friend of mine named Sheila that he, along with Yig and Mel had killed many children. Yig said that he loved to hear the kids beg for mercy before he shot them in the eye."

Evers spat, "Bastards."

I blenched.

Evers scowled. "What happened to Sheila?"

"A month after Nate spoke with her, he shot her in the nose, killing her."

Evers' jaw muscles tightened. "Yow. Why did she trust Nate?"

Tira sighed, then wiped tears off her cheek. "Sheila told him she was looking for her daughter and described the teen. Nate said he knew where the girl was."

Evers blinked. "It's too bad that Sheila was so desperate."

Tira exhaled, a sad expression on her face. "Yes."

Harris snarled, "Nate, Yig and Mel deserved to die."

Tira kicked one of the corpses. "I hate these assholes."

Frank remarked, "Harris, don't make this personal. This is an assignment, nothing more."

He exhaled, an irritated expression on his face. "Yes, sir."

Sylvia gnashed her teeth. "Let's find CZ."

I said, "Let's find the other prison camp first."

Sylvia grumbled incoherently, an angry expression on her face. Our members tramped on.

After climbing over five more hilltops, all of them covered by shiringas, a blurred woman's face, a bad connection, materialized in my lenses. She cried out, "We're . . ." Without warning, this stranger's face vanished, and her voice was replaced by static. I told the others about this.

Frank scowled. "The same thing happened to me a second ago. That was Communications' Officer Melan. My guess is that her police cruiser, the Fedo, was trying to communicate with us before their ship touched down near this spot."

Ahead, about a thousand feet above the tree line, a triangular police cruiser dropped out of a cloud, then zoomed toward us. Without warning, it plummeted and disappeared behind the palmettos.

Harris winced. "My guess is that the Fedo just crashed."

Frank announced, "Keep up the pace. We have to find out if that is correct."

After circling around a fifteen-foot-high, sixty-foot in diameter Dwot web, I said, my heart pounding, a terrified response, "They aren't attacking."

Evers asked, "Why?" Our group passed a chasm. A cracking grew louder.

Tira shouted, "The gorge is becoming wider."

My body went cold, a mortified response. To our left, dirt, bromeliads and palmettos dropped into it. Everybody dashed to the right while the ground beneath our feet shook harder.

Harris' foot went over the edge. Tira grabbed his hand, pulled the officer up, and both of them along with everybody else leaped over fallen thorn trees.

Harris yelled, "It's hopeless." Within seconds, our group reached solid ground and kept going.

As chills ran down my spine, I glanced over my shoulder. Sixty yards behind us, vines along with underbrush tumbled over the chasm's edge. I looked straight ahead while our group rushed between lilies. A few sprayed a cloud of droplets.

Sylvia announced, "Don't inhale the mist or you'll pass out and die."

Harris retorted, "Don't bullshit me."

Sylvia snapped, "Shut up and follow my advice."

He spat, "You should shut up. I won't."

She exclaimed, "What an asshole."

Frank called out, "We must focus on reaching the prisoner camp."

Within minutes, our collective stepped over animal skulls and leg bones.

Harris asked, "What killed them?"

Tira inspected them with her tiny wrist-mounted scanner, a terrified expression on her face. "Airborne tetrodotoxin. That's my guess."

Harris frowned. "Why aren't we ill?"

Tira scowled. "My best guess is that our group doesn't live in this spot. Keep moving, or everybody will get sick and die."

Harris asked, "Are you sure about the tetrodo, whatever it's called?"

Tira glared at him. "Tetrodotoxin. Not one hundred percent. All right, stay here, smartass."

Harris asked, "How far is it to a safer spot?"

Tira grimaced. "It's hard to say. Once we reach another spot, I'll probe it with my scanner."

Frank coughed. "My stomach hurts." He stopped. "The helmet and face mask won't come out of my collar. I can't avoid the organism."

Tira put her arm around his waist. "I'll help you. Keep going, or you'll die."

Sweat began trickling down his temple.

Thirty minutes later, our group came upon kapoks. Tira called out, "According to my scanner this area is safe."

Frank sighed, then halted. "I feel dizzy . . . need to rest."

Sylvia coughed. "My head is spinning. Stopping to rest is a great idea."

Faraway, a two-foot-long missile rose above treetops. I pointed at it. "An Interceptor is coming this way."

Harris glanced in that direction, a shocked expression on his face. "Where is it?"

I blinked, irritated that he wasn't paying close attention. "It's between those wimbas."

He flinched. "Now I see it."

Tira blurted, "Son-of-a-bitch. It'll be here in a few seconds."

Evers announced, a mortified expression on her face, "I'm surprised that somebody noticed us."

CHAPTER FORTY-NINE

The projectile hit the nearby ground, missing Evers by three feet, and exploded. Everybody dove to the ground while dirt rained down on us. A grinding became louder.

Harris asked, "What's making that noise?"

Tira announced, "A digger."

Harris scowled. "A what?"

Tira explained, "It's a . . ." The machine's nose-mounted corkscrew popped out of adjacent dirt, interrupting her explanation.

Harris asked, "What the hell?"

The entire vehicle rose out of the ground. On its top, a ninety-three fired. A mortar shell, one that made a high-pitched zinging, whizzed by us. The projectile struck nearby mushrooms, then blew up.

Just about everybody discharged their weapons. Our group's laser beams and ammo bounced off it.

Tira blurted, "Shit."

Frank's launcher whooshed. Its missile struck the digger, went off and tore the left side of the machine off. Inside it, on the slumped forward operator's neck, blood gushed out.

Sylvia raised a fist. "Got the bastard. Great shot."

I nodded, hands trembling.

Sylvia announced, "I need to piss. Will return soon."

Several moments later, I said, "She's been gone a long time."

Tira frowned. "Something is wrong. Normally, it only takes her a couple of minutes."

I said, "Let's spread out and conduct a search." Everybody departed. I pushed aside neck-high creepers, hiked past bromeliads and stepped over three-inch long orange slugs, gastropods that honked. Faraway, in the darkness, an unseen creature cackled. To my right, on leaves, hummingbirds squeaked. In the other direction, a foot-long praying mantis crawled across a branch, then gulped down a cockroach.

Ahead, hidden behind a fifteen-foot wall of vines, Tira announced, "I found her."

I shoved the plants aside, stepped over Gaoot droppings, rushed between wimbas and halted next to Tira as she stooped over Sylvia. On the front of Sylvia's neck, blood trickled out of gunshot wound.

I whispered, "A sniper did this, might be close by."

Tira remarked softly, "Yes. Bullets damaged her vocal cords, kneecap, and ankle. She can't stand or talk."

Harris arrived, then crouched, and placed bandages on all three wounds.

Tira asked, "Are those any good?"

Harris replied in a low voice, "Yes."

Tira aimed her scanner at the injury. "Chances are that mutated airborne marburg virus have entered the wounds. She'll die in twenty minutes."

Harris murmured in her ear, "The bandages' nanorobots will repair her vocal cords, then suture the wounds in two minutes. It will take them about eleven minutes to destroy all the virus."

Tira responded quietly, "We have to leave this area immediately. It's full of Gaoots. I'll carry Sylvia."

Everybody grabbed our injured friend, placed her on Tira's back, and we departed.

Our group tramped through a walking palm grove. On the dark ground, thousands of two-inch long beetles, insects with squinting eyes on their backs, climbed over leaves.

Harris said, "We left the sniper behind."

Tira remarked, "That's my guess."

I asked, "Sylvia, how are you?"

She replied in a hoarse voice, "Although my body aches, I'm feeling better."

Tira offered a brief smile. "That's great."

Ahead, a six-foot-tall Qio man in a dirty tunic, a stranger with a smart rifle, stepped out from behind a towering wall of creepers. At the same time, he aimed it at us.

Just about everybody discharged their weapons. He turned, then rushed behind the plants. Evers, Harris and I chased him. Not far beyond Monkshood, he jumped over a waist-high leaf and sped up.

Evers blurted, "He's quick."

I spat, "Yes."

Harris exclaimed, "Run faster."

The stranger darted inside a wimba trunk.

Harris said, "He's either a three D hologram or his suit cloaked him."

Evers scowled. "I've never seen any cloaking suits."

I said, "I haven't either. Forget about chasing him. Let's go back."

Evers frowned. "He might have been created to lure us away from the others."

I blinked, worried. "Maybe." Our group retraced their steps.

Harris glowered. "Let's hope he isn't following us."

I glanced over my shoulder. "The only thing I see is the jungle. The only thing I hear is our footsteps." I looked straight ahead.

Harris added, "We should pay close attention."

Evers looked to the right and left, her brow tight. "I only notice our footsteps and leaves rustling in the wind."

Harris glared at her while he bit his lip.

She glowered. "Why are you staring at me?"

"I want to make sure you're paying attention."
She shook her head, a frustrated expression on her face.
He looked to the right, his brow furrowed in concentration.

We reached the others and told them what happened. Frank rubbed his face. "He was probably a hologram, designed to lure us away from the camp."
Harris snapped, "He might be following us."
Frank barked, "Knock it off. That's an order."
Harris winced. "Yes, sir."
Frank added, "Although IT keeps trying, every cloaking device they've created has failed. Let's go."
Harris grumbled incoherently while everybody departed.

Within minutes we came upon a poorly lit spot in the jungle, one with hundreds of skulls, thousands of empty rib cages, and numerous pelvic bones in it. I cringed.
Tira blurted, "Yuck."
Sylvia blenched. "I've never been to this area before." Without warning, a ten-foot-long hornet zoomed over the treetops, then dropped a humanoid skeleton. It crashed to the ground, then broke apart. At the same time, the giant insect flew away. "There's your answer. My guess is that the hornets drop their finished meals here. But I'm not sure why they use this location." Our crew trekked.

CHAPTER FIFTY

Everybody came upon towering kapoks. Not far beyond them, I noticed about twenty one-story amber buildings, along with a few gray ones, dwellings that were surrounded by about sixty ten-foot-high poles. Several feet behind a pole, inside the top of a thirty-foot-high tower, a Qio woman aimed her rifle at us and fired.

All of us rushed to the left and went behind palmettos as ammo struck nearby dirt. Tira announced, "This is Noen." Our group discharged their weapons. Laser beams struck the Qio woman, and she fell.

Tira whispered, "The fence is electrified. If you rush between the poles, you'll get shocked to death." Sylvia climbed off her back.

Evers asked, "Sylvia, can you walk?"

She muttered, "Yes, slowly."

I squeezed the trigger. Bullets struck two poles. Both crackled while sparks shot out of them.

Tira announced, "Great shot. The fence is disabled. Watch out for guards." Everybody rushed toward it. Two human men in uniforms darted out of an amber building, guns blazing.

Ammo from our crew struck both. They screamed, took a few steps and keeled over.

Men, women and children, bony figures all dressed in rags, began pouring out of several amber buildings. My lenses sent neutrinos into their minds, and some particles returned. Joni, Glenn, Yinnie, Bill and Rex were here. I blinked, surprised and grateful.

Evers said, "Jason, you're alive. That's great."

Tears ran down his cheeks.

Zesa and Marti trudged out of the crowd, coming this way. Zesa, a shocked expression on her face, stuttered, "I-I thought we, we were going to die. Tha thanks for rescuing us."

I grinned. "My colleagues helped." I mentioned their names.

Harris kept staring at them, a horrified expression on his face. "It's hard to believe that anybody would treat you so badly. Zesa and Marti, would you like food and water?"

Marti's cracked lips started trembling. At the same time, she nodded.

He and Frank gave them energy bars, food that changed its composition in order to revive their bodies' current weakened state.

Evers took a deep breath, a panicked expression on her face. "Are Chloe and Sean here?"

Zesa paused, then drawled, "Yes, both are." A thrumming grew louder. She pointed at the sky, her hand shaking. "They're coming."

I blinked, surprised, then looked up. "Who is coming?" Two gigantic hornets flew over treetops, moving in this direction.

Marti cried out, "Them."

Tira shouted, "Shit."

Frank hollered, "They're huge."

Sylvia bellowed, "I hate them."

Both descended, flapping hard. Beneath them, the crowd scattered, trying to escape. One wasp seized a girl. Every member of my group fired. The insect screeched. *Eaaaa.* Without warning, the airborne pest let go of her, and both hornets flew away.

Zesa trembled. "Ma more hornets will be coming soon. They they come once or twice a day, grab inmates and tah take them to parts unknown. I day despise them."

Frank scowled. "Did the guards stop them?"

Marti spat, "No. They just stood and watched."

Evers frowned. "The guards are monsters."

Zesa stuttered, "The the guards rarely feed us. And and when they do, they only give us tiny scraps of bread."

Evers shook her head. "Horrible."

Frank asked, "Where are the hornets coming from?"

Sylvia replied, "I'll take you there. We should kill as many as possible because they keep breeding. At some point, there will be so many that we can't destroy them."

Harris glared at her. "How do you know where they are?"

Sylvia snapped, "I just know. Shut the fuck up and pay attention."

Harris gnashed his teeth.

Evers blinked. "What about the prisoners? They need food and protection from bandits, Kolo's troops and robbers."

Marti replied, "Several inmates know how to find wild vegetables." She explained that since the fences had been destroyed, the prisoners could locate food.

Harris scowled. "Can you protect yourself from bandits, Kolo's troops, and robbers?"

Zesa stuttered, "Sa some prisoners can. Give give them weapons." She called out two names. A human man and a Qio woman rushed up to her. She told them about her plan. Both nodded.

Frank gave them rifles. Our group, Harris, Frank, Evers, Tira, Sylvia, two of Sylvia's friends and I departed.

Harris scowled. "I have mixed feelings about handing out firearms to amateurs."

Sylvia blurted, "They're fearsome warriors. Quit complaining."

Harris glared at her. "I'm not complaining. I'm pointing out the obvious."

Sylvia turned toward him, then took a step until her face was an inch away from his. At the same time, she barked,

"You don't know them like Zesa does."

Harris snapped, "They're dirty, tired prisoners . . ."

Sylvia took a swing at him. He ducked, and her fist grazed his shoulder.

Frank announced, "Stop arguing. Harris, that's an order. We must destroy the hornets."

Harris bit his lip. "Yes, sir."

Sylvia grumbled, an angry expression on her face, then stomped off.

CHAPTER FIFTY-ONE

Our group reached the gorge we had passed. In it, thousands of gigantic hornets buzzed.

Tira announced, "The noise they make pisses me off."

I cringed, repulsed by it. Four missiles shot out of Frank's handheld launcher. Below us, all four detonated. Orange flames swept over the insects. They screeched. *Eeeeooooo.*

I winced as a blast knocked me backward, a couple of inches. Several of the hornets rose. The inferno engulfed most of them.

Tira pointed upward. "Several are escaping."

Evers asked, "Where are they going?"

Sylvia replied, "I think I know."

Harris asked, "How would you?"

Sylvia glared at him. "I took an online class in entomology, one where I studied hornet behavior."

Harris shook his head. "One online class doesn't make you an expert."

Sylvia asked, "Have you ever studied entomology?"

Harris snapped, "No."

Frank said, "Sylvia, lead the way. Your limited experience is all we have."

She nodded.

Harris gnashed his teeth.

Everybody came upon the bone graveyard. Harris glanced to the right and left. "I don't see any hornets. Sylvia, you were wrong."

"Listen, asshole. We're not finished." She pointed ahead. "Look behind that hill."

Harris groused, "Sounds like a bunch of crap to me."

I said, "Let's go." Our crew marched past skulls and ribs.

Harris spat, "There's no sign of them. This is a waste of time. They're probably headed for Noen."

Sylvia said, "Harris, keep your voice down."

He scowled. "Why should I?"

She replied, "If the hornets are here, they'll hear us and attack."

He exhaled and murmured, "Okay." Our colleague stepped on a rib. It cracked.

Sylvia whispered, "Be quiet."

Harris' brow tightened while he inched forward. Within seconds, he placed his left foot on the ground, inches from a clavicle.

Tira glanced at him, then nodded.

He frowned and kept going. Everybody reached the top of a hill, glanced down, but only noticed bones.

Harris shook his head while grumbling to himself. Sylvia pointed at a hill, one that was on our left. Our troop hiked toward it, then stepped over scapulas, femurs, metatarsals, and mandibles.

I cringed.

Evers winced.

Frank kept staring at the bones, a shocked expression on his face.

Tira shook her head, a disgusted expression on her face.

Sylvia blenched.

CHAPTER FIFTY-TWO

All of us reached the top of a hill, looked down and noticed eight huge hornets, ones that were tending eggs. Everybody fired. The insects screeched as ammo tore them and the eggs to pieces. *Eeooooy.*

Harris exhaled. "I was wrong. Sylvia, how did you know they were here?"

"Some of the bones had flesh on them. The insects love to eat it."

Evers asked, "Why are the bones here?"

Sylvia replied, "There aren't any Gaoots, Dwots or other predators nearby. So the hornets bring their half-finished meals to this spot and finish eating them."

Harris scowled. "Why did they lay their eggs here?"

Sylvia responded, "It's a safe area."

Harris frowned. "Why aren't there any predators nearby?"

Sylvia remarked, "The hornets scared them away."

Harris glared at her. "How do you know they scared them off?"

"I along with two of my friends saw them do it."

Tira blurted, "I'm one of those friends. I saw them do it."

Harris paused, a surprised expression on his face.

The next morning, Sylvia told me that Uncle Joe, a Noen prisoner, had died a week before. Then she added that Chloe, Sean, Jason, Rex, Yinnie, and Glenn wanted to stay at Blo for a few weeks. During that time, she told Jason about Rosa's death. As he started weeping, she hugged him and pointed out that he could talk to her anytime about his mother's passing.

The following evening, Frank shared new information with me. "According to a Detective Irm, a colleague who spoke to me within the last few hours, if Anna didn't kill us, Kolo told her that one of his assassins would shoot her daughter, Chloe, in the head."

I winced. "What else did Irm say about this?"

"Most of your neutrino probe's information regarding Anna were correct. Only the conversation between Kolo and Anna was missing."

"What about Wo Ta?"

"That was a pseudonym Kolo used sometimes when he emailed secret messages to some of his henchmen."

I blinked, surprised "Overton? Was it a town or a person?"

"That was a code name for Kolo's plan to destroy Lasho with the accelerator."

"What about the shipment?"

"It was a bio-circuit, equipment that improved the accelerator."

Two weeks later, during a meeting with Harris, he told me that four evenings ago, three geneticists, professionals who had studied epigenetics for years, showed him a 3D hologram, a tool that pointed out that for unknown reasons some of the hornet's genes had switched on during Lasho's expansion. As a result, the insects, which were one-inch long, became larger. All three scientists, part of the team that built this moon, didn't know that its construction would affect the insect's growth in unforeseen ways.

The morning after my discussion with Harris, when Evers and I boarded a spacecraft, bound for Cirok, she spoke to me about new events. Chloe, Sean, Jason, Rex, Yinnie, Joni, Marti, Sylvia, Tira, Zesa, Wendy, Bill, Glenn and Nellie decided to stay at Blo for several months.

The End

You may also enjoy the following from eXtasy Books Inc:

Brynin
Thadd Evans

Excerpt

It was the year 1014 as the OTA Corporate Empire spread out over eight planets.

On screen, coordinates brightened. We were more than two light years beyond the edge of the OTA Empire.

Below the coordinates, the accelerometer indicated that ST7, our eighty foot long, thirty foot wide, tear drop shaped starship, was still maintaining a velocity of 157,203 miles per second.

Greg, a medium height, slender man with a narrow face entered the bridge and sat down. Greg, who had a doctorate in Astronomy, worked for OTA as a mapmaker. After seven years, he told his manager that he was tired of eighteen-hour days with little time off, and OTA fired him.

After speaking to OTA and Opco Corporation Human Resource managers, and OTA spacecraft captains at over six hundred locations, the only job he could find was working as my navigator. And since I was the sole proprietor of an independent company, a cargo starship shipping organization with no ties to OTA or Opco, hiring him wasn't a problem.

In addition to that, for several years, Greg had created spheroid holographic planispheres, three-dimensional star charts, navigational guides which were visible through an oval window. Every planisphere was different. Some contained the brightest stars. Others displayed comets, moons, asteroid belts and constellations. In every case, the observer could change the planisphere's latitude and longitude, making it possible for the current user to study charts more easily.

Because my ship wasn't following well-traveled OTA routes, most navigators were afraid of working for me. Several had told me that if ST7 broke down beyond Yopla, a distant planet, no one would rescue us. Luckily, Greg didn't care about that.

Near the top of his screen, aligned vectors, coordinates that were created when laser beams ricocheted off five distant planets, Yot, Minq, Nym, Bir, and Sios, returned to our ship, creating part of a galactic map. Although we used the vectors to make two and three-D maps, not all the beams came back. As a result, there were over 6,302,511 holes in the maps.

On many occasions, we filled many of them with less accurate ultraviolet and RGB scans. The problem with ultraviolet and RGB, red, green, blue light, was that the light itself curved as it passed Alpha Centauri A, Alpha Centauri B, Yot, Minq, two planets and six moons, Nasm, Caz, Onme, Ryet, Meis and Norom. Because of that, those distorted scans created faulty star charts.

Near the bottom of the screen, a tiny piece of asteroid dust whizzed by the port wing like a bullet.

Beyond that wing, just over 81 million miles from us, near the top of Alpha Centauri C, hot gases exploded, and shot toward us.

Greg said, a worried expression on his face, "If those hit ST7, the hull may burn up."

I shoved my hand through floating text and the ship veered starboard—missed the edge of the Dena asteroid belt by several feet. "If it wasn't for your vectors, we would have smashed into that belt."

"Thanks. Unfortunately, we're not out of trouble yet."

I blinked. "We're moving away from Alpha Centauri C."

Greg nodded.

On screen, an ultraviolet scan of the solar winds and Nooipl, a planet, and its magnetosphere, enlarged. The winds and the magnetosphere were spreading out. Steering through them would be more complicated.

In the center of a map, a cloud of asteroid dust, particles that were eleven miles from the port side, began moving toward the ship more quickly.

According to a Bayesian model, there was a 31 percent chance that the dust would hit us. However, these odds were based on old servers, computers that used sixty-one rows of poorly aligned mirrors.

I shoved my hand through text—sixteen statistical models appeared. "All these models are inaccurate because the servers are overloaded."

"It's the same old problem. We're up shit creek."

At the bottom of a monitor, the ship's servers were slowly recognizing recent probes of turbulent asteroid clouds, 877 exabytes of information.

Text warning flashed. Hard Drive Capacity Exceeded. Like before, its storage capacity had been reached. Right now, there were 451,000,000,000,000,000 bytes of data on it.

After comparing turbulence densities from two servers, a video of the ship's port side hull enlarged. Scratches covered every inch of the hull. Close to the edge of another screen, the starboard side brightened, making it easier to see.

From aft to the bow, most of the protective layering had been torn off. The entire hull would have to be resurfaced. However, the aging nanorobots, spider-like devices, might break down before they finished. In the past year, they removed paint more slowly because their conduits had been exposed to boiling and freezing temperatures.

I thought about the unfamiliar moon, Brynin, our next destination. Who lived there? I wasn't sure.

ST7 passed 14.1, the ninth planet in the R1 system and new coordinates along with videos appeared. Massive dry craters covered every square mile of 14.1, a lifeless planet. There weren't any towns or settlements. It was best to avoid it.

An unknown male voice came out my earplugs. "Cap . . . Jaso . . . Wel . . ." The sound was replaced by white noise.

"Greg, did you hear what he was saying?" I frowned.

"Just a few words through my earplugs. But most of it was garbled." He blinked.

Near the edge of a screen, a video of P L Five, the planet that Brynin orbited, magnified. In the northern hemisphere, clouds moved across a vast ocean, one that was bordered by a long coastline. Close to an empty beach, 42.358N latitude-71.06W longitude, the tide rolled in. But the rest of the screen was empty. It was impossible to tell who lived close to the beach.

"Have you received any radio signals from P L Five?" I cleared my throat, worried.

"No. Although there are some distorted voices at two hundred-twenty Kilohertz, they don't make any sense." His face tensed up as he leaned forward.

On screen, at 51.22N-51.44W, near the center of a vast ocean, there weren't any boats or ocean liners.

At the top of a monitor, behind our ship, the solar sail opened, and we began decelerating. If we slowed down too fast, ST7 would break apart.

"You'll watch the solar sail full time?" I paused.

"For eleven minutes. Then I have to create newer vectors." He tightened one fist, concentrating.

"Understood."

An unfamiliar voice came out of my earplugs. "This is Uma, calling from Brynin, the only safe moon left. LN warships have landed on the other moons, RO, Litor and M3."

Chills ran up my spine. "Greg, did you hear that?"

"Yes. Trouble. " He exhaled, ill at ease.

ABOUT THE AUTHOR

May, 2016, I moved to Sacramento, California. I'm retired, used to work in market research. When I'm not writing science fiction, I draw, read, watch movies and listen to music.
My website-> http://thadde.cnc.net/w/wr.html

www.ingramcontent.com/pod-product-compliance
Lightning Source LLC
Chambersburg PA
CBHW061558170626
46811CB00001B/245